THE BALD

Dickon Levinge

THE BALD MONKEY

FICTION4ALL

TABLE OF CONTENTS

Chapter 1: Henry

Henry did not consider himself to be overly precise or controlling about many things in his otherwise chaotic life, but this was his haven. His isolation chamber, where time became meaningless and the memories he visited became the present. His cocoon. He immersed himself in the warmth of the red bulb and inhaled through his nose. Relishing the sharp, vinegarish scent that wafted from the stop bath tray – which he had lined up exactly between those containing the developer and the fixer. Taking care that each solution was warmed to the optimum temperature.

Like everybody else in his profession Henry had, for his day-to-day work, switched over to digital formats years ago. Lazily snapping dozens, sometimes hundreds, of images on a job. Knowing that at least a few of them would be good enough to appease his aesthetically challenged clients. Scattergun photography for the birthday bashes he couldn't stand, the corporate events that made him seethe and the lavish weddings he so detested. Oh, God, the weddings. How he dreaded those most of all. Ugly people in uglier outfits grinning inanely with unfounded, alcohol-induced optimism. But at least they paid well and enabled him to continue with his more artistic endeavours – along with the absurd mission on which he had, in recent years, become increasingly fixated.

It was this vanity on which today's darkroom session touched. The negative he chose came from one his older, more precious files. Black and white. He slipped the celluloid strip into the enlarger, snapped the gate onto the frame he knew so well and brought into focus the inverse image of a smiling couple sitting outside a floating restaurant. A converted passenger ferry, from the 1930s, moored alongside the Embankment. The London Eye framing them with a diffused halo against a darkening sky with silver-edged clouds. A bottle of champagne in an ice bucket, along with three glasses, sat on the table before them.

Henry placed the photographic paper onto the base plate, flicked aside the red safety filter to give it a three second blast of white light, then moved over to the baths. He slipped the exposed sheet into the developer and, for what must have been at least the hundredth time, savoured the memory's gradual return. Instinctively, it was Arabella he watched appear. The wisp of hair at her temple that she could never quite tame. The tiny, fine line at the corner of her mouth. The one he used to call her smile crease. As the richness of the image deepened, he took a set of rubber-tipped tongs, carefully removed the print from the developer tray and transferred it into the stop bath. His younger self stared back at him. Straggled hair still full and dark. A joyful, vibrant smile. The only sign of age were his glasses, newly acquired that week.

Then he clenched his jaw when, as always, his attention was stolen by the reflection of the photographer in the left lens of his new specs. Marion. Arabella's sister. It was she who had introduced Henry to Arabella some six months before the photograph was taken. Which was the only reason that, at times, he almost forgave her for the basic error of capturing her own reflection in such an important, momentous image. At times. And only ever almost.

Henry took a second set of tongs, removed the photograph from the stop bath and eased it into the fixer. As it rested there he focused on the main subject of the image, the detail that gave it such immense value. Henry's and Arabella's hands clasped together and held above the champagne bottle. Outstretched towards the camera and showing off the diamond ring that Henry had presented to her just hours before. The first portrait of them as an engaged couple. The only record of that precious milestone in the great love story that was their marriage – until it was so abruptly ended.

A loud, demanding jingle wrenched Henry back from his past. Cursing himself for forgetting to switch it off, he removed his mobile phone from his pocket and scowled at the lurid screen. 'I'm making arrangements myself, 'a text message read, 'You should have done it years ago. Shame on you'.

Henry seethed. *Speak of the Devil's daughter.*

No word from Marion for nearly six years and, now, the third message in as many days.

He snatched the photograph out of the fixer bath, rested it on a table and, bending down, examined it under a loupe. He focused on the reflection of Marion behind the bulbous, intrusive lens of his old Nikon F2, which she'd clearly had no idea how to use. How could she have missed her own reflection?

He removed the negative and, again with the loupe, inspected it with a frustrated squint. Over the years Henry had tried, many times, to remove Marion's trespass the old-fashioned way, by blocking and dodging in the darkroom, but never with an adequate result. He always ended up deadening his own expression. His all important, sideways glance towards his beautiful new fiancée. Finally, he supposed, he'd have to resort to the cold and soulless digital method.

Henry ripped the photograph in two and tossed it in the bin.

"Drew!" he bellowed as he threw open the door and marched back into the harsh, glaring reality of the present.

Drew, his young, earnest assistant, sat in front of a cinematically huge computer screen perched on the only tidy desk in the room. Henry handed over the negative strip and said, "Frame sixteen, second in from the left. Scan, clean and set it up for me to work on later, will you?"

Drew replied with a serious nod, which seemed at odds with his fixed smile, and carefully took the strip in his hand – taking care only to touch the sides.

"I'm out for the evening," Henry added. "Lock up when you're done." He picked up a thick, battered file from the maelstrom of paperwork and glossy images that was his own desk, tucked it under his arm and left.

Chapter 2: The Bald Monkey

Henry slapped the file down onto the bar, knocking over a saltcellar. "Shit." He took a pinch with his right forefinger and thumb, threw it over his left shoulder, repeated the action twice and finished the ritual with three sharp knocks on the polished oak surface. As he mounted the barstool, he looked up to see Michael, the septuagenarian landlord whose healthy complexion and thick waves of white hair could have easily fooled anybody into thinking he was a youthful sixty, grinning back at him.

"Still at that malarkey, are you, Henry?" Michael quipped in a musical, Connemara lilt, "You'll be avoiding stepping on the lines between the tiles when you're coming in, next."

Henry glanced down at the polished, porcelain squares that checker-boarded the entire pub, then looked back to Michael and humoured him with a forced smile.

"Pint?" Michael asked.

"Please," Henry replied, then turned his attention to the file. He flicked it open and leafed through an array of faded documents, old maps and photographs of dank, brick lined tunnels. As Henry studied one of the maps a massive hulk of a man wearing workman's trousers and an old donkey jacket, plonked himself onto the neighbouring seat. He glanced at Henry's file and rolled his eyes.

"Oh, for fuck's sake," he grumbled.

Henry flicked the newcomer a sideways glance just as Michael appeared with his pint of ale.

"Cheers, Michael. One for Des here too, if that's okay."

"I'm sure it is," Michael curtly replied, regarding Des with a less friendly expression than that with which he had greeted Henry. "Snakebite, Desmond?"

"Yeah. And a shot of tequila." Des squinted down at the map. "I've gotta feeling I'm gonna need it."

Michael looked to Henry for approval, which duly came in the form of a smile and a shrug.

"Go on, then," Des reluctantly asked, "Let's see what you've got."

Henry grinned and pushed the map towards his friend," I think we missed a section."

"Did we."

"We did. Here." Henry circled a small square on the map with a China marker. Out towards the edge and near a thick, blue curve that signified the River Thames.

"That's Embankment. I took you down there yonks ago. Fucking years back."

"Language at the bar, Desmond. We're a family establishment in here." Michael chided as he placed Desmond's drinks onto the bar.

"Sorry, Michael," Des replied in the tone of a grumpy teenager. Then he cheerily asked, "Groucho been in yet?"

"Please don't call her that," Henry groaned.

"Still sixteen minutes to go," Michael replied, gesturing to the wall clock which read sixteen minutes to six.

"Fuck, we're early today."

"I'm serious, Desmond. If you're going to use that sort of language then you can move to a table and keep the volume down. In fact, you should do that anyway. It's going to get busy later and I'll be needing the bar space."

"Yeah, alright," Des replied, the teenage angst back in his voice, even though the giant of a man was well into his fifties. Although not as well into them as his grey stubble and life-beaten face might have suggested.

Henry gathered up his file and his drink. The duo moved across the spacious room dotted with high, round tables and barstools to an opulent, red leather corner booth.

Sixteen minutes later Sonia – a tall, thin, pinstriped woman with a mop of jet-black hair and thick, black eyebrows above thicker, blacker, plastic framed glasses perched on the bridge of her prominent nose – bounced through the front door. She looked around the pub, saw Henry and Des sitting in the booth, frowned quizzically and then approached Michael. After exchanging pleasantries with him while he poured her a large gin and tonic, she took her drink and loped across the room to join the two men. "What are we doing here? Why aren't we at the bar?" she matter-of-factly enquired with a clipped cadence possessed by the ghost of an Eastern European accent.

"Dizzy's fault," Henry replied with a wicked grin, "He kept swearing so Michael exiled us to the tourist section."

"Arsehole," Sonia scolded, glaring at Des as she sat, "I hate not sitting at the bar. That's where all the action is."

"Wouldn't have mattered," Des sulked, "Michael said we'd have had to move, anyway. Says it's gonna get busy tonight."

"Yes, Des. Busy. As in action!" After taking a long sip from her drink she looked down at the table, spied Henry's document and excitedly added, "Ooh! You're off on another of your expeditions!"

"No, we are not," Des snapped.

"Yes, we are," Henry corrected.

"When are you going?" Sonia grinned.

"We ain't," Des insisted.

"When are you going?" Sonia repeated.

"Tomorrow night," Henry smiled.

"Oh, for fuck's sake." Des knocked back his tequila with a frustrated gulp.

"Pick you up about eight outside here, Dizzy?" Henry cheerily suggested, to which Sonia let out a loud, cackling laugh.

"Yeah, all right," Des sighed. "Better make it nine, though. I've got a job on."

Henry and Sonia ceased their laughter, shared a quick look and quietly sipped their drinks, the atmosphere suddenly taking on a more solemn air.

"Nine will be fine, Des."

"Last time, Henry. Promise me."

"Last time, Dizzy. I promise. There's nowhere left to look. Anyway. Come the end of the month it won't really matter. Marion's calling it."

Then it was Sonia and Des's turn to share a look of concern.

14

"It might be for the best, Henry," Sonia tentatively suggested.

Henry's jaw flexed but he passed no comment. He forced a smile and cheerily asked, "Another round? My shout."

"Well, now, that sounds just marvellous!" Sonia beamed.

"Yeah. Don't think I can, though." said Des, taking the other two by surprise. Then they saw that he had locked his gaze on a small, wiry man with sharp, darting eyes behind spotless, wire frame glasses. Evan, who stood at the end of the bar, summoned Des with an aggressive jerk of his bony head.

Des finished his snakebite, swilling the last sip around his mouth as if it was mouthwash, nodded his goodbyes and stood. The other two watched as he joined Evan – Des towering over him and yet appearing smaller, almost diminutive, as they exchanged a few words while Evan discreetly handed him a thick, grubby envelope. As Des left, Evan threw Henry and Sonia a hard glare, before retreating to a high table and reading a tatty, heavily thumbed copy of The Sun.

Sonia and Henry turned back to face each other, both with grim faces. Until Sonia smiled, and in a light, airy voice declared, "Tonight, dear Henry, I am of a mind to get rat-arse pissed!"

Chapter 3: Thanksgivings and Misgivings

Shortly after closing time Henry and Sonia rolled their way down the hill that is the straight, wide and tidy Gloucester Avenue. A boulevard running the length of Primrose Hill that's more akin to the thoroughfare of a rural village than one in the centre of a great metropolis. Henry staggered only slightly, and that was mainly due to him having to support Sonia who, several gins and a bottle of wine later, had been more than true to her declaration. Sonia rambled, as she usually did in her inebriated state, yet still managed to remain coherent. On this occasion, she rebuked Henry for not pulling his weight in helping her prepare an exhibition of his work that her gallery was set to host at the end of the month, in three Thursday's time. The last Thursday of November.

"That's Thanksgiving, you know." Henry slurred. Then he frowned as he wondered if he might, in fact, have been a little more drunk than he'd given himself credit for.

"I couldn't give a toss, Henry!" Sonia snapped. "Why would I give a toss about an American holiday? You know how I feel about Americans these days."

"I thought he was Canadian?"

"Oh, it's all the same, fucking thing! They're all bastards. And they all celebrate Thanksgiving."

"Actually, Canadian Thanksgiving's on a different day. I think it's a month earlier."

"Jesus, Henry, what part of me not giving a toss don't you understand? I'm trying to make a serious point, here!" By the time Sonia was making her serious point they had reached the bottom of the hill, meandered through a small alley and were just turning onto Regent's Canal's towpath. Left, towards Camden. "The early invitations went out yesterday. The space is empty, waiting, and you haven't even chosen half of the photographs, let alone had them printed and framed!"

Henry nodded in serious agreement as he moved around Sonia, placing himself between her and the water as she slipped and stumbled a little too near to the edge for his comfort.

"I mean, it's serious, Henry. Oh, I see what you did there. Thanks. And don't change the subject!"

"I didn't change the subject."

"Yes, you did. You were banging on about bloody Thanksgiving. Which is not the reason you chose that date for the show. And you know it. And, by the way, the rest of us find it a little weird."

"Oh, God, not this again."

"Yes, this again. I mean it, Henry. It's creepy."

"It's a coincidence. You always have these events on a Thursday. This year, that date just happens to fall on a Thursday."

"Ha!" Sonia snapped, stopping both of them in their tracks by reeling on him with an accusatory finger-stab and a gotcha expression. Then she looked away and frowned, wondering if she had actually caught him out on anything, before realising she probably hadn't. So she smiled, linked her arm through his and allowed them to continue on.

Sauntering and swaying under the rounded, brickwork arch of a small bridge and past old, converted warehouses – once factories and storehouses, now expensive flats and extortionate coffee shops. "All I'm saying is that you need to get on with it," she mumbled, then fell silent as they walked over a humpbacked, pedestrian bridge that crossed the canal.

They passed the lock gates, weaving between and stepping over late-night drinkers, hollow-eyed homeless people and a determined busker, at least as drunk as Sonia, who strummed an old guitar with only four strings while groaning out the garbled lyrics for Fairytale of New York.

"A bit early in the year for that number, isn't it?" Henry said as he slipped a five pound note into the musician's open guitar case. The player looked up with wide, vacant eyes and gave a grateful, toothless smile.

Sonia randomly declared another loud and victorious, "Ha!" before, again, resting her head onto Henry's shoulder and, her eyes half closed, allowed him to guide her onto the next main road.

Two hundred yards further on they came to a halt outside a red-bricked, Victorian warehouse, the door of which was surrounded by colourful, ceramic tiles. Most of the tiles were cracked and the building's brickwork appeared in desperate need of repointing. It seemed to be the only structure in the area that had not, in recent years, been renovated. Above one of the windows, with a white, empty room beyond, hung a sign which read The Sonia K Gallery.

"Got your keys?"

Sonia rummaged around her leather backpack, found an oversized bunch of keys, fumbled with them while trying to get one into the lock and then stared down, slightly swaying, as they fell through her overly relaxed fingers. Henry bent down to pick them up. Then he stopped still when he saw they had landed on the manhole cover just outside the window. He gave slight shudder, eyeing the steel plate with a feeling of dread, before taking a quick breath, retrieving the keys and unlocking the door.

Sonia smiled, gratefully, then looked up at one of the first floor windows and dramatically said, "Living above the shop. Has it really come to this."

"I'm afraid it has," Henry replied with an equally theatrical flair. It was a well-rehearsed exchange that he and Sonia had conducted many times and, as always, it continued with Sonia smiling warmly, wrapping her arms around Henry's waist, drawing close to him and whispering,

"Are you coming in?"

As he always did, Henry placed his hands on her shoulders, gently eased her away from him and quietly replied, "No, Sonia. I am not."

Sonia shook her head, disappointed but unsurprised, and said, "It's been six years now, Henry."

"Nearly seven, Sonia."

"Ha!" This time she knew she had him. "Exactly! Nearly seven years, Henry." Henry said nothing. Sonia then folded her arms, leant against the doorframe and, after taking a thoughtful moment, quietly added, "You know, this might be the last show I get to do here."

"What? Why?" Henry said. The usual doorstep conversation now taking a new, worrying digression.

"Oh, the usual. Money. Thanks to the American. Canadian. Whatever. Shit-bag. And, just look around," Sonia gestured, with a wide arc, at the surrounding buildings. All pristine, new and soulless. "Bankers to the left of me, developers to the right. And, here I am."

"Stuck in the middle –"

"Stuck in the fucking middle!" Sonia raucously laughed. Then she leaned in towards him again. This time to give him a warm, affectionate hug. "You need to start being less passive about everything, Henry. Get more proactive."

Henry smiled as she returned to her normal agenda of how to fix Henry.

"And I don't just mean about the show." She gave him a kiss on the cheek and retreated into the gallery. "Although, don't get me wrong. I do mean mostly about the show," she laughed. And was about to shut the door when she turned back to face Henry with a hard, sullen expression. Quietly and soberly she said, "I'd kill him, you know. If I could."

"Who?"

"The Canadian. If I could, if I knew where the hell he was, I would hunt him down and I would kill him. Strangle him. Were the opportunity to arise, I'd wring his devious, thieving, beautiful bloody neck." She held a dead-eyed stare for a moment, then snapped back to her usual smile as she gave another wink, clacked her tongue and blew Henry a final kiss. "Night, Henry. And fucking get those prints organised."

Sonia closed the door and Henry stepped back to watch the various lights turn on and off as she made her way through the gallery space, up the stairs and into the small, top floor flat. Satisfied she was relatively near her bed, he made his way down the road. At the first crossroads, while waiting for the light to change, he turned back and looked up at the gallery. The stained glass window above the worn out door. The cracked tiles and the neglected brickwork.

Nearly seven years, he thought. Remembering that night when his life, or at least all that was worth living it for, came to an end.

Chapter 4: Six Years, Eleven Months and Five Days Ago

Arabella smiled down at the finely crafted bracelet which Henry had just gifted her. The charms, hand etched by one of London's finest artists, comprised of a crucifix, a Star of David, a crescent moon and a fat Buddha, just to cover any and all religious bases. A four-leaf clover, a horseshoe, a baby elephant, a happy pig and a tiny rabbit's foot, to bring as much luck as possible. A club, an ace, a diamond and a heart because, apparently, as well as being a fine artist, the creator was also a notorious poker player. And, finally, a tiny disc inscribed with the number ten. This last item Henry had asked to be added both as a commemoration and because the number of original charms totalled thirteen. Which, he thought, rather defeated the purpose of them being lucky.

"Henry, it's beautiful. Is it silver?"

"Nope," Henry grinned." Guess again."

Arabella gave him a cockeyed look.

"What metal is for a tenth anniversary?"

The corner of her mouth curved with a half-smile of curiosity. She shook her head.

"Tin! It's tin!"

"Tin. That's so you," she smiled.

Henry raised his old Minox spy camera, his own lucky charm which he had carried with him since his teenage years, and snapped a candid shot.

The final shot.

"Aren't you going to put it on?" he asked.

"Here," Arabella extended her wrist. "You do the honours."

Henry carefully fastened the bracelet. Then, holding her hand in both of his, he softly kissed the back of her wedding ring finger. As he did so a thunderclap shook the empty glasses on the table. They both looked towards the window, which was streaked with beads of heavy rain. "I'm afraid it's going to be a wet walk home if we can't find a taxi."

"The walk home will be lovely," Arabella replied, gently squeezing his hand before withdrawing her own as the waiter arrived with their bill.

While Henry paid, Arabella turned her attention to her phone, scrolling through various missed messages. Once Henry had settled payment and they were leaving, Arabella walked slightly ahead of him with the phone pressed to her face. "Yes, it's tin," she explained to the other party, "That's the metal for a tenth anniversary. Can you believe it? So thoughtful. So Henry. ...No, Chinese."

Henry caught up with her as a head waiter opened the door for them. Outside, the black sky sparkled with streams of heavy rain caught in the streetlights.

"No, we couldn't get one," Arabella continued on her mobile. "We're walking back. Oh, it's not too far. It'll be lovely. I'll see you soon, yes? Bye, now." Arabella hung up, pocketed her phone and linked her arm through Henry's.

"Marion?" Henry guessed.

"She says happy anniversary and hopes to see us soon." Arabella kissed him and the two of them,

23

laughing and with their heads held low, dashed out into the storm.

They pushed their way through the flooded streets of Camden. Wading uphill through cascades of water and laughing at the ridiculousness of it all. An occupied taxi came past, its pavement-side wheels catching the edge of a pool and throwing a wall of water over them which raised their guffaws to the heights of hysteria.

"Come on, quick! I want to see!" Arabella shouted. She ran to a small scaffold in front an almost derelict looking building. The Sonia K Gallery. Sheltered under the scaffold above the doorway, she attempted to brush water off herself. She looked into the front window and saw a row of black and white photographs leaning against the blank walls, ready to be hung. "Oh, look!" she piped. "Sonia's already started setting up! Is that why you wanted to walk home tonight? So we could have a sneak preview?"

"Well, it is on the way. I'm afraid I just didn't bank on this storm coming in."

"So then, get under here, silly. Before you drown!"

Henry took a step forward, then stopped.

"What are you waiting for?"

Henry glanced at the ladder, leaning against the scaffolding outside the first floor window. Set up for Sonia to mount the sign advertising his latest, and biggest, exhibition.

With a wicked smile Arabella said, "The ladder, Henry?"

"Bad luck," Henry replied with a self-deprecating shrug.

24

"Oh, Henry," Arabella laughed, "You and your silly superstitions." By way of making a point she stepped toward the ladder, wading through the stream of water that ran over her brand-new boots.

"'Bella, please be careful."

She laughed and with a wide-eyed, mischievous grin said," I do love –"

And as she stepped under the ladder, Arabella disappeared into the water. Swallowed by an open manhole and flushed into the bowels of London.

Chapter 5: Dizzy Des

Three days before Arabella's death – or, as Henry insisted on calling it, her disappearance – Des sat in his usual place at the long bar in The Bald Monkey. On any ordinary day he would barrel in at around six o'clock, still in his work overalls, slap his gigantic hands on the bar and bellow, "Michael, me auld fella," trading his North London growl for a cringingly bad Irish accent, "Sure, isn't it pint o'clock!"

Michael would shake his head and, with a wide grin, pour Des his usual pint of Guinness while Des regaled him, and anyone else who cared to listen, with whatever tired old joke he had heard on the site that day. Which was usually as bad as his Irish accent and just as offensive. Des would time the joke, purely by instinct, so that the punch line would coincide with the exact moment his pint had settled. Then lean against the bar, drink a good three inches from the top and strike up some friendly banter with whoever happened to be standing closest to him. Often a complete stranger who would, invariably, buy him his next drink.

After his third or fourth pint, Des would then leave to spend the rest of his evening with Angie, his perpetual fiancée. They had been living together for the better part of eleven years, nine of which they had been betrothed, but they kept putting the wedding off because they liked the idea of being engaged. "It's fuckin 'romantic. Innit." Des would reply whenever anybody asked him to explain.

In recent weeks, however, Des had been going elsewhere on one or two evenings of the week. To visit his new girl, Becca, having told Angie that he was having to work double shifts on account of the extra workload involving the Crossrail delays. "Happy days, yeah?" Des would chuckle, when he confided the secret of his clandestine affair to any pub stranger who would stand him a pint.

Three days before Arabella's accident, Des arrived at The Bald Monkey, not at around six o'clock, but at opening time. He stormed in wearing a thunderous scowl, slumped in his usual place and ordered a pint of Guinness with a whisky chaser. As he nursed the pint and sipped the spirit he mulled over the events of the previous evening, when he went to see Becca to find both her and Angie sitting in the living room. Both furious. Both with packed suitcases. Both suitcases containing his clothes. It seemed that one of his recent fellow drinkers and confidants may have been a stranger to him, but was not a stranger to Angie.

Des nursed the first round, and the second, but on the third he picked up the pace. He furiously drank his way through lunchtime, then the afternoon, and by the time the five o'clock post-work crowd began to trickle in Des had become the man at the end of the bar that everyone did their best to avoid. Everyone apart from a young couple. A brash and confident estate agent who arrogantly showed off his brand-new Rolex to his pretty, wide-eyed girlfriend. As he did so the glare from the watch flashed in Des's eye.

Des squinted, threw the young man an angry look and said, "Fucking leave it out, will ya? Tosser!"

The estate agent turned puce and took a step away. But his girlfriend rounded on Des and snapped, "Don't you talk to him like that, you fat pisshead!"

Des slid down from the barstool, rolled towards the couple and loomed over them. After a moment he frowned at the estate agent and growled, "I know you, don't I?"

"I don't think so." The estate agent downed his drink and took the girl by the hand." Come on."

Des watched the young man lead her through the front door. As they exited, he placed the boy in his mind. He slammed his empty glass onto the counter, stormed out to follow and caught up with them as they were about to cross the road. "Oi! You! Tosser with the flash watch!"

The estate agent turned to face Des, moving his girlfriend behind him, and began, "Look, you've probably just seen me here before. I don't –"

"Yeah, I've seen you before. But not in here. You work in that estate agents down on Hartland Road. Don't you."

"What about it?"

"With Angie. You know Angie. Yeah?"

"Yeah," the boy nervously croaked." Yeah, I know Angie."

"What you been saying to her, then?"

"Mate, I have no idea what you're on about."

"Don't you 'mate 'me! What you been sayin' to my Angie, hey?" Des screamed, leaning down and

pressing his puffed out, crimson face into the boy's –
pale and terrified. "What you been saying to my
Angie!"

As the boy stepped back Des cocked his colossal
fist and slammed it into the side of his cheek – which
shattered with a sickening crack.

When he woke the next morning, the first thing
Des noticed was that his wrist had been shackled to a
bedframe. He looked down at his hand. Caked in
dried blood. The knuckles stripped down, almost to
the bone. Then he started to remember, but only
vague snapshots through a furious filter of delirium
and alcohol. The girl screaming and begging him to
stop while his massive, powerful fists flailed, as if
controlled by some horrible outside rage. The
choking, gargling of the young man while his bloody
face became more disfigured with every hammer
blow.

Des's gut gave a violent twist when he saw his
victim in a bed across the ward. Unconscious, his
head and face a great ball of blood-sodden bandages.
His sobbing girlfriend holding his weak, limp hand.
It was then that Des noticed the matching gold bands
and a modest, diamond ring. Not a girlfriend. A wife.
The watch, Des would later find out, had been a
wedding present which she'd given him on their
honeymoon – from which they'd just returned the
day Des had attacked the young newlywed. The boy
hadn't even been in the country when Angie found
out about Becca.

When it came to his day in court, Des pleaded
guilty to the charge of Grievous Bodily Harm and

was sentenced to eighteen months, nine of which he served. It was in prison that Des earned the moniker Dizzy Des. So dizzy that he could hardly remember how he got there but he copped to the charge anyway, the other inmates laughed. Chiefly Evan, who had heard about Des in the prison yard, sought him out and befriended him. They were from neighbouring estates in North London and, all being well, would probably be getting released at the same time. Evan was finishing a much longer sentence for attempted murder.

Shortly after his release Michael, conditionally and in no small part due to Sonia's advocacy, allowed Des back into The Bald Monkey. But he never treated Des with the same fondness or trust. Gone was the jovial, gregarious giant with the broad smile who greeted everyone with a bellowing laugh and a risqué joke. In his place sat the morose beast who slumped over his new drink of choice, snakebites with tequila chasers, while sneering at the world. Now unemployed and unemployable. Except by Evan, who appeared as a new, semi-regular a few weeks after Des's return. He'd slink in, his head on a swivel, mumble a quick word to Des at the bar, then have a quiet pint in the corner while reading a red-top tabloid and holding other muted, nefarious meetings. Des would then slope out and go about whatever dark, violent assignment he had been tasked.

Henry did not discover all of this the first time they met. It came out in drips and drabs. Smaller revelations becoming outright confessions over the years of their friendship. The first time they met, two loan drinkers sitting side-by-side at the long bar, all Henry discovered was that, up until some recent troubles, Des had been a foreman for a construction company. Much of his work was on the London Underground but most of it, Des said as he took a long draw from his snakebite while nodding down at Henry's map, had been in the London sewers.

"Really. Well, I'd quite like to buy you a drink, then."

"Been a long time since anyone in here's done that," Des cryptically replied, then nodded his grateful acceptance.

The two then sat for hours, pouring over the various maps that Henry had gathered in recent months, while he explained to Des the terrible fate that had befallen his beautiful wife. And confided his desperate hope that, by some miracle, she may have survived.

"No chance, mate," Des replied in a sombre, gravely timbre. "See this?" He pulled the map towards him and pointed with his thick, calloused index finger to a red line that ran under the circled spot, where Arabella had vanished, and out towards the river. "That's a trunk line, that is. One of the old big boys built by the Victorians. You and me, we could walk through one of those side by side. I could reach for the ceiling and still have a foot between my hand and the brickwork. And I'm nearly six-six, I am. Now. On a night like you're talking about, with all that rain and flooding? That's going to be at full capacity. All the gates open. And it's gonna be fast. Fifty thousand —"

"I know. Fifty thousand litres per second," Henry said, leaning back and sipping his ale. He'd heard all of the numbers and statistics before. The colossal speed at which the subterranean torrent would have been moving. How all of the safety sluices would have been open to full capacity. How it would have only taken minutes for Arabella, her body battered and broken, to have been washed though the entire pipeline and out into the River Thames. And with the river swelled and the tide heading out at full flow, carried into the Thames Estuary.

Yet there was one part of the equation that still gave Henry hope. The time factor. That it would have only taken minutes for her to have made the journey, all the way from Camden and out into the river. If that was where she ended up.

Becoming more excited at what he considered to be possible, although admittedly highly improbable, scenarios, Henry pulled the maps towards him. Using a paper straw as a pointer he showed Des the various diversions, junctions and reservoirs that broke away from the trunk sewer between the gallery manhole and the river. Any one of which she could have been carried into. Any one of which might still hold a clue to her survival. Or even, he found himself forced to admit, her body. Then, at least, he would know for sure and be able to finally lay her to rest. If only he could get down there to explore.

Des knocked back his tequila shot, considering Henry's proposal. Then he followed that up with the last two inches of his snakebite, which he swirled

32

around his mouth and swallowed with a satisfied gasp. "Dangerous work, that is," he finally said with a note of authority. "Not entirely legal, either."

Henry shrugged and signalled to Michael for another round.

"So. You're looking for a guide, then. That it?"

"Guide. Advisor."

"Someone to stop you getting yourself topped."

"Would be most appreciated."

Des let out a short, loud belly laugh that Michael reacted to with a brief smile. He then reached for his fresh pint and was about to continue when something behind Henry captured his attention. He leaned in and quietly said, "Hey, Henry. Wait until you see this bird. Comes in here every day at eight minutes past six on the dot, and she's the spit of Groucho Marx."

"Oh, shit." Henry hurriedly tidied the maps into their file.

"Only, you know," Des continued, either ignoring or not noticing Henry's reaction, "More of a looker, if you know what I mean." Then he called out, "Alright, Groucho?"

"Oh, piss off, Dizzy," Sonia retorted as she bounced towards them and cheerily added, "Henry Glass in a pub! I never thought I'd see the day."

"Well, you've been banging on about this place for years." Henry added Sonia's Hendricks gin with Fever Tree tonic to his tab, while Des looked on with amused confusion, and the three sat together for what would become the first of many such gatherings.

Chapter 6: Eek! Eek!

The morning after Henry had delivered Sonia back to the gallery he woke up on his sofa. The final photograph of Arabella, snapped with his old Minox, lay beside him on a glass table – alongside the whisky bottle he'd emptied as his nightcap. He pulled himself up, took the print and padded over to the longest wall in the room, which was covered with a collage of images that chronicled his and Arabella's life together. They were arranged in order, from the day that Marion had introduced them to that last, wonderful meal just minutes before her disappearance. Henry pinned the shot back in its place, at the end of the visual timeline, then looked back to the early days. A print of their engagement portrait. The champagne. The ring. The smile. The reflection in his glasses.

Marion's reflection.

Henry bristled. Then he remembered that he had asked Drew to scan and load the negative into the computer so he could try and digitally erase the interloper. He turned towards the office and saw that the light was on. He could hear the clacking of typing from within and, tiredly, shuffled his way towards the door.

Drew, looking particularly bookish, sat bolt upright while he typed at what always impressed Henry as a phenomenal speed. He opened his mouth to ask Drew when he got in but Drew beat him to the first word.

"I uploaded that photograph for you. And I spoke to Sonia. She says she's still waiting for a shortlist of images for you to edit down for the exhibition. I made a long list for you. I just thought it might save a bit of time, especially with that big wedding job coming up next week. Anyway. I'm just replying to Sonia, now. I hope that's okay." Drew smiled. A polite and earnest smile which Henry always found slightly disconcerting. It seemed to be all teeth and, although the corners of his mouth would rise higher than almost anyone else's Henry had seen when grimacing, the eyes always seemed to remain unaffected. Rather thoughtful and a bit sad.

"I'm taking a shower," Henry groaned, mainly as a suggestion to himself and because he suddenly felt in dire need of the Solpadeine Max in the bathroom cabinet.

Once refreshed, Henry prepared for the planned excursion with Des. The first time they had gone underground, a few weeks after their fortuitous meeting in The Bald Monkey, Henry had found himself woefully unprepared. After a three-hour investigation of the trunk line under the gallery he'd emerged with a ruined pair of RM Williams boots, a befouled Barber jacket and several bruises on his forehead. In response he had, over the years, put together a kit to ready himself for any and all subterranean eventualities. It included such items as a heavy pair of waterproof, LL Bean walking boots, a selection of climbing ropes, an even bigger selection of torches, one of which was designed to fit onto his miner's helmet, a heavy duty boiler suit and, just to be safe, a diver's dry suit which he would wear underneath. The dry suit he kept a secret, having already suffered enough ridicule from Des and Sonia as, over the years, his 'Excursion Equipment Kit', as he called it, had taken on ludicrous proportions – and which he once made the mistake of abbreviating to the acronym EEK. From that moment, whenever they saw him fully kitted out, Des and Sonia would raise their hands and, with wide eyes and wider grins, loudly scream, "Eek! Eek!", in high-pitched squeals.

He had also invested, just before the second mission, in a Nikon Nikonos-V underwater film camera to document the journeys and, he rationalised to himself and to Sonia, put together a potential exhibition of London sewers. Perhaps to accompany a photo essay, or even a book.

Having readied his EEK, Henry saw he had some time to spare and so attempted to Photoshop the engagement image – until he realised that the previous evening's excesses had rendered his vision and mental focus far too impaired to even attempt such a task. He lay down to sleep off the rest of his hangover.

By the time he woke, the time was already approaching nine o'clock. Henry cursed himself, along with Drew for leaving without waking him up, then leapt up and started to pull on his dry suit. Never a quick or easy job, especially as Henry had gained a few pounds since purchasing the painfully tight-fitting garment four years previously. The extra time it took, together with the frustrating minutes spent lacing the boots, meant it was already well past nine when he donned his miner's hat, pulled on his new high-vis jacket and, finally ready to go, marched towards the door – just as a sharp, officious knock came from the other side. "Shit. Yeah, alright, Dizzy! I'm coming now!" He yanked open the door." Mate, I'm sorry."

To which Marion haughtily replied, "Oh, we're mates now, are we?" Closely followed by a perplexed, "What on God's green Earth are you wearing?"

Henry stood utterly still. His feet as firmly fixed to the steps as his stare was on the face that, earlier that day, he had attempted to digitally erase. After fully registering her presence he replied, he thought quite calmly and cleverly, "What on God's green Earth are you doing here?" Although, as he heard himself utter the words in a quiet, quavering timbre, he realised it sounded more childish and petulant.

"Your text."

"Text." Henry vaguely remembered starting a text about three refills into the previous evening's nightcap. He then rolled his eyes upwards, remembering that he was wearing the miner's helmet, as well as a high-vis jacket and a satchel full of ropes and, thinking it would be best to circle back to the text issue, said, "I suppose I should explain the outfit."

"No need. I just remembered. How could I not remember. Although, I really had hoped you'd given up these antics years ago."

"Oh, bollocks!"

"I beg your pardon?"

Henry pushed past her and ran over to an old, short wheelbase Land Rover Defender. He inspected the back, which was a mere inch from a low wall, and the front, which was about the same distance from an E-Type Jaguar under a tarpaulin. "Bastard neighbour! Bastard neighbour's parked me in again!"

"Well, just knock on his door," Marion suggested, and couldn't help cracking a small smile.

"No, look. All the lights are out. He's gone off to his swanky house in the Cotswolds. Bloody second homeowners, I hate them." He rounded towards the house opposite his own and screamed, "This is not a city for part-timers! Bastard!" He then turned back to face Marion and, while taking a few deep breaths to calm down, noticed that she was looking at his battered and bruised Land Rover with a wistful smile.

"I can't believe you've still got the old girl," Marion muttered, and then added with a small chuckle, "God, how Arabella hated this car."

"No, she didn't."

Marion cocked an eyebrow and raised a defensive hand.

"Anyway. It's not going anywhere tonight."

"I'm amazed she's still able to go anywhere at all. Still. You clearly have somewhere to be so maybe we should do this another time."

"No, no, the text. It's all coming back to me, now." Henry lied, "We should talk about it. Here's an idea. Why don't you give me a lift and we can discuss it in your car?"

Marion responded with a long, unflinching stare of incredulity.

Five minutes later Marion, with Henry gripping the sides of the passenger seat, flung her red Fiat 500 around the corner and screeched to a halt outside The Bald Monkey.

"Jesus," Henry gasped. "I'd forgotten."

"Forgotten what?"

"Never mind." He tapped the window and waved at Des, who stood outside smoking.

Des frowned, flicked away his cigarette and came towards them. He opened Henry's door, looked into the back seat of the tiny hatchback, then back to Henry and said, "What's this, half an Uber? Some sort of clown car you nicked from the circus? How the fuck do you expect me to fit back there, then?"

"Oh, charming," Marion said to Henry. "Are all your new friends this congenial?"

While Henry moved the front seat back as far as he could, then let Des sit there while he squeezed into the rear, he made the introductions.

"The Marion?" Des asked.

"I suppose so. Why. What have you heard?"

Des expelled an all-too-long whistle, the kind a mechanic does when he's 'never seen one that bad before', and swiftly changed the subject to Henry's tardiness. Marion then requested a destination which Henry, with only a hint of guilt, revealed as the Embankment.

"Jesus. There are such things as Taxis, you know. Or full-sized Ubers that don't look like clown cars."

"Yeah, alright. I am sorry about that one."

Drifting away from the conversation Henry wondered, as he often did, how differently his life would be if they had taken a taxi the night of his tenth wedding anniversary. Or an Uber. Or even a clown car, stolen or otherwise.

"Henry!" The cry came with a tap on his window.

Henry turned with a start, knocking his miner's helmet to a jaunty angle, and from the darkness outside saw Sonia leaning towards him. She raised her hands, widened her mouth into a cross between a grin and an expression of mock horrification, wiggled her fingers and screamed, "Eeeeeek!"

Chapter 7: Wet Wipes and Leather Boots

Des lifted a square, checker-plate steel cover using an elaborate key he had purloined from his former employers. He glanced up at Marion, who had agreed to wait for Henry and Des and give them a lift home. But first she stood, quite fascinated, and watched them descend into the city's depths.

"Aren't you a little underdressed for these kinds of adventures?" she asked Des, noticing the sharp contrast between his simple overalls, steel capped boots and modest torch when compared to Henry's Great Explorer's outfit.

"No, Marion," Des sighed as he began his descent. "I'm afraid I am not."

"We'll be about forty-five minutes," Henry huffed, "An hour, tops." And he followed Des down into the shaft.

A few moments later Henry stepped onto the wet, slime covered floor of the sweating, brick lined tunnel. He flicked on his brand-new Victoper Wesho head torch, set to the full six thousand lumens, revealing a stunned and blinded Des just inches from his face.

"Jesus, Henry! Where the fuck did you get that? NASA?"

"Sorry," Henry whispered, turning the brightness setting down from Landing Lights to Opening Night Spotlight. "Shall I lead the way?"

"With that thing? You'd better. I'm gonna be seeing nothing but the afterglow for days as it is. Pillock."

"Sorry."

"And you don't have to whisper. I tell you every time. There's nobody else down here."

"You never know."

"Believe me. I know," said Des – still blinking while he stepped aside for Henry to take the lead.

Henry clicked his head torch up a couple of notches to Police Helicopter Searchlights and, referring to a map he held in a heavy, transparent plastic envelope, confidently announced, "This way."

"There is only one way," Des grumbled. He inhaled through his nose and twisted his face in revulsion as he caught the pungent aroma of sulphur, rot and decay. "Christ, you never get used to that." He produced what he considered to be the only essential piece of any sewer excursion kit, a small tub of Vicks Vapour Rub, and dapped a generous dollop under each nostril.

A few hundred yards down the line they came to a high, Gothic arched crossroads. More reminiscent of a grand cathedral than an underground sewer. The turn to their right had been bricked up, according to Henry's research, well over seventy-five years ago. The one ahead, he also knew, was the continuation of the trunk line from which they had arrived. The very one that ran under the outside of Sonia's gallery and emerged as an emergency overflow at the Embankment – less than a hundred yards from where they stood. One which they had, many years ago, investigated from the exit point into The Thames to almost this intersection.

The tunnel to their left, to which Henry now turned his beam, was a much smaller passage, and the entrance to the alcove Henry wished to investigate.

"I tell you. That girl's a menace on the road," Des said, attempting to break the eerie silence with idle chit-chat. "I'd have been impressed if I hadn't been so fucking terrified."

"Well, if you won't wear a seatbelt."

"You really think the seatbelt on that dodgem would have got around me, even if I did have room to reach for it? And why did she drive us, let alone agree to wait for us up there, anyway? I thought you two had been on the outs for years."

"We have. We are. And I don't know." Henry returned his attention to the new, much smaller tunnel, the beam of his light catching the warm steam that lightly swirled around them. "Probably just curious. She's like that. Okay, this is it." He crouched and stepped into the archway of what was, as far as he could surmise, the last recess of the system in which Arabella could possibly have come to rest.

The two shuffled along the narrowing passageway in single file, Henry bent down and Des uncomfortably stooped. After twenty or so feet, Henry came to an abrupt stop and flatly said, "Shit."

"Yeah. Everywhere."

"No. I mean, look." Henry stepped to one side and Des to the other, so he could look forward, and saw that just ahead of them the tunnel was completely blocked by a fatberg. A solid mass of

43

congealed cooking fat, mostly deposited by London's finest West End restaurants, combined with an assortment of detritus and debris that had made its way from the city's sinks, baths and lavatories over the years. Feminine hygiene products, prophylactics, nappies and a colossal amount of wet wipes. The plastic based wet wipes, Des had once told Henry, were the worst culprits. They seemed to have a way of binding with the fat in a way that can make them nearly impossible to move or even break up. Often, especially in these larger tunnels, they would also contain larger flotsam that had been washed down from the streets through storm drains and other entrances – such as items of clothing, teddy bears, even small pieces of fly-tipped furniture. Des once claimed that he had found a king size mattress lodged in one, with the fitted sheet still attached, but even Henry thought that was a stretch.

"Well. That's that, then," Des sighed, sounding almost as disappointed and dejected as Henry felt. He patted Henry on the back, stiffly turned around and, using his own pitiful torch, lumbered back towards the main tunnel.

"I'll get some shots. Just for the record." Henry took out his camera and snapped off a few frames. As he clicked the shutter for the third shot, something in the beam of his headlight caught his attention. He took the camera away from his face and stared down at the bottom of the grey, glistening lump and saw, protruding from the mass, a lady's boot. He recognised it immediately, even with just the foot and ankle showing, as a knee-high boot with a Cuban heel. Lamb skin and made by Burberry. The exact same type of boot which Arabella had worn on the night of their tenth wedding anniversary. Not just the very same type of boot. The very same boot.

Arabella's boot.

Henry slipped the camera back into his satchel and, with eyes wide and as if in a trance, moved towards the boot. Arabella's boot.

Behind him, hearing nothing, Des felt a sudden twinge of concern. He managed to turn his head to face behind him and called, "Henry?"

Henry, entirely focused on the prize for which he had spent seven years searching, heard nothing other than the blood pulsing though his ears. His mouth dry and hand shaking, he reached forward and grabbed the ankle. He could tell, from the feel, that there was still a presence inside. In his heart, he knew it could only be her skeletal remains, but he still felt compelled to retrieve her. To, in some way, in any way, hold her again. He could feel his eyes burn and his cheeks moisten with tears as he pulled. It wouldn't budge. Henry placed his foot on a nearby ledge for support and readied himself for another attempt.

Des tilted his head, squinted and, thanks to the brightness of Henry's light, could see his friend gripping the boot. "Oh, fuck. Henry! For Christ's sake, don't do that!"

Henry pulled with all his might, barely hearing and certainly not registering Des's panicked screams. The boot moved. Slightly. Just a fraction. Then an inch. Then, as a stream of stagnant, malodorous water ran from around it, several inches. Finally, in a breathtakingly quick moment, the entire fatberg opened up around the massive hole the removed boot had left behind. A jet of rancid, fetid water and detritus knocked Henry off his feet and, as the jet became a torrential river, swept him back down the tunnel. Chunks of disintegrating fatberg crashed into and slipped past him. Each congealed, discarded remnant of human waste as stale and rotten as he had been warned.

Finally, Henry came to rest back in the crossroads of the trunk line, sitting on the floor with his back against the wall. Sodden and dripping, he looked up to see Des sitting opposite him. Staring at him with an utterly dumbfounded gawp. Like him, waist deep in waste. West end, Michelin star piss and shit. The effluent of the affluent.

After taking a moment to find his bearings, Henry remembered the boot. His prize. With a mild, teary-eyed smile, he held it aloft. He tried to shout, *Look! Look, I found it! I found her!* but his vocal cords were frozen. Whether through the excitement of the discovery, or terror from the fatberg flood, he could not tell. All he did know was that he couldn't speak. Then he noticed that Des's gawp had become a stare, not of any sort of victory, happiness, or even relief that their quest had finally ended in a victory of sorts, but rather despondence. Rebuke. Almost, Henry thought, fury.

Des flicked his eyes towards the boot, gesturing for Henry to do likewise.

Henry rolled his gaze upwards and saw that the boot was worn, not by Arabella, but by the leg of a battered, plastic mannequin.

Marion sat in her car watching as, nearly half an hour earlier than they said they would and moving a little sluggishly, the men re-emerged. She watched as they secured and locked the metal plate and then slowly, with hunched shoulders and downcast silhouettes, plodded their way towards her. As they neared, she started the engine and turned on the lights. Only then, when they were caught in the Fiat's high beams, did she see them glistening. Soaked through, dripping, and Henry with something that looked suspiciously like a long, dead fish dangling from his right hand. "Oh, not bloody likely," she muttered, shaking her head and shifting into first. She inched the car forward, rolled down the window and, as she drove past them, smiled sweetly and said, "You can take the fucking tube."

Chapter 8: Sonia K and the American

Five days a week, Monday through Friday, Sonia would smile her way into The Bald Monkey at precisely six o'clock every evening. Knowing exactly how long it would take her to amble from her gallery, along the towpath and up the hill, she would ensure that the last visitor was out of the door by half-past five at the latest. This would give her fourteen minutes to tidy the gallery and ready herself for the evening, ensuring that she would be locking up at sixteen minutes to the hour. A slow but purposeful walking pace would see her arriving at The Bald Monkey at precisely six o'clock. Sonia liked routine. Sonia demanded order.

Often, especially when she was hosting one of his shows at her terribly hip Camden gallery, she would invite her dear friend and neighbour Henry to join her in her favourite pub, and he would always decline on the grounds of 'not being a pub person'. Which Sonia always found a little weak and a lot disingenuous since, when they met back in the 1990s at St Martins Art School, she and Henry spent most of their time and all of their grant money in the den of reprobates that was Soho's Coach and Horses. It wasn't until he met and married Arabella that he began to shun the public house in favour of trendy wine bars and private members' clubs.

Sans Henry, Sonia would perch on a stool at the bar and chat with the other locals and regulars. Almost always ending up in either howls of laughter or furious argument with Des – the life and soul of the bar whose forgiveness she'd valiantly championed when, following his disgrace, incarceration and release, Michael had threatened to ban him for life.

Upon arriving, Sonia would order a single Hendrix gin with Fever-Tree tonic, to be served in a goblet, half-filled with ice and three slices of cucumber. This she would nurse for half an hour before ordering a second, identical drink. Thirty minutes after that, she would switch to a medium sized Sancerre, which she would sip for twenty-two minutes, giving her the required eight minutes she knew it would take for her to stroll round the corner to her home.

At eight o'clock on the dot she would walk through her front door, ready to enjoy a gourmet meal, prepared to five-star standards, by her loving partner: a former tech investor from Seattle who had retired young and now found his joy and fulfilment as Sonia's adoring househusband.

This routine continued for nearly five years – until one evening, about six months before Henry and Des ventured down to the tunnels under The Embankment to retrieve a Burberry boot from a mannequin, Sonia arrived home at precisely eight o'clock in the evening to find there was no gourmet meal prepared to any standards. There was no loving partner. There were, instead, empty closets, a cleaned out safe and a set of keys on an otherwise bare kitchen table.

"At least the fucker left the keys", became Sonia's bitter jibe in the following weeks, while she propped up the bar consuming her three large gins and tonic followed by a bottle or two of whatever white wine was on special, between around six o'clock and closing time. Changing the locks would have been an expense she couldn't have afforded: as well as cleaning out the safe, the American had emptied the bank accounts. He had even managed to take out a six-figure loan on her house, forcing her into foreclosure and to move into the studio flat above her gallery.

Over the months that followed, Sonia conducted her own, private investigation into the mystery that was her American househusband – an activity for which she soon discovered she had an uncanny knack. Perhaps because it mostly required the two qualities Sonia had always possessed in abundance: tenacity and perseverance. The first thing she discovered was that he was, in fact, a Canadian househusband. The second was that the latter part of his description was invalid on account of him already being married without divorce to at least two other women – one in Ireland and the other in Australia.

The third truth she unearthed was that he was not a tech investor and that nobody by the pseudonym he used had ever even lived in Seattle. Rather, he was a convicted confidence artist from Calgary who, shortly before she met him, had served three years of a five-year sentence in a United States penitentiary for wire fraud. He had taken investors' money, failed to make the promised trades, lied about it and attempted to recoup the projected profits with other, high-risk dealings. He had failed. Miserably. In many cases, catastrophically. Homes had been lost, lives had been ruined and there was even rumour of a suicide.

The final reality, which Sonia had still to truly face, was that he had disappeared without a trace. Every lead, every clue, every hint of where he had gone just led to one blind alley after another. But still, Sonia was determined to, one day, find the American. The Canadian. The whatever he had become next – whose actual name was as meaningless as his current alias was untraceable. And when she did, Sonia had every intention of killing him.

Chapter 9: Something Deeply Iffy

Henry, Des and Sonia sat on their usual stools at the long bar. On the corner, with Henry at the curve and the other two flanking him at right angles. Both Des and Sonia were howling with laughter, Sonia with tears streaming down her face.

"And he kept the bloody boot!" Des yelped, finishing his tale of the previous evening's escapade. "I mean, mate. Why did you keep the boot?"

"It's a reminder of what might have been." Henry gestured towards Michael and pointed at his empty pint glass. "Anyway," he turned to Sonia and, in a desperate attempt to move the conversation elsewhere, brightly asked, "How did it go with Drew? He brought the photographs over. Yes?"

"He did," Sonia replied, her laughter dissipating and a frown of curiosity appearing in its stead. "He is an odd fish, isn't he?"

"Ha! Tell us something we don't know," Des laughed.

"What do you mean?" asked Henry.

The previous day, while Henry nursed his hangover and prepared for the debacle that was to be the tunnel search with Des, Drew delivered the first consignment of framed photographs to the Sonia K Gallery. A group of five portraits – three from Henry's Notorious Londoners project, taken a little over a decade ago for The Evening Standard's ES Magazine. As a general rule Henry hated portraiture, particularly those taken in the soulless confines of a studio. He'd only agreed to this selection, and a few others, to be included in his retrospective because they'd all been shot in the subjects' homes. Sonia had insisted that these five prints were included because they were all reasonably high-profile subjects which she thought she could sell for a song – particularly one of them – which was of the once, and very briefly, famous actor Magnus James.

James had starred in a highly successful mini-series in the early nineteen-eighties, in which he gave a stellar performance as a lothario stage actor torn between the women he loved and the morphine he craved. He won several awards and it seemed he was destined to become the next major star of stage and screen, until his next two shows revealed that James had not been acting at all and was incapable of playing anything other than himself: a womanising heroin addict.

Within a few short years, instead of a famous actor, he became an infamous boulevardier. That he had remained ever since. Even as a septuagenarian James still revelled in his own excesses and, more importantly to Sonia, his own ego. She knew that James would respond to an invitation to any gallery opening that featured his image – especially if the invitation included a handwritten note tantalisingly divulging that it was to be positioned in a place of prominence. She was also reasonably sure that when he saw that the print was a limited edition of five, each to be sold at a very respectable four and a half thousand pounds, he would not be able to resist buying one himself. Especially once sufficiently lubricated by the generosity of her free-flowing refreshments.

"Henry's insisting that, if we must have these portraits, they have to be in the basement," Sonia said to Drew when he arrived at the door with one of the poster sized prints held carefully in his soft hands. "This way." She took another of them and lead him into the gallery.

Drew followed Sonia, at her usual brisk and busy march, down the length of the main, ground floor space. At the end of the room a rickety, wooden stairway took them into the basement, which was about a fifth the size of the first floor and, designed as a butchery, still adorned with the original red and green tiling. As he gingerly descended, Drew noticed that the top of the set of steps were slightly separated from the wall.

Sonia, already down in the basement, saw his glance of disapproval and curtly said, "Don't worry. That'll be repaired before the opening. It's an old building."

"Yes. It is more than a little creaky."

"As I said. It's an old building. Now. Over here." She pointed to the back wall where she had leaned the photograph of Magnus James. " We're going to put this Magnus in the middle, and the one you've got at the end. Obviously, you can't hang them on the wall so you're going to have to procure some easels to display them on. London Graphics in Covent Garden should be able to sort you out. Can you handle that?"

"Of course."

"Good." She handed him a wad of notes. "This should be enough. But make sure you keep the receipt. You'll be returning them the day after the opening night."

Drew frowned and shook his head in what Sonia felt sure was a gesture of rebuke.

"Well, what the fuck am I going to do with five easels?"

Drew shrugged. Then, his resting face returning to a toothy smile, nodded his agreement. He took the money and ascended the stairs while Sonia watched and wondered, as she always did when they met, what exactly she made of Drew. They rarely interacted, except when she happened to visit Henry at his home during office hours – which was less frequent since she had lost her house that had made them neighbours. However, she had been present when Drew arrived in Henry's life, just over four years ago.

It had been late in the afternoon on the last day of the last show that Sonia had hosted for Henry. The exhibition had been focused around a photo essay about London's Victorian sewers that Henry had put together during the preceding year – which Henry had been using as a cover in the early days of his search for Arabella. As they were about to close and Henry was readying to load some of the many unsold prints into his Land Rover, Drew appeared and nervously introduced himself to Henry. He carried with him an old and battered copy of Henry's first photographic book from his war photography days. Drew explained to Henry, in a clearly scripted but

55

rushed monologue, that he had recently graduated from university and, although he had studied for a career in business, had become disillusioned with the idea. Some time ago he had discovered a passion for photography, primarily from looking at Henry's work, and he offered himself as an assistant.

Watching on, Sonia found the spectacle highly amusing. Henry had never had an assistant in his life – apart from when his sister-in-law used to help him out but that was just for fun. The idea of him telling someone else what to do was, to her mind, hilarious. She'd once heard him thank an automated checkout teller in the supermarket.

The idea did, initially, make Henry very uncomfortable, but Drew persisted. He offered to help Henry remove the photographs from the gallery and load them into the Land Rover and Henry hesitantly accepted. As they worked at striking the show Drew continued to pitch himself and eventually wore Henry down – most notably by offering to work at minimum wage and no travel expenses. This Sonia found astounding as, during the general chit-chat, it had come to light that Drew lived out in Watford. The tube alone would take up most of his income.

Perhaps he's not all there? she'd thought. And still thought to this day.

"What do you mean, an odd fish?" Henry asked, while Des ordered another round and charged it to Henry's card – as penance for the previous evening's underground shenanigans.

"I mean odd, Henry. Just plain odd," Sonia replied. "I can't quite put my finger on it. He's so... Earnest. So serious. And, Jesus, that smile."

"Yeah, I know what you mean about the smile," Des interjected, pushing the various beverages along the bar. "It's creepy. Looks like the fucking Joker."

"He does not look like the Joker."

"Brian Cox, then."

"Or Brian Cox! I think it's a nervous thing."

"Oh, nobody's that nervous," Sonia came back in, "But okay, never mind the smile. I mean, what is his story? Seriously. How long has he been with you now, Henry. Three? Three and a half years?"

"Nearly four."

"Nearly four years. I remember when he arrived at the gallery. Passionate about photography. Wanted to learn under you. Yes?"

"Yes."

"And how's that going?"

"Very well. He's incredibly well organised, a first class photo-editor and makes a superb cup of coffee."

"No, I mean the learning about photography bit. I know he's a great assistant, God knows you've come to depend on him enough, but what about the other end of the bargain? How's his own work progressing?"

"Fine. I gave him one of my old film cameras a while back. Olympus, I think. God knows, I wasn't using it anymore. He says he's getting on well with it."

"He says. But you haven't actually seen any of his work."

"He's not ready to share it."

"Not ready to share it," Sonia slowly repeated, leaning back, folding her arms and regarding Henry with a squint of suspicion. "You know I asked him to join us here for a drink today. After we'd finished hanging more of your photographs. He wouldn't come."

"He never does."

"Now that really is a bit suspect," Des chimed in.

"I gave up asking him for a drink or a meal after the first three months. Maybe he's just not a pub person."

"Oh, where have I heard that before," Sonia scoffed, rolling her eyes. "But, anyway. Let's recap. He never comes for a drink. You've never seen his work. What are you paying him, these days?"

"Same as when he started."

"You haven't given him a raise in four years?" Des bellowed." You stingy fucker!"

"Desmond!" Michael shouted, from the other end of the bar.

"He's never asked for one."

"Never asked for a raise?" Sonia's voice dropped an octave." In four years this young man has never asked for anything more than minimum wage. Has never, really, socially interacted with you. Has never asked for your opinion on his own portfolio which, after four years, must be reasonably substantial. I mean, Henry, by the time you were his age you'd already finished your career as a war photographer."

Henry just shrugged.

Sonia unfolded her arms, drained her gin and tonic, then leaned her elbows on the bar. She clasped her hands together, rested her chin on her knuckles and, while giving Henry a long, thoughtful stare, slowly declared, "There is something deeply iffy about this dude."

"You think there's something deeply iffy about every dude," Des replied, knocking back his tequila shot and gesturing towards Michael.

"He's got a point there, Sonia," Henry said, then added, "You never used to, you know."

"Yes, well. I used to have a home," she snapped. Then she squinted past Henry, and, with a bright smile, cheerily said, "Perhaps we should move to one of the booths."

"Why?" Des asked. "I thought you hated not sitting at the bar. Where the action is and all that."

"Usually, yes. But I suspect the action is about to come to us." Then she grinned, nodding towards the door and said, "And four sitting at the bar is a little awkward."

The other two turned towards the room. Sonia beamed with excitement while Henry heaved an exhausted sigh and Des let out one of his extra-long, mechanic's whistles as all three of them watched Marion stride towards them.

The four of them settled into the corner booth, with a bay window facing the street behind a bench seat and one of the pub's many, cut-glass mirrors along the perpendicular wall. Henry and Des ordered another round of their usual tipples with, at Marion's suggestion, a bottle of white wine for her and Sonia.

As if I wouldn't have ordered a bottle, anyway, Sonia thought. Silently disgruntled at having to now share.

"So. You got back on the tube okay, then? Not too busy?" Marion asked after a long, uncomfortable silence.

"Yeah, no thanks to you," Des huffed.

"Oh, you are joking."

"The tube was fine, Marion," Henry calmly interjected." We even had an entire car to ourselves."

"I'll bet you did!" Marion chortled, giving a slight snort that made Henry smile. "And, was it my imagination, or were you carrying a dead fish, Henry? Looked like a salmon."

"It was a boot," Des grinned. "Burberry, apparently. Lamb skin with a Cuban heel."

"What on earth did you want with that?"

"It's a reminder of what might have been."

Henry and Des went on to describe their return journey via the more conventionally traversed underground tunnels. Each one interrupting the other with his version of events. Des rebuking Henry for removing the mannequin leg and nearly drowning them in London's finest sewage, when he had been warned several times over the years that such large items being removed like that can often lead to the collapse of the 'berg, and Henry arguing he had been warned that it could happen sometimes.

"Sometimes. Not always," Henry insisted.

They argued on the issue for an hour or so, leaving Sonia and Marion to roll their eyes and grin at each other at the ridiculousness of two grown men debating the finer points of sewer investigation

60

etiquette. Until Des, without a word, finished his drink and left them for the bar.

"Where's he off to?" Marion asked.

Neither Henry nor Sonia replied. Instead, they watched Des, his head bowed, interact with Evan. His nefarious summoner, who now handed Des an envelope.

As Des walked past them to leave, pocketing the envelope containing his orders and cash payment, they gave him their customary goodbye nod which, as usual, he returned with red-faced embarrassment.

"Okay, then," Marion said." Ask no questions, as they say."

"Probably for the best," Sonia agreed, "And if you'll excuse me, I see the handsome woman and her pretty young boy have taken our usual place at the corner of the bar. I must go and remind them those stools are only on loan. Marion, I shall leave you the rest of the wine. Enjoy." She gave Henry a wink and a click of her tongue, while cocking her head, then upped and left for the bar.

Marion poured the remaining wine into her glass, which turned out to be slightly less than a dribble, threw Sonia a look of rebuke and gave Henry a sarcastic grin.

"I'll get you another," Henry said, offering her a soft smile. "It seems I'm firmly in the chair this evening, and I have a feeling we're both going to need some mental lubrication." Henry shifted to leave the booth, placing his hand flat on the table.

Just before he stood Marion leaned forward and placed her hand over his. Henry flinched and looked at her, as she looked back at him with an equally soft smile and gently said, "She's dead, Henry. She's not missing. She's dead. And she has been for seven years. And at the end of the month, on that seventh anniversary, as soon as the council office opens its doors, I'm going in there to make that declaration official. I'd much rather do it with you, but I'm doing it. It's time to lay her to rest. If not physically, at least in our hearts."

Henry nodded, feeling his eyes moisten and his teeth clench. He pulled his hand away, shuffled over to the bar and ordered the drinks.

Chapter 10: The Morning After

"Your shirt's on inside out."

"What?" Henry sat hunched at the red vinyl-topped bar of his favourite Soho haunt, sipping a proper English ale. One of the many pleasures he'd missed during the five months he'd just spent in yet another war-torn, failed state. That along with not being shot at. As he reached for the beer, he noticed the loosely open cuff of his tatty, Ralph Lauren shirt, the stitched seam on the outside. "Ah, yes. I didn't notice until it was already on and I was about to do up the buttons."

"Then why didn't you take it off and put it back on properly?"

"Couldn't do that. Bad luck."

"Come again?"

"Well, not bad luck, per se. If you put a shirt on inside out by accident, it's a sign of good luck for the day to come. But if you then turn it back the right way around, you've lost whatever luck was on its way."

"I see. And has any such luck come your way so far?"

"Maybe," he shrugged. "Too early to tell, really." Then he sat up straight, extended his hand and said, "Henry."

The girl nodded, bouncing a jet-black ringlet hanging over the right of her wide, dark blue eyes, and cheerily replied, "Marion."

Now, two decades and at least one lifetime later, Marion stood in front of Henry's collage while cradling an oversized mug of hot coffee. She focused on the early images, in which she featured more prominently. Noting that after the wedding photographs she appeared less and less. She stepped closer to the wall and homed in on the early picture of Arabella and Henry holding their hands towards the camera, showing off the wedding ring, with the London Eye framing them in the background.

"I thought I could smell coffee," Henry groggily said, and Marion turned to see him standing in the doorway. Still in his pyjamas with his dressing gown lazily wrapped around him. Marion smiled as she noticed it was inside out.

"Your assistant made it for me," she replied, adding in a whisper, "What's his name again?"

"Drew. You spent the night, then."

"You insisted." Marion nodded towards the sofa, on which lay a neatly folded blanket and a large pillow." Said I wasn't in a fit state to drive. Probably right, although I have to say I was in a more fit state than you. Do you drink that much whisky every night, Henry?"

"Is that any of your business, Marion?"

Marion shrugged, as if to say it wasn't and to imply she didn't really care." Coffee's in the kitchen. Still plenty there. I'll be out of your hair as soon as I've finished mine." Then she turned back to the photograph and continued, "I seem to remember you were a bit miffed about this one. Something about my reflection." She leaned in close and squinted. "Although, I have to say, I can hardly make it out."

"I don't know what you you're talking about." Henry turned to go to the kitchen, then paused and tentatively added, "You can stay for a while longer, if you like. Maybe have some breakfast?"

"Lunch, I think you'll find."

"Let's split the difference and call it brunch, then, shall we?" Henry retorted, then went to fetch his coffee.

Marion looked back at the wall, scanning the images and twisted her lips into a bemused grimace as she muttered, "Your very own shrine. Wouldn't you have just loved that, little Sis."

Henry insisted on showering and changing first. Then he realised that he didn't have any actual food in the house, which meant him having to go to the shops. By the time he even started to prepare the meal, brunch had become a decidedly late lunch. While Henry chopped and fried onions, along with potatoes, eggs and bacon, Marion sat at his kitchen table leafing through Henry's proofs for his upcoming exhibition. She stopped at one and gave a small, wistful smile.

"I remember you showing me this. When we first met."

Henry moved away from the stove and looked over her shoulder. A gaunt, heavily lined face with hollow, haunted eyes stared back at him. He looked to be in his early-sixties and held a battle worn machine gun in his hands, but loosely and without any real conviction. More through desperation and fear than anger. As if he would have been much more comfortable had the weapon been a stack of books.

Or a cooking utensil. Or a child. Anything other than a tool of death and destruction.

"Yeah," Henry replied in a dry, hoarse whisper, "Me too." Henry had shown the photograph to Marion in her flat, a few days after they had met in the Soho pub. The man had been Henry's guide for a few weeks on what was to be his final frontline assignment. He remembered that, in a previous life, the reluctant warrior had been a well-respected lecturer in humanities. Until the university was bombarded – after which he was taken to a crowded, shelled out football stadium and given the choice of either a gun in his hands or a bullet in his head. That had been about three years before he and Henry had met, when he had just turned forty. Before the war years had etched his face with deep crevices of unwanted and undeserved memories. Before he became Henry's guide. Before he was finally shredded by machine-gun fire while at Henry's side, saving Henry by taking all the incoming fire that had been spat towards both of them. Henry, still numb and in a state of confusion, had also taken photographs of the man after the attack. Images too gruesome for any publication. Too horrific for even Henry to look at again, after the first and only time he printed one of them – an image which would be forever imprinted on his own mind.

Henry remembered everything about the man, he'd told Marion all those years ago. How he had three children, all killed in the conflict. How he had not seen his wife since the day he was conscripted, but prayed for her every morning when he woke and every night before, when he could, he slept. Henry

66

remembered every detail – except the man's name. It was when he made that confession to Marion that Henry finally broke down. Fell into her arms and cried, uncontrollably, for what seemed like days.

"I'm off, now," Drew interrupted, snapping both Henry and Marion back into the present. "I put your kit together and left it in your office."

"Kit?"

"For tomorrow. The Thompson wedding?"

"Oh, bollocks!" Henry slumped back into his chair. He had completely forgotten. Although how the Thompson wedding, of all jobs, could have slipped his mind he could not fathom. Danny Thompson was an arrogant, self-important windbag who annoyed Henry intensely, but he was also a colleague to whom Henry owed much of his success. A former newspaper editor, Danny had employed Henry for much of his work, both as a frontline snapper and beyond. In fact, his final war zone assignment was for Danny – when he took the photograph of his old, nameless friend. Henry glanced back down at the soft, defeated eyes, then flipped the photograph over.

When he had set up his own business, Danny had been one of the first to hire Henry – for his own wedding. A lavish, high-society affair where the wealthy, the titled, the important and the self-important competed for favour with the recently ennobled Sir Danny Thompson and his aristocratic bride, Felicity. Many of the photographs were used in *Tatler*, *Hello!* and just about every glossy purveyor of social pornography on the pre-internet newsstands. Since then, and to their credit, Sir Danny and Lady Felicity had stayed loyal and regular clients. Over the years Henry had taken several family portraits, covered many a lavish birthday party, and regularly photographed all three of their children as they grew from spoiled little brats to entitled little shits.

Tomorrow, it was the turn of their eldest, Diana, to be married. Henry had completely forgotten and had arranged for Drew to spend another day helping Sonia set up for the exhibition. To arrive without an assistant wouldn't just make the job twice as hard, it just wouldn't look right.

"Can you get all the photographs over to Sonia before?" Henry asked.

"No chance. Most of them are still at the framers, and Sonia wants me to help her hang them. Plus I've got to go into Covent Garden and pick up five easels."

"Five what?"

"Easels. Of course, we could put Sonia off until the day after."

"No, we can't do that," Henry sighed, then muttered, "Well, we could, but it would be more than either of our lives are worth."

"Thompson," Marion chimed in." You don't mean Danny Thompson, do you?"

"His daughter. How did you know that?"

"I helped you out at his wedding, remember? God, that was an age and a half ago."

"That it was," Henry said, giving Marion a thoughtful squint. Then he leant forward and tentatively asked, "I don't suppose you're free tomorrow?"

Marion let out a loud laugh, ending with a louder snort, before she realised Henry was serious and, her eyes wide and mouth agape, replied, "Really, Henry?"

"Well, even if you could just give me a lift. It's out in the sticks and Drew's going to need the Land Rover."

"So, Uber it."

"I'm sure Sonia wouldn't mind putting it off another day," Drew interjected, sounding distinctly tetchy.

"And the last time I gave you a lift you tried to get back into my car while you were covered with half of London's excrement."

"I can assure you, Marion, the only excrement present tomorrow will be the human variety."

"Yes, I remember Sir Danny and his cohorts."

"There'll be champagne."

"And I'll be driving."

"You will? Fantastic! I'll really owe you one, Marion."

Marion opened her mouth to protest further, but then she caught Henry's sharp, bright eyes. For a split second she saw a spark. A roguish flicker that she hadn't seen for many years. She sat back and, matching Henry's earlier, mischievous squint, raised her palms in surrender.

Having successfully drafted Marion into assisting him for the following day's job and bidding her a good evening, Henry was feeling rather good about himself. He wandered down the road to The Bald Monkey. His intention was to enjoy a quiet, solitary pint – until, as he walked in, he saw Des sitting in his usual place at the bar, but looking pale and ashen. Small, Sonia sat beside him and, looking almost as perturbed, caught Henry's eye and beckoned him over.

"How is everyone?" Henry asked.

"Up shit creek, Mate," Des replied. "Well up shit fucking creek."

Michael, standing tall and stern faced behind the bar, passed no comment on Des's dry throated expletive.

Chapter 11: The Drummer Boy and the Ad Man

"Who's the new bird?" Evan asked Des, his high-pitched voice tinged with lasciviousness. He stared over at Marion who, from the corner table, was looking back at them, asking Henry and Sonia where Des was going.

"Nobody," Des replied. "Old friend of Henry's."

"She's fit." Evan handed him an envelope under his newspaper. "Make him pay or make him bleed. I mean it, Des. You need to go hard on this one, now. He's just taking the piss. Break his hands." Evan handed Des another package under the table: an old, rubber handled claw and ball hammer.

"Jesus, Evan. I can't do that. How's he supposed to pay you if he can't make a living?"

"Yes you can and that's not your fucking problem."

Des felt his mouth dry and his throat close as he quietly replied, "Come on, mate. You know I don't do that. Lumps and bumps. That's my brief."

"Yeah, well your brief's just been expanded. Mate." Evan's eyes flashed with a wild, savage flare. A flare that instantly died down to a glint as he took a breath. "Consider it a promotion, Dizzy." He patted the pocket Des had just slipped the envelope into and quietly added, "Comes with an extra ton."

Acid bubbled from Des's gut and into the back of his throat as he walked out into the night air. He waited until he was around the corner, and away from the streetlights, before opening the envelope. Inside there was a scrap of paper, on which Evan had scribbled an address using a thick, carpenter's pencil, along with six hundred pounds. A hundred more than usual. The envelope was creased and tatty. The wrinkled scrap of paper had been roughly torn from a spiral notepad, and the payment came in a random selection of denominations. Each note old and ragged. Grubby.

The address, which Des already knew, was near Broadway Market. Part of the Regent's Row estate that ran along the bank of Regent's Canal. It was about an hour's walk, mostly along the towpath, apart from the stretch that went over the Islington tunnel, so Des decided to take the journey on foot. The exercise would do him good, he told himself, but was really so he could get his blood pumping and his adrenaline surging. To get into character. Get mean.

The seemingly endless stream of speeding cyclists along the towpath did much to spur him on and stoke his rage, although this time he made sure to not prematurely lose his temper. The last time he made this walk at night, to the same destination but with less violent intent, he encountered one Lycra-lout too many. Des hadn't meant to actually hit him. He just thrust out his arm to give him a scare. And give him a scare he did, when the cyclist caught Des's elbow straight in his throat. At which point the bicycle flipped upwards and over them both, while the bicycle-boy carried out a backward somersault that took him straight into the canal. Still full of fury, Des had picked up the buckled pushbike, hurled it into the cut and then readied himself to pull the spluttering, thrashing cyclist out of the water to carry out a pummelling. He probably would have done so, were it not for the distraction of a group of youths who found the incident hilarious and were raising their phones to start filming a YouTube clip that, undoubtedly, would have both made Des an internet sensation and returned him to the clink. For a moment he thought they were kids from the local estate and made a quick lunge towards them, brandishing a balled fist accompanied by a mean glare. Then he saw how they froze with wide, terrified eyes and that one of them, a young man with bright purple hair, carried a portfolio case. He realised they were just some students from the local art college and not really worth the punishing. "Fish him out," Des ordered with a low rumble, pointing at the panicking cyclist who, exhausted and confused, had finally made it to the bank but kept slipping back in as he struggled to find purchase against the slippery flagstones.

Tonight, Des pushed on without incident, dodging the bicycles and just allowing each encounter to feed his frustration. Fuel his irritation. To turbo-charge his aggression and pent-up anger so he was cocked and ready to fire when, eventually, he arrived at the flat. There he marched through the front door, glancing up at the CCTV camera above a sign that read The George Orwell Building, secure in the knowledge that it had been disconnected some years ago. He stomped up the shabby, neglected stairs to the second floor and squared himself outside Flat 2a, from which the gentle, rhythmic sound of a snare drum playing along to soft jazz music emanated. Des hammered his massive, leather gloved fist against the centre of the door. Three slams, spaced about half a second apart, each giving the previous the moment it needed to reverberate around the apartment with both menace and inevitability. He stood listening. The drumming stopped and the music came to an abrupt halt. Des hammered again. Three more thumps. This time slightly harder. Slightly slower. Followed by a frightened silence. "Come on, Tommy," he called in a tired, firm voice. "Charlie Parker didn't turn himself off."

The lock clicked and the door opened ajar.

Des took a long draw from his pint, draining the last third in one swallow.

"What did you do?" Henry asked.

"Nothing," Des replied, waving his empty glass towards Michael. "I didn't do anything. I couldn't. I just had a word with him. An actual word, you know. Talking. Told him he needed to get the cash pronto. He said he had something coming up so I told him to lie low for a few days while I try and sort things with Evan." He glanced across to the darkest corner where Evan sat, pursuing his daily tabloid.

"I take it Evan is as yet unaware?" said Sonia.

"Oh, you reckon, do ya? I told Evan I'd done one hand because he'd managed to give me five hundred and I gave it to him out of the money he'd paid me. Didn't believe me, though. I mean, he took it, but he didn't believe me."

"How do you know?"

"I just knew, alright? I could see it in his snaky fucking eyes. And, because he said that next time

74

he'd pay me half before and half after the job's done. And next time he's gonna want a lot more than just breaking the poor kid's hands."

"So? Why don't you just tell the little pissant to sod off?"

"Because then I pay with my kneecaps, Henry."

"Seriously?"

"That's what he said. And, before you ask, yeah. Yeah, I believe him. Given where and how I met him, I believe him."

"Jesus, Des. I knew you were walking a fine line but... Jesus. You knew about this, Sonia?"

Sonia shrugged. She and Henry turned and faced the bar, while Des tensed, as Evan rose from his seat and swaggered towards them. Needle eyes on Des.

"Alright?"

"Yeah. Alright." They both nodded and Evan walked on, leaving the pub. Des let out a deep breath, turning to face the bar. Nothing on tonight. No need for a quiet word. Some time bought. Not much, but some. Maybe a week, until he's sent back to pay another visit to Tommy. Or some other poor unfortunate.

The three sipped in unison, then sat in silence. Each contemplating Des's predicament. Des full of consternation and regret. Wishing he could put the clock back to a time before Evan had come into his life. Before he'd lost control of himself with that poor estate agent. Before he'd lost control of himself and had that affair.

Henry searched his mind for a way he could help his friend. To help him get away from the whole sordid, sickening situation. To help him escape.

Sonia, eyeing the place where Evan had sat over her tumbler of gin, followed a more pragmatic train of thought and wondered if there could be a way to just remove Evan from the equation. To remove Evan altogether, she joyfully fantasised with an impish smile. It wasn't as if the world would ever miss him.

Henry caught Sonia's smile and, thinking the moment could do with a respite of levity, was about to enquire when a hollow, baritone laugh reverberated around the room – and he bristled. The other two shared a sidewise glance and Des, thankful for the distraction he knew was about to come, winked.

Henry swivelled around to face the room and glared over at the laughing man, his black designer suit stretched across his greedy paunch, who sat at a round table with three younger, thinner versions of himself. Henry ignored the sycophantic, grinning acolytes and just glared at the laughing man, noting the ridiculousness of his ornate, heavily tinted glasses in the dim light of the pub. Henry glowered at him – the owner of the Jag. The 1967, 4.2 litre, Series 1, E-Type Jaguar in British Racing Green. Mint condition, but permanently hidden away under a drab, if bespoke, cover. Outside Henry's house. Nose-to-nose with Henry's Land Rover. Terry. Terry the Ad man.

"Bastard." Henry hissed.

"Bastard."

"Fucking bastard." For the first time in the evening Des let out a chuckle.

"I'm going to go and talk to him."

"No, you ain't."

"Yes, I am. I'm going over there and I'm going to give him a piece of my mind."

"No, you're not, Henry. I know it. Des knows it. And you know it. You're going to sit here and you're going to stew. And you're going to drink. And you're going to complain and moan about your dastardly neighbour with the E-Type you say you hate but, secretly, you love, admire and, let's face it, covet."

"Covet's a bit strong, don't you think?"

"No, Henry, I do not think. Do you think, Des?"

"Not one bit, Sonia."

"No, not one bit. The main reason you hate him so much is because you yearn for that car and are convinced he doesn't deserve it."

"Well, he doesn't deserve it! It's just another investment for him. The only time he moves the poor thing is if he wants to show it off to one of his gullible clients or have it appraised. I mean, the man goes out to the country every other week and what does he do? Takes the bloody train."

"Maybe he's worried about the environment."

"Oh, don't be so ridiculous! He's in advertising, for Christ's sake!"

"So you admit it."

"I admit nothing."

"Well, there are many reasons to hate him," Sonia mused. "He is, as you have many times pointed out, obnoxious, rude, disingenuous, arrogant, loud and, generally speaking, an outright arsehole."

"Yes!"

"Yes. And, occasionally, he parks you in."

"Always."

"Often. Let's say, often, he parks you in."

77

"Often. As in, at this moment."

"Indeed. As in, at this moment. Which is why you intend to go over there and give him a piece of your mind. Correct?"

"Correct. Right after this drink."

"Right after that drink, dear Henry, you will have another drink. As shall I, as shall Des. And we will sit here and listen while you plan exactly what you want to say to your odious neighbour, and how you're going to say it. How you need to be firm and assertive – but don't want to come across as rude, petty or confrontational, so need to be as polite as possible. I mean, you are neighbours after all. You don't want to end up engaged in some sort of ongoing feud."

"Well, there is that."

"Yes, there is that. Which is why sometime into the fourth drink you'll decide that, perhaps, the best course of action would be to leave a note. Stick it on the car for the next time he uses it. Or, if you need him to move it immediately, pop it through the letterbox."

"Not a bad idea."

"It's a very good idea, Henry. You've had it many times. But you won't do that, either."

"I might."

"No, you won't. You'll think about it, when you're at home. Peeking through the blinds to see if he's moved it of his own accord. Peeping across at his house to see if he's still here or back in his country home. Then you'll give that awkward smile and little wave when you find that he is still here, happens to be looking out of his window at the same time and you've caught each other's gazes. At which point, as you always do, you'll wonder if that's a good opening for you to pop across the road and ask him if he wouldn't mind parking his car a little further back, just a few inches, so you're not parked in. But, again, you won't. Because, well, it would just seem a little awkward, wouldn't it. Is all this familiar, Henry?"

"No."

"Yeah. Oh, yeah. This is very fucking familiar."

"And then, one day, you will need your car."

"I'll need it tomorrow."

"Well, there you are. So. What will you do?"

"I'll have to go and speak to him."

"No, you won't. What will he do, Des?"

"He'll send Drew."

"You'll send Drew." Sonia raised her glass and, with a wink and a tongue-clack, clinked it against Des's, while Des let out a belly laugh and gave Henry a hearty pat on the back.

Shaking his head, Henry turned a sidewise glare towards his abhorrent neighbour, Terry the Ad Man, and again hissed, "Bastard."

Chapter 12: Something Old, Something New, Something Borrowed, Something Green

"What are you doing?"

"Drew's having Terry move his E-Type to get to the Land Rover," Henry replied, sheepishly peeking through the Venetian blinds. Marion came up close behind him and leant in to try and get a view.

"She is very pretty, you must admit."

"What? Who?"

"The E-Type."

"Oh. Yeah, I suppose so. Pity she never gets any exercise. Poor thing. Careful! You might get seen."

"Seen by whom? And stop whispering, Henry. We're in your living room, for God's sake."

Henry ignored her and concentrated on Drew talking to the odious neighbour – the latter wearing a brash silk dressing gown and holding an oversized, steaming mug with 'No1 Geezer' blazoned across the side.

Smug bastard, Henry thought.

Drew's head bobbed and his face came into the light – which gave Henry a start. He knew what Sonia and Des meant about that smile. All teeth and vacant eyes. Interestingly enough, Henry thought, just like the ad man to whom he now spoke and, astonishingly, laughed. He'd never laughed like that with Henry before. Did they know each other beyond the occasional move-your-bloody-car conversations? Is that why Drew never shared his work with Henry?

He'd been showing it to the ad man instead. Pitching himself as a commercial photographer. They were probably having a good chuckle about it now at Henry's expense. Oh, snap out of it, Henry. Stop being so paranoid. "That's Sonia's department."

"What's Sonia's department?"

"What? Nothing. He's coming back." Henry quickly moved away from the window. "Well?" he casually asked, raising his own cup of coffee – now cold, in a mug with nothing blazoned on the side.

"Fine," Drew replied. "He's going to move it now, then I'll be off. Unless you need a hand loading your kit into Marion's car?"

"Oh, that would be very kind of you, Drew."

"No, thanks. You'd best be getting on," Henry said. "We'll be fine."

Drew shrugged, flashed them a toothy goodbye and left. Henry moved back to the window and watched Terry move his car a couple of inches forward, cursing him for not having done that in the first place, and then the two shake hands. The pleasantry irked Henry, and he felt his blood near the boil as Drew climbed into the Land Rover which, momentarily, started up with a tired, throaty cough, accompanied by a blast of black smoke from the exhaust. The emission settled after a few moments while Drew sat still, allowing the ancient engine to crumble and mumble while warming up.

"Good God, Henry. Gertrude's sounding terribly bronchial. When was the last time you had her seen to?"

"Who?" Henry came away from the window and turned his attention to his kit, which Drew had

81

organised into two aluminium cases and a tripod bag near the door. As he inspected, he remembered, and gave a warm smile. "Of course. Gertrude. I'd forgotten you used to name cars. What's your Fiat 500 called?"

"First of all, she isn't just a Fiat 500. She's a Fiat 500 Abarth 659. The Ferrari tribute model."

"I am aware. 1.4 litre turbo. 2009, I think?"

Marion smiled, seeming impressed for a moment, and then gave him a suspicious squint. "You Googled that. Didn't you."

Henry mirrored both her squint and her smile. "Shall we get these loaded?" he said, looking down at the kit bags.

"I see your avoidance tactics haven't become any less transparent over the years. And, no. You can get these loaded, since you prematurely dismissed your actual employee before press-ganging me. I'll meet you in the car. Whose name, by the way, is Lilith."

"Because she's a demon on wheels?"

"Damn right."

An hour and a half later, having made record time, Marion snapped the gears back, pressed her foot to the floor and all one hundred and sixty of Lilith's horses galloped up Sir Danny Thompson's ornate, topiary lined driveway.

"Let's avoid making too much of an entrance, shall we?"

"What's happened to you, Henry? You used to be such fun," Marion jibed, then bit her lip when she saw Henry flinch. A line nearly crossed. She lifted her foot and Lilith's team shifted down from gallop to canter.

On either side of the freshly tarred driveway, lush green conifers stood tall – but tamed to the will of their owner. Each one's natural growth cropped and chopped to form a perfect cone. Uniform, depersonalised and strangely resembling a collection of oversized awards or trophies. Each had been decorated with white ribbons looped from tree-to-tree, guiding the guests to the top of the hill where the red-bricked Thompson Mansion stood.

"Jesus, Danny," Marion sighed with a smile.

Henry relaxed and they both started to laugh. Marion, again, lifted her foot and Lilith coasted up the end of the driveway through a Romanesque archway – also decorated with white bows. When they arrived at the front of the mansion, they found themselves streaming with tears.

The tears quickly dried up when, as they parked, they were greeted by a bouncer poorly disguised as an usher who leaned his wide-jawed face into the open window, scanned the kit bags and gruffly informed them that staff needed to park around the back.

Once parked in the stable yard, alongside caterers' vans and idling limousines, Henry unloaded the cases. Without missing a beat Marion opened them, checked lenses and mounted them to the bodies she knew Henry would require.

"I have to say," she said as she worked, "Drew really does do a good job of organising."

Henry agreed. But as he watched her couldn't help but notice how easily and efficiently Marion slipped back into the role. She seemed to know exactly the right pieces of kit he'd need and which lenses to match. In this case, two Leicas: one with a portrait and the other a wide lens. She also took out one of his backup cameras and suggested that she could take candid shots while Henry focused on the more formal. "Even though I haven't picked up a camera in an age and a half."

The lush front lawn, perfectly flat and mowed to exactly three quarters of an inch, played host to the early arrivals. Gaggles of groom versus clutches of bride. The bridal cliques all looked like cast members from a royal wedding: the women dripping with diamonds and the men donning the finest Savile Row suits. The groom's rabble, on the other hand, appeared to be straight from an Essex-based reality show. Shaved heads, necks so thick that none of them could quite do up their top shirt buttons and blue trousers straining around sinewy calf muscles – all wearing their Rolexes slung low and held slightly out for display purposes. They also, Marion noticed to her amusement, appeared to have found a surplus of moccasins while suffering from a shortage of socks. She was about to comment as much to Henry when she noticed that the back of a bulbous scalp nearby was tattooed with what appeared to be a perfect square. Marion raised the little Canon to her eye, zoomed in and saw that it was, in fact, a QR code. Again, she let out an amused snort and turned to share the moment with Henry, only to find herself alone. Henry had moved to a flock of the bride's guests and was charming them into a group shot of wide smiles and raised glasses. Marion turned back to the scalp with the intriguing square and, swapping the Canon for her iPhone, inched towards it. A zoom, a swish, and a series of cloud-based connections later a link opened up to the wild, psychedelic world of Show Us Yer Tats.

Marion flicked through the web page's images: goblins and ghouls, seahorses and sea monsters, brawny heroes and busty heroines. Marion was hardly a fan of tattoo culture but even she had to admit that the work was stunning. There appeared a particularly impressive image of a samurai warrior, fully armoured with his sword drawn and ready for battle, colourfully inked across a bronzed, muscular back.

"That one's mine," the smooth rasp was close enough for her to feel warm, peppermint breath against the back of her neck. She turned to face deep blue eyes under a shaved scalp – the back of which, Marion assumed, was QR coded.

"The tattoo itself or your work? I'm guessing it could hardly be both."

"You never know. I might just be that good."

Marion responded with an unimpressed head tilt.

"The ink's mine. The artist works for me. My shop. Show Us –"

"Yes, I saw. Classy."

"Innit?" he grinned, raising a flute and sipping. "You got any ink?" He flicked his eyes up and down, too quickly to cause offence but just slowly enough to make both his interest and his curiosity clear.

"I do not."

"Shame."

"It is not. I don't get on with needles."

"Oh, neither do I. Not the medical kind, anyway. Last time I got a shot I nearly fainted."

"Must have hurt, though. The tattoo, I mean."

"Like a bastard." He glanced at her camera, "You an influencer, then?"

"What? Oh, no. Just helping out a friend." Where is Henry? She took a furtive look about and saw him at the far end of the lawn, wrangling a party of bridesmaids into a gazebo.

"I'm Ron."

Marion replied with a polite smile, then glanced back to the gazebo and watched Henry directing the bridesmaids. Trying to set up that perfect shot he always sought. Looking from her angle, she reckoned he was trying to get the house in the background, with the green hill rolling down into the valley and the sixteenth century, flint walled church nestled below – where the service would take place in a couple of hours. She watched him gesticulating, almost falling backwards and, she knew full well, purposefully playing the fool to coax out genuine smiles. Including one from her.

"You've got great teeth."

"Jesus," Marion sighed.

"Mar!" Sir Daniel Thompson, a rotund and silver-headed incarnation of the dark haired and devilish Danny Thomson she had known a little under two decades ago, came barrelling towards her. "Marion, as I live and breathe."

"Alright, Danny?" Ron said.

"Yeah. Alright, Ron. Shouldn't you be looking after your boy?"

"He's our boy now, Danny."

"Don't remind me. And don't call me Danny. Now, piss off to the bar and get me a drink. Whisky. Something for Marion too. Glass of bubbly, Mar?"

"I'm working." She held up the camera. "Driving, too."

"Ah, that won't be for ages. Besides, Henry can drive you back. Can't you, Henry?" He looked past Marion's shoulder and she turned to see Henry close behind – his Leica with the portrait lens held up and snapping as she smiled. The camera came down and he asked,

"Can't I what?"

"Drive."

"Of course I can drive."

"Debatable," Marion snorted.

"I can drive you home, if you like," Ron chimed in. Moving close to Marion and holding a flute towards her. She instinctively took the glass by the stem.

"Where's my scotch, then? Never mind." A tuxedoed waiter came by with a selection of whiskies, vodkas and gins. Danny took one and, as he raised the glass to his lips, shook his head and said, "Plonker. Ron, here, is the best man and brother of the useless sod who's about to steal my precious daughter away from me. Also happens to be one of the most successful tattoo artists around. Apparently that's a very big deal these days."

"Actually, I'm not an artist myself. Just a canvas and a salesman."

"Yeah. Thinks he's the Ralf fucking Lauren of body art. Don't you have a groom with a hangover to go and look after, Ronald? Go on. Off you fuck."

Ron flushed slightly but, when Danny followed with a wry grin and a wink, replied with a soft smile while slowly shaking his head. He turned to Marion, gave her a polite nod with another smile that could only be interpreted as, 'I'll see you later', and headed towards the mansion.

"Subtle," Marion said.

"Na, but he's alright. And I was only half taking the piss calling him a wannabe Ralf Lauren. That boy's got a move or two in him with the sales banter." Danny drew a cigarette from a nearly empty pack with his blue, booze-bloated lips. "More than can be said for his half-wit brother."

Marion was about to respond when Henry interjected, "Well, perhaps we could get on with the job now. If we've finished flirting with the guests?"

"Say again, Henry?"

Danny grinned at the sharp exchange.

Marion raised her camera defiantly towards Henry and snapped a record of his confusion, before throwing him the same, sweet smile she had earlier offered Ron.

From the back of the immaculate sixteenth century church Marion snapped a few photographs of the crowd as the last of the guests filed in. One had Henry, standing off to the side at the top of the aisle, in her frame while he photographed facing towards her. She wondered if he'd mind her uploading that image onto her new favourite Facebook group, Photographs Of People Taking Photographs Of Other People. Then she realised she'd first need to explain to Henry exactly what Facebook was. The idea made her laugh out loud, much to the annoyance of the Duchess sitting on the bride's side a few feet away from her. As she winced an apology she clocked Henry gesturing towards her, pointing towards the approaching bridal procession.

Marion took another series as they passed her. In one of them Danny looked back at her and, with a fixed grin, raised his eyebrows. It was an expression that she didn't remember Danny ever wearing before, at least not when she knew him. It was, she thought, almost a look of vulnerability. Not an expression this much respected, but mostly feared, pit-bull of Fleet Street would be known for. She lowered the camera and smiled back. After they had passed, Marion let the camera fall to her side and, now away from any further action, became a mere spectator. She looked up to the groom and his best men – for some reason he had two, one of whom was Ron – when she noticed that his posture was a little off. Where everyone else stood upright with heads held high, the groom slumped. His head gave a wobble, then dipped to the point of hitting his chest, and his other best man gave him a sharp dig in the ribs. The groom reacted with a start, nearly toppling over and was only saved by Ron gripping his arm.

That's why he's got two best men.

Clearly, Danny hadn't been joking when he said that Ron had a hungover brother to look after.

He isn't going to make it. She smiled, guiltily excited at what terrible things might occur within the next few moments.

Marion's mischievous thought rapidly proved to be a terrible prediction when, as the bridal procession ended and the music stopped, the groom turned to his wife-to-be and gave her a wide, loving smile – which instantly collapsed into a grimace of horror before, within a microsecond, all colour drained from his face, his eyes popped and his mouth opened wide to release a torrent of viscous, fluorescent-green vomit.

Chapter 13: A New Day

"What kind of an idiot does that?" Danny asked. Finally calm.

"A man who doesn't want to get married. A man who doesn't have the guts to call it off and so, instead, self-sabotages."

"When did you get so wise and fucking deep?" Danny sneered. He poured another malt for himself and offered to top up Henry's glass. Henry shook the offer off: he'd had enough for one night, he insisted.

The two had been sitting together, alone in the ballroom, since the mass exodus nearly twelve hours previously. After Danny had looked down at his daughter's beautiful, elegant dress, drenched in a slime of semi-digested, lime-based cocktails and chilli chips, before swinging a right hook that knocked his almost son-in-law down into the aisle.

As Danny stood over the unconscious villain of the moment, Ron and the other best man holding him back, he looked down at the guests. All standing utterly motionless, staring back at him. At his befouled daughter. With a twist of his gut, he noticed the cameras. Every guest, each of the two hundred and seventy-eight of them, held aloft some sort of device. Phones, Cameras, iPads. Snapping, filming, streaming.

Christ, the streaming.

Could this humiliation be going out, live, cross the globe? Of course it could. Of course it was. He looked to the side and saw that the only person who didn't seem to be taking any photographs was the official photographer. His old friend, Henry. His only ally of the moment.

Danny felt his blood heating up again. He knew his face must have been beetroot red as he felt his cheeks burn. He stepped forward, ready to order the gawking rabble before him to fuck off home when, from behind him, he heard a quiet, mournful sob. He turned to see Di, his beloved first born, looking back at him. Utterly broken. He stepped towards her, took his jacket off, wrapped it around her and then, quietly and with whatever dignity he could claw back, marched her back down the aisle.

Twelve hours later, while Danny and Henry sat at the bride and groom's table alone, Danny doing his best to work his way through enough alcohol to intoxicate two hundred and seventy-eight guests, Di was fast asleep, he hoped, in her own, childhood bedroom – from which Danny had made sure to remove any and all devices that could connect to social media. On the table between him and Henry stood a small stack of memory cards, the only official images from the event.

"Should've asked. Marion get home okay?"

Henry nodded that she did.

"Can't have been best pleased about you dragging her all the way out here for nothing."

"I think she's just worried about you. You know what she's like."

"What."

"A worrier. She worries about other people."

"That she does." Danny's reply had a slow, knowing drawl.

"What are you getting at?"

"Well, I mean. We all remember how she looked after you after…. You know. After you got back from that last foreign job. When it went tits up."

"You mean the one where you left me in the shit after it all went tits up?

"Yeah, well." Danny looked down with what could easily have been mistaken for embarrassment by anybody who didn't know him. He then refilled his own glass and topped up Henry's, who this time made no objection. "Those are the risks, yeah? Anyway. What I'm saying is, she was there. Wasn't she? I mean, that's when you met her, right? And she saw you through all that shit."

"I suppose she did."

"And then you ended up marrying her sister."

"That I did."

"And how did she feel about that, Henry?"

"What do you mean?" Henry was beginning to lose sight of Danny's direction.

"I mean, how did she feel? You getting together with her sister, after she'd met you and spent all that time looking after you?"

"What are you talking about? She was thrilled. She introduced us, Danny. Got us together."

"Is that what she did. Matchmaker Marion, yeah?"

"Yeah. If you want to put it that way."

"Okay. Matchmaker Marion it is." Putting an end to the topic, Danny looked down at his iPhone, sitting next to the memory cards from Henry's cameras. "What do you think's going on out there, Henry? On the Internet. The World Wide fucking Web. Bad enough it nearly destroyed my business. Now it's going to humiliate me and my family. God knows how many of those snaps and clips are floating around out there in the ether. The cloud. The digital fucking abyss. Half of them being pushed to go viral by the Buzz-feeders, the Insta-Influencers and the Tick fucking Tokers. Some of those bastards have been out to get me for years. Just waiting for a chance to bring me down."

"Probably because, at some point, you fired half of them."

"Only if they deserved it," Danny grinned and let out a dry chuckle. "Which, I can assure you, was a lot more than half of them."

"Why do you care?"

"What do you mean," Danny's laughter trailed away, "why do I care?"

"I mean, look around you. Look what you've got. Look what you've achieved in your life. Why do you care what a bunch of strangers think, or what they post, about you?"

Danny leaned back and regarded Henry with soft eyes. With slow, deliberate thought he replied, "I care, Henry, precisely because I have achieved all of this. Built it up from the ground. From the dirt. From the shit. You know, I remember when we first met, Henry. I liked you straight off because you were such a go-getter. So gung-ho. You knew what you wanted and you wanted the front line. The action. The adventure. But it wasn't because you were hungry, or because you were desperate to pull yourself up in

94

life. You already had all that. The posh schools. The nice family. I mean, you live in your mum's old house. Yeah? Nothing wrong with that. I never resented that in you or anyone, never have, because it's exactly what I wanted for my kids. Only more. And, you know what? That's what I gave them. Through pure drive, determination, aggression and, yeah, I'm sure some people would say, a certain amount of cuntishness, I got that and more. This mansion. The flats in London and the villa in Spain. That's where my daughters have been brought up, while going to the posh schools, even posher than the one you went to, and I'm fucking proud of that. More than proud. I don't think I would have wanted to bring up a child in the shit-hole estates and streets I was dragged up through.

"So. When I see one of them, my precious Di, make the mistake of marrying a man who's just a step above where I came from but doesn't have the self-discipline to stay sober, or even just get moderately drunk, on the night before his very expensive and even more public wedding, it breaks my heart. And it angers me that, even though she's been brought up with only the best surroundings, her humiliation is going to be so public. She doesn't deserve that."

The two sat in silence for a moment. Then Henry reached for the bottle, topped up both of their glasses and replied, "Given the circumstances, I think we can both agree that you can be forgiven for your occasional acts of cuntishness."

The sky began to brighten, illuminating the pristinely set tables dotted around the ballroom, each place setting untouched, and Danny suggested they move outside for a round of sunrisers. They decamped to the gazebo, where Henry had earlier photographed the bridesmaids, and watched the sun come up over the valley. They looked down at the village nestled within and the little, flint walled church that now looked utterly tranquil in the cool, blue dawn. After a while Danny suggested that Henry should share some breakfast with him, but Henry thought he'd better get back. Aside from anything else, he was fairly sure that Danny's daughter would be waking soon and, more likely than not, be in need of some fatherly support. Danny concurred and said he'd arrange for his driver, Matt, to drive Henry back to the city.

Much appreciated, Henry replied, as he recalled the other melodrama of the wedding day. The side show that, in the interest of respecting Danny's disaster in comparison to his own minor hiccup, he had elected to not mention. But which now, as he watched Danny stroll up the hill and back to the house to wake and fetch Matt, he began to mull over and dwell upon.

"You didn't take any photos on your phone, did you?" They were standing beside Marion's car, about to load Henry's camera gear.

"No, of course not," Marion replied, slightly affronted as she handed Henry the memory card from the Canon. "Well. Just the back of the best man's head."

"Oh, yeah," Henry mumbled. "The illustrated man-child." As he was about to pluck the card from

Marion's fingertips, she pulled it back and curtly replied,

"What do you mean by that?"

"By what?"

"That. What you just said. About Ron."

"Ah. It's Ron."

"Well, that is his name."

"Yeah. Hasn't exactly covered himself with glory over today's proceedings, has he."

"Hasn't he? As far as I can see he's had a pretty shitty time of it, actually. He had no idea what his brother got up to last night, did you know that? Did you know that it was him who introduced them? After Di had visited his shop and he persuaded her not to get a tattoo across her neck because he knew her father would kill her and that she'd regret it further down the line?"

"Strange business strategy for the Ralf Lauren of body ink."

"What are you going on about? It isn't like you, Henry. Or at least it never used to be."

"Good point. How would you know what is or isn't like me, Marion? We've hardly spoken to each other for the last six years."

"And now I'm beginning to remember why."

"Okay. Let's just drop it and get out of here." He lifted his camera bag towards the back seat when Marion closed the back door.

"No, really. Why is it that you've taken umbrage against this guy?"

"I haven't, Marion. I'm sure he's a lovely person and that you'll get along famously."

"Jesus Christ. Seriously, Henry?"

"Seriously what?" He looked on, utterly bewildered, as Marion got into the car and started the engine. "Marion. What the hell are you doing?"

"I'm going home."

"What? Why?"

"You bloody work it out!" She hit the floor and peeled away, spitting gravel at Henry and swerving around the bouncer disguised as an usher.

The bouncer then approached Henry to retrieve the memory cards and said, "The boss was wondering if you'd fancy joining him for a drink. He's just put Di to bed with a fist full of Xanax and I've got a feeling he's looking to tie one on." Henry nodded: who could blame him. And suddenly, he felt he could do with a snifter himself.

By the time Matt was pulling up in front of Henry's home it was nearing lunchtime. Henry knew he should have been exhausted and hung over but all he felt was a strange combination of physical exhaustion and mental alertness. He was weighing up the options of lunch at home or down at The Bald Monkey, when spotted Lilith parked nearby. And Marion sitting on his step.

Henry thanked Matt for the lift, alighted from the Mercedes and joined Marion on the top step. After a moment Henry said, "You know, that's the second time his week you've given me a lift and then stranded me."

"Yeah, well," Marion replied, "The first time you were covered in shit and the second you were talking it."

"Fair point," Henry nodded. Then, with a stretch and a yawn, asked, "Pub lunch to make it up to you?"

"I could eat. And, by the looks of it, you need to." Marion stood while Henry groaned and forced himself to his feet. As they made their way down the hill he glanced over at his Land Rover, returned to her usual parking spot beside Terry's E-Type. Once again, nose to nose.

"Let it go, Henry," Marion gently cajoled.

Henry responded with long, tired groan and they continued down the hill.

Arriving through the doors of The Bald Monkey a couple of minutes later, Henry and Marion found Sonia sitting alone at the bar.

"Sonia," Henry smiled.

Sonia returned a sullen gaze, which she flicked back and forth between Henry and Marion. She'd been sitting at the bar, sipping a weak gin and tonic and trying to decide how she was going to deliver the information she'd discovered while they had been at the debacle that become the Thompson wedding. Trying to work out how she could tell them the deep secret she had unearthed. The identity of the person responsible for Arabella's death.

Chapter 14: All in Good Fun

Six years, eleven months and thirteen days ago, during the biggest storm that London had seen for nearly twenty years, a group of up-and-coming engineering students played what they called The Great London Treasure Hunt. While most sensible people were at home, hunkered down in their living rooms with heaters blazing and shutters bolted, these new friends, recently inducted into the elite Engineer's Collectors Club at their prestigious university, rose to the challenge of their older peers and set out to procure various items of engineering and historical significance from across the great city of London. These were to be retrieved and delivered to the group leader, dubbed the Chief Engineer, no later than midnight. Failure for a new member to deliver an item meant expulsion from the club, which had been in existence for well over a century and a half, and all of the privileges that it offered: mostly an opportunity to occasionally and recklessly carouse with a group of like-minded individuals. Members and, more importantly, former members who might be in a position to offer post-graduation employment.

The winner would be heralded the guest of honour for the rest of the evening's merrymaking, which usually went on until well into the following day. They would also have their item returned by one of the fellow participants, usually the person who came back with the least interesting artefact. It was, after all, just a bit of fun. No permanent damage was allowed and all 'borrowed' objects were to be replaced post-haste.

The first two participants both appeared with sundials from Greenwich. A most proletariat choice, the Chief Engineer judged, and far too easy for the challenge. Both suffered instant disqualification.

The third contestant presented an etching of the great paddle steamer, The London Engineer, which was built in 1818 and operated out of Nelson Dock. The framed etching, dated from the time of the ship's launch, had been procured from the wall of a pub near the dock – a tavern famous for its collection of maritime memorabilia. A pedestrian item, at best. Especially when it was discovered that the freshman was a local to that pub and friend of the landlord.

It certainly proved less impressive, and far less controversial, than the next prize: a blue plaque commemorating Isambard Kingdom Brunel. Nobody could deny that it definitely met the criteria, being both historical and engineering related. But the sheer audacity, the gall, the utter disrespect of removing such an item, even for this illustrious event, caused much concern. It verged on blasphemy.

The subject was still under hot debate when the final entrant, a known rising star amongst both his peers and professors, returned with what was immediately declared the winner. An artefact that more than exceeded both criteria, being both of great historical and engineering note. And the work that must have gone into acquiring it – the research to select such an apt example, the requisitioning of the special tools needed, the logistics in collecting and transporting such a heavy, awkward item in the dead of night. Particularly in the dead of such a dismal night. All were hugely impressed.

Although none of those who now applauded and celebrated him were surprised as he stood before them, leaning against his prize – a wrought iron, Victorian manhole cover from one of the original, trunk sewer hatches. The date on which was also the same as the year the Engineer's Collectors Club was founded. It hardly came as a surprise because anyone who studied with or taught him knew that this dynamic young man, this fountainhead, was as ambitious as he was charming, gifted and imaginative.

They all knew that Drew was destined for greatness.

Henry sat still. Silent. Pale. Marion beside him, shaking. Tightly gripping his hand. Her fingernails almost drawing blood. Sonia, having told what she'd discovered but not yet how, sat facing them. Equally still. Waiting.

Finally, Henry spoke. "I'm going to kill him."

Chapter 15: Sonia K, Private Eye

"You're not killing anyone and you know it," Des said, having been briefed on Sonia's revelations. He had arrived at his usual time, just before six, and didn't know whether to be more surprised to find that Henry, Marion and Sonia were all sitting together at the bar in morbid silence, or that there wasn't an alcoholic beverage to be seen. It wasn't until he jovially put the last wrong right by ordering in a round and received little to no reaction that he realised that something was terribly awry.

Now, having moved to the social shelter of the corner table and heard the same tale from Sonia that she had told Henry and Marion, he felt just as disquieted. Although, perhaps not quite as stunned. His recent years of encounters with villains and malcontents from across society's darkest spectrum had immunised him against any sort of shock regarding the depravities and dishonesties of human nature. "Trust me. I know killers and you ain't one." He glared across the room to Evan, who sat alone in his usual table in the darkest of corners. Then he flicked his eyes to Sonia as she was about to object and firmly added, "Either of you. Anyway, Groucho. How'd you find all this out?"

"I asked around."

"You asked around. What, you just went door-to-door and asked random strangers if they'd ever heard of some bloke called Drew, who you've always thought was a bit dodgy, and then, low and behold, someone said, 'Yeah. I know Drew, and you're right. Dodgy as fuck.', before spilling the beans."

"First of all, Dizzy, there was nothing random about it. When you spend the better part of three years attempting to chase down the whereabouts and identity of a missing ex-husband who's taken you for all your worth you do pick up a trick or two when it comes to the art of investigation. And second of all, it wasn't a bloke who spilt the beans. It was his ex-girlfriend."

This slightly took the wind out of Des's sails who, failing to think of a response, engaged his mouth by sucking down a couple of inches of his snakebite and thoughtfully swilling it around his mouth.

The new revelation further intrigued Henry who, in the five years he had worked for him, had never been aware of Drew ever having a girlfriend. The relationship, Sonia explained, had been over for some time before Drew arrived in Henry's life. And the girl in question had been with Drew on the night of the storm. Indeed, she was one of the students participating in the ill-fated treasure hunt. The one who'd appeared with Brunel's blue plaque.

Her name was Gail. The two woke up together the next morning in Drew's flat, having celebrated Drew's victory while commiserating her failure. It had fallen upon her, as the loser and as punishment for her heresy, to return all of the bits of loot to their proper places. The couple looked across the room to where the bounty was stacked – her with dejection and Drew swelled with far too much pride for her liking.

However, being a man in love who knew his place, he agreed to help her through her day's chores. They thought it best to wait until nightfall to replace the more illicit thefts, such as her plaque and his manhole cover, and decided to return the sundials and the etching during the day. The etching around noon so they could enjoy a pub lunch. It was as they made their plans that they both received text messages from the Chief Engineer: 'Have you read the news? Get over here asap'. There was a link attached.

According to Gail, Drew sat still, cross legged with head bowed, staring down at his phone for what seemed like hours. Reading and re-reading the story. Double checking the address. Was it really the same manhole cover? Reviewing the timeline and dates. Could it be an old story, sent by one of his fellow students to wind him up? Was it even a real story? Or fake news. He prayed for fake news as he followed various threads and sources. He checked, double checked, countlessly checked them all. All the same. All the same story. Throughout the hours he sat more stories emerged, with further details and descriptions of the vanished woman and her distraught husband.

Then he came to the updated story on the Evening Standard site: not only their names, but a photograph of them. Eleven years old and taken on the day they got engaged. They looked so young, only a few years older than Drew was at the time, and dynamic. Hands clasped together, showing off the ring, with the London Eye in the background, framing them like a halo.

Only then did he shut off the phone, pull the covers up over his head and desperately try to will himself into unconsciousness. Maybe, just maybe, it was all some terrible, horrific nightmare from which he would waken. If he could just sleep.

Since Drew was obviously going nowhere, all those involved with the treasure hunt came to him. A group decision had to be made – one that had to be unanimous, the Chief Engineer maintained. He attempted to do so with a strong, stern tone of leadership but, according to Gail, his voice had such a crack it was as if puberty had reversed. This was when Drew finally sat up. They had to go to the police, he declared. They had to take responsibility for what was, he was sure people would understand, a genuine accident. A silly prank which had gone horribly wrong. Gail agreed. She took his hand, kissed him gently, and wholeheartedly agreed. They had to do the right thing. Even if the others weren't going to come with him, she would accompany Drew to the police station to confess and face the consequences. They would leave the others out of it, if that's what the others wanted. But she would stick with Drew.

Really? Asked one of the other students. Gail thought his name was Newton, but she couldn't quite remember. She'd only met him during these forty-eight hours and it was possible that they called him Newt, not as a shortening of his name, but because of his slightly amphibian features and greenish, clammy complexion. He leaned forward, narrowing his eyes, and went on to question the wisdom of going anywhere near the authorities. Even if Drew and Gail did agree to leave the others out of their confession, there would surely be some sort of investigation. Various interrogations and cross-examinations. The truth, most certainly, would out. And then all of their lives, their futures, would be finished. Stolen. Just because of one, silly mistake – the consequences of which none of them could really have foreseen.

The others reconsidered. Most notably the suddenly adolescent Chief Engineer. Even Gail, she'd admitted to Sonia with more than a little sense of shame, was swayed by the thought of facing the future with a permanently sullied reputation. She tried to convince Drew, but he remained adamant that they had to do the right thing. Until Gail pleaded with him. What of their future together, she implored. After the others left, she continued to beseech, to beg Drew to come around to silence.

Eventually, he acquiesced.

But over the weeks and months that followed the Drew she had met, the charismatic star of his peers whose intellect and creativity was matched by none, admired by all and envied by some, slowly disappeared. Melted away to be replaced by a morose, quiet, brooding doppelgänger. It started a few days after they had carted away the manhole cover, along with the other incriminating evidence, and thrown them into the depths of the Thames. To join his victim, Drew had said as it splashed into the water below Hammersmith Bridge.

In the weeks that followed Drew became obsessed with Henry Glass, the man whose life he knew he'd ruined. He went to the opening of the exhibition, which had gone on regardless of the tragedy that had occurred outside the venue's front door just a couple of weeks earlier. In her honour, Henry had said in his short welcoming speech. For Henry's sanity, the young Drew had overheard Sonia say to one of their mutual friends. Drew had bought a copy of the exhibition's accompanying book.

It was the same book which, three years later, when Drew appeared at the same gallery to ask Henry for a job, he had Henry sign. When Drew had told Henry what a hero he was to him. How he had always wanted to be a photographer because of Henry's inspiration.

The truth was, according to Gail, during those three years Drew's guilt became unmanageable, and his obsession with Henry unfathomable. He followed each and every one of Henry's professional activities. He neglected his engineering studies, and switched to a less challenging business course, in favour of messing about with cameras. Finally, he made a vow that his life had to be dedicated to making amends to Henry – even if Henry would never know.

Drew graduated by the skin of his teeth instead of the honours that had been expected of him. By this time his and Gail's relationship was long over, but they were still in touch. It was just a few weeks after his graduation that Drew arrived at the Sonia K Gallery – as it turns out for the third time – and asked Henry for the job. That was the last straw for Gail, when she finally broke off all communication. Because it wasn't a job that Henry was looking for, according to her. It was redemption. Worse than that – to her mind, it was a bizarre, twisted form of martyrdom.

"He was right," Marion finally spoke. "They should have gone to the police. They should have gone to the police then, and that's what we should do now."

"What would be the point," Henry said. "It was seven years ago. All we have is a second-hand story. A rumour, at best. And all that does is point towards an accident."

"It was a little more than an accident."

"Not to them. Not to any outsider."

"Yeah," Des came in. "Besides. Coppers are only interested in anything that'll up their stats. CPS is worse. There's no percentage in it for the plods or the suits."

"Jesus." Marion knocked back the rest of her wine. "So, what do you want to do. Kill him? I mean, actually, really kill him? We're not criminals, you know."

"He is."

"Oh, fuck off, Groucho!"

"Well, you are, Dizzy."

"Jesus Christ, I've got to see him," Henry said, more to himself than the others. "To work with him. Tomorrow. Tomorrow morning, he's going to show up at my house. My home. The one I shared with Arabella. And I've got to look him in the eye." He looked to Marion. "How do I do that?"

Sonia took his hand. "You don't," she said. "Don't see him. Not for a few days, anyway. Until you can maintain some sort of composure. Send him a text, right now, and tell him to come to the gallery. Tell him I need him to help me set up the show. It has the added benefit of actually being the truth."

Henry took a beat to think, then nodded in agreement. He retrieved his hand from Sonia to finish his drink and, as he slammed the glass onto the table, saw that Marion was gripping his other hand. Not holding it with affection, to either give or ask for comfort, but gripping it as if it were the edge of a cliff from which she was dangling. As if, should she let go, she would fall to certain death. Her knuckles, and Henry's flesh around her pressed fingertips, were bloodless and white. Henry was pretty sure it should have hurt, then realised his hand had gone completely numb. He took his free hand and rested it on hers, giving her a mild smile.

Marion relaxed her grip. "I need to go," she said. "I need to go home."

"I'll walk you to the car." Henry stood and, with nothing more said or to say, he and Marion left Des and Groucho.

Momentarily, Des took a large gulp from his snakebite, swilled it around his mouth and, after swallowing, leant forward towards Sonia and whispered, "You're not going to whack him over the head and bury him in the basement, are you?"

"No, Des, I am not going to whack him on the head and bury him in the basement!"

Des let out a dry laugh – which abruptly stopped when Sonia added,

"These things take planning."

Chapter 16: The Six Ps

"We're going to have a private party." Sonia told Drew, having summoned him down to the basement.

"Oh." Drew sounded a little worried. "Isn't it a little late to send out invitations?"

"Yes, well, I'm sure if we get a move on we can rise to the occasion. Meanwhile, we need to make a few tweaks to this space. Turn it into a VIP section. Of sorts."

"Okay." Drew's consternation increased.

"Problem?"

"No… Well, no. Not a problem as such. It's just…" He allowed the sentence to drift away and, staring up at the door, tapped his index finger against his pursed lips. Another little trait, like the smile, that Sonia realised she found deeply annoying. She wondered if it was one of the many tell-tale signs of a psychopath. She decided it had to be, then remembered that she was in the middle of a conversation and snapped,

"Well?"

"Well, it's just. I've been a bit worried about the basement section, as things are. Don't you think there might be some health and safety issues?"

"What? Health and safety? Health and bloody safety, Drew? What are you talking about?"

"The stairs."

"The stairs."

"The stairs." Drew paused, bracing himself for Sonia to contradict him. The only response he received was a cold, demanding glare that he could only hold for a few seconds without having to look down, when said, "They're very narrow." Again, he paused. He looked back up to see that Sonia's stare remained fixed, and so he continued, "And a bit rickety. And old."

"It's an old building. We've been through this."

"Yes, I appreciate that, but perhaps it might be worth having them fixed up, just a little bit, if you're going to use it for events?"

"It's also a Grade One listed building. I'm not allowed to have it 'fixed up, just a little bit'."

"Grade Two."

"What?"

"Grade Two. This is a Grade Two listed building." The nervous quaver in Drew's voice suddenly settled, and he added with a quiet sense of authority, "If it was a Grade One you'd be right, you wouldn't be able to touch any of the original fittings or fixtures without permission. But with a Grade Two you should be alright. Besides, that stairway is hardly original. Looks to me like it was added sometime in the nineteen-seventies."

"Okay." Sonia raised a hand. "Okay, Drew. I'll see what I can do. But it'll have to wait until another day. Meanwhile, I'm sure you're capable of being careful enough to bring down a couple of trestle tables and the easels. I mean, you were fine with the prints?"

"Of course, Sonia. It's not me I'm worried about. And, sorry if I'm seeming a bit pedantic. It's just..." Again, the sentence petered away, along with Drew's sudden flurry of confidence.

"Just what."

112

"Well. I just want the exhibition, especially the opening night, to go as well as possible. You know. For Henry. I know how much it means to him."

"Oh, I'm sure Henry's going to find the evening an overwhelming triumph and hugely cathartic." Sonia looked at her watch. "I'll be gone for the rest of the afternoon. You okay to handle this, now?"

Drew nodded.

"Good." Sonia ascended the rickety stairway and strutted down the centre of the space, her Western heeled cowboy boots clacking against the concrete floor. She flashed a look down the gallery to see that Drew was, already, fetching a trestle table and bringing it downstairs. Up until the previous evening she would have put it down to diligence, his personal loyalty to Henry and a solid work ethic. Now, she had no idea.

"Little. Bloody. Shit," Sonia spat as she filled her wine glass to as near the top as she could. "It's almost as if he's onto us being onto him. I wonder if he is. I wonder if he's playing us."

"For God's sake, Groucho, what are you on about?" Des asked. "And why are we sitting here in the corner when it's just the two of us? I miss our normal spots." He looked longingly over at the bar. A dark, rich length of oak with a row of eight seats – six along the front, one on the rounded corner and one on the short end, tucked against the wall. That was his favourite place. Where he could lean against the wall, rest his arm on the bar and hold his drink, while facing Henry on the corner and Sonia on the outside – because she needed the space for all those

113

big, dramatic arm movements. He looked at the rows of bottles against the back wall – behind Michael, who leaned across and spoke to some overly enthusiastic interloper carrying a Union Flag tote bag. Four shelves of bottles, all bright and polished, highlighted by the immaculately kept mirrors and lights behind them. Then he looked above them to three more shelves reaching all the way up to the coffered ceilings. All crammed with bric-à-brac and curios. He was sure he'd seen all that before, but never really taken proper note. Perhaps because he was always at the bar and just that little bit too close. "Bloody hell, it's like fucking Bargain Hunt up there."

"Bargain Hunt? What are you talking about, Dizzy?"

"What? Nothing. Just mumbling. What are you talking about?"

"Drew."

"Oh, Christ." He knocked back his tequila and slammed the glass onto the table. "Now look what you made me do. I've gone and taken my shot too early. Now I'm going to have to get another one. And I can't even just raise my hand and wave to Michael. Because we're all the way over here and I'm going to have to get up and walk all the way over there."

"Oh, the trials and tribulations we must face on a daily basis. And what do you mean, too early?"

"I always leave my shot until the very end. Right before the last sip of my snakebite."

"Jesus. You're beginning to sound like Henry. Look, I'm sorry that we're sitting here. It's just more

114

discreet, that's all. And from now on, until we finish, discretion is everything."

"Until we finish what?"

"Until we finish Drew."

"Jesus." He skulled the rest of his pint in a series of deep, angry gulps. Then calmly rested the empty glass next to its smaller partner. Then he inched forward slightly and quietly said, "Look, Sonia. Don't get me wrong. I want to end the little shit just as much as you do. Henry's probably chomping at the bit to see him six feet under. But killing people isn't that easy, Groucho. Not killing them and getting away with it, anyway. Trust me. I met a lot of people who've tried, and I don't want to end up back where I met them. If you know what I mean."

"I know you have, Des. And, tell me, what's going to happen when your vile little employer asks you to kill that poor drummer you let off so lightly the other day?"

"It won't come to that." Des looked across the room, to one of the smaller tables off to the side where Evan sat reading his red top rag – as usual, so crumpled he must have found it on the tube or retrieved from a skip. "Tommy's got his gig. He'll pay up, with interest, I'll square things with Evan and that'll be that."

"You don't sound entirely convinced."

Des fell silent. The massive man replied with nothing more than a diminutive shrug.

"What if I were to tell you, my dear, Dizzy Desmond, that I have an idea that could take care of Drew, solve your Evan problem and, perhaps, even alleviate a few of my own troubles?"

"I'd say it sounds to me, my lovely Sonia, like you've finally gone cuckoo."

"Not gone cuckoo, Des. Just cultivating a notion. Ruminating a plan, you might say. At least, the early stages of one. It'll take all three of us to actually make it happen. Possibly with some outsourcing to a trusted friend or two. All we have to do is be discreet, careful and, above all, adhere to the rule of the six Ps.

"Yeah, okay. On that note I'd also say that it's your round, Groucho. But since I'm now empty, you've got half a bottle of wine and Henry's fuck-knows-where, I'll hike my way over to the bar myself. Hopefully, I won't die of dehydration on my way there or need a sherpa to get back. Where is our boy, anyway?" He stood, collected his empties and was about to move away when he turned back and asked, "And, what the fuck are the six Ps?"

Chapter 17: London in the Snow

Arabella had always looked amazing in black and white. But never more so, Henry thought, than when it was snowing in London. The last winter they'd had together it had snowed for nearly a fortnight. Every morning Henry and Arabella would waken to a fresh, white blanket of silent softness covering the street view from their bedroom window. Henry loved snow. The muffled quietness gave him solace and the strange, flat brightness from a sunless sky gifted him a special kind of light that only appeared, at least in his city, rarely. And when it did it almost never lasted more than a day or two.

This winter, however, it stayed with them for a magical eleven days. With Henry, anyway. Arabella couldn't stand the accompanying chill. It gnawed at her bones, she would grumble. After the first weekend she could take no more and, once the incompetents finally freed the airports of ice, went to stay with a friend in warmer climes. Three weeks in Hawaii, she declared, would renew her spirits and warm her soul. Her friend always wintered there and had been begging her to visit for years so, given that London had become a suburb of the Arctic, this seemed as good a time as any. Three weeks seemed a bit long to Henry but Arabella made the point that if you're going to travel that far, flying nine hours to Los Angeles and a further five to Honolulu, and then yet another island hop to Maui, you may as well make the gruelling journey worthwhile. Besides, the first three days would be spent jet lagged in bed – and she'd be home in time for Christmas.

Henry agreed. Henry would always agree to anything that would help, please or bring happiness to Arabella. Although, sadly, she didn't make it back in time for Christmas. Her friend, it turned out, had other friends visiting for the holiday season. They'd invited her to spend Christmas and New Year in LA's Hollywood Hills. 'It would be fantastic if you could come over and join us', she had said to Henry on the phone, but Henry couldn't. He had various regular jobs over the silly season – it was always his busiest time of the year.

Arabella had forgotten. She'd see him back home on the third of January, not a day later, and promised to bring him back a bobble headed Hula girl for the dashboard of his Land Rover and an I Heart Hollywood T-Shirt.

Henry wore the T-shirt, now faded, riddled with holes and frayed away at the neckline, as he looked down into the developer tray and felt that magical day return – the day before she flew West. The unmanageable curl, a jet-black ringlet, balanced the natural frame of her face perfectly as it hung down from her black mink hat and nearly touched the collar of the chinchilla coat. An unpopular fashion choice, Henry among others would occasionally point out, but one that Arabella would rationalise by arguing that the outfit was a family heirloom, inherited from her grandmother, which had been a vintage piece even when she acquired it. It would be a shame to throw it away purely in the interest of some absurd

118

collective guilt trip plaguing modern society. Aside from that, she would add with a sly smile, these poor animals gave their lives just so that she and others before her could look spectacular. Surely, the sacrifice must be respected.

Her dubious, if heartfelt, rationalisation didn't always go down well but, as he looked at the print drying on the line, Henry had to agree that she did look spectacular. The high contrast of the textured coat, the black hat and ringlet. Arabella's piercing, daring stare straight down the lens. The bright, luminous whiteness of the snow-covered hill and bleached cityscape behind her.

Henry took the print from the drying line, shook off any excess water and then left the darkroom for the living room, where he stood in front of the collage. He paused for a moment, carefully studying the timeline and making sure he chose the right place. Momentarily, he located the general area – just after a series of party snapshots celebrating their ninth wedding anniversary, and just before a group shot of the two of them reunited at a black-tie gala with some Americans who had come back to London with Arabella. Henry pinned the photograph on the wall, stepped back and, for the first time since he had heard the news about Drew, smiled.

Satisfied, Henry looked over to his phone charging on the mantelpiece, next to the boot recovered from the mannequin, which he noticed was flashing. A text from Des: 'Where the fuck are you?'

Chapter 18: Cage Fight

Des sat back in his favourite spot, leaning against the wall with his drinking arm on the bar and his fingertips resting on his pint. He held his phone in his other hand, grinning as he watched a video.

"Anything good?" Henry asked, attempting to feign enthusiasm as he took his seat and waved towards Michael.

"Bloody awesome, mate. It's you. I'm watching you!" He turned the phone to Henry, who felt his stomach clench as he saw a shaky shot of Danny's almost son-in-law vomit, swiftly followed by Danny lunging forward and punching him to the ground. "I mean, you're only in the background, but mate. That's you, right? How do you know him?"

"We used to work together."

"Seriously? That's amazing. Publicity shots I suppose, yeah? Wish I'd known I'd have asked you for an autograph. God, he must have been well hung over for that old geezer to have been able to knock him over like that."

"Wait. Who are you talking about?"

"Sammy Roberts. Who are you talking about?"

"The old geezer. Danny Thompson. Known him for years. Who the hell is Sammy Roberts?"

"Seriously? You've never heard of Sammy 'The Speedster' Roberts? Well, allow me to educate you, my son." Des returned to his phone and began searching for other videos.

The first clip Des showed Henry was one of Sammy's early press conferences. Standing with his shoulders slightly slumped and his eyes low, at first glance he looked like a scrawny kid in a pair of baggy shorts. Until, upon closer inspection, Henry could see that rather than scrawny he was wiry. All sinew and muscle. And although low, his eyes were aware. Alert. Darting around the room, as if scanning for the nearest threat. The fight he was preparing for, Des informed Henry with a note of awe, lasted all of thirty-eight seconds. He moved with such breathtaking speed that his opponent barely got in a single punch before Sam Roberts cracked him a series of such swift, savage blows – a volley from his fists followed by a high, backwards kick – that he fell to the canvas without even raising a fist. Sam Roberts became Sammy The Speedster.

Des then showed Henry a montage of Sammy's career to date. A series of battles between him and a cast of equally sinewy young men either throwing kicks and punches or wrapping their limbs around each other, then twisting until one or both reached some sort of breaking point. It was sweaty, bloody, noisy and, Henry imagined, smelly. Des chuckled all the way through while letting out an occasional, "Oof! That's the way it's done!"

"Are there any rules in this?"

"Nah, none that really count for anything. I mean, you're not allowed to hit each other in the bollocks."

There followed a shot of Sammy speedily kneeing his opponent in exactly that region and declaring an immediate victory.

"And there's weight divisions. You know, like boxing. Your boy Sammy's a super lightweight. But he's got the speed of a lightweight and the strength of a light heavyweight. That's what makes him so dangerous."

Henry noticed that as his career developed so did the artwork on his body. In his early bouts he just had simple, blue-lined work. A star on his shoulder. On the other shoulder a more expertly drawn rendition of 'Pinhead', the leader of the Cenobites from the Hellraiser films. Henry would later learn that it was an attempt, in his early days before his speed became so legendary, to try and lure fans into nicknaming him The Hellraiser. Or The Cenobite. Instead, as anyone could have predicted, the crowd taunted the young rookie with jeers of 'Pinhead! Pinhead!' As he won more fights the jeers became cheers, his profile heightened and the tattoos became more elaborate. A pair of wings, after he won his first major belt, appeared on his back.

Henry had always heard that a person's tattoos could be considered a biography. Each one detailing or representing a milestone in their life. He wondered what Sammy's complete story was. What each etching represented – apart from the obvious ones, such as series of gold bands around his right upper arm. Each for a championship he had won. Although he did question why one of them, rather than gold, was jet black. He smirked when he noticed a small QR code on his neck.

"Sammy The Speedster," Sonia interjected as she appeared over Henry's shoulder, "What a legend!"

"Am I the only one who's never heard of this guy?" Henry handed Des back his phone.

Sonia shrugged, "Shall we adjourn to the corner table?"

"Oh, come on, Sonia. We're fine here," Des grumbled.

"We have things to discuss, Des. Plans for Henry's opening night. And as I tried to explain to you yesterday," she grinned to Henry, "Prior preparation prevents piss poor performance."

Des rolled his eyes while Henry gave a wide grin. The pithy phrase had been one of his mantras in his early career. One he would repeat constantly while preparing his kit for an assignment, checking and double checking that each piece of equipment was accounted for, in its place and properly cleaned. That every battery was fully charged. It was an expression he introduced Sonia to, two decades ago, when she was putting on his first show. Introduced her to and indoctrinated her with. Always remember the six Ps.

"Oi. Dizzy."

Des turned pale. They all turned to face Evan.

"A word."

Henry had been right about the pungency, although not its precise nature. He had expected the stench of sweat and adrenaline to waft from the cage. Instead, the fetor emanated from all around. As it does wherever a large group of people, particularly when dominated by men, gathers in congested proximity. He followed Sonia as she elbowed through the crowd, spearheading their way towards the front row on which she had insisted – while Henry kept a mental tally of the malodorous mix.

Sweat. Nicotine. Halitosis. All offset by a plethora of sharp, acrid deodorants and colognes.

Perhaps, Henry thought as Sonia finally stopped at their seats, he'd been focusing on the aromas in order to avoid taking too much notice of the onslaught of assaults on his other senses. As they moved down, pushing through an audience enthralled by the battles already underway, various faces scowled and threw him angry glares. Furious eyes and clenched, unshaven jaws – each sending similar messages. What are you doing here? Don't you fucking shove past me!

This is not your world.

Henry had never been a fan of crowds. At least, not since he'd spent so much time among the ones that were shooting at each other. Now, as he felt various clammy, hot strangers pressing against him from all directions, each one screaming with glee and excitement at two people who looked as if they were doing their best to kill each other in the name of entertainment, he remembered that the only thing worse than a normal crowd was a baying one. An excited rabble that could so easily be inflamed into an angry mob. A riot waiting for a trigger.

Henry had most definitely left his comfort zone at the door.

"What the fuck are you doing?"

Henry felt a moment of alarm, then realised the question had come from Sonia. "What do you mean? These are our seats, aren't they?"

"Yes, but you're not supposed to actually sit in them. People'll think you've never been to one of these before."

124

"I have never been to one of these before."

"Alright, but you don't need to broadcast it," Sonia said in what probably would have been in a hushed whisper were it not for the cacophony – which she immediately joined by leaning towards the cage and screaming, "Break his fucking jawbone!"

Henry stood and, along with Sonia, took a look around the general area and steps up to the exits. "Do you see him?"

Sonia shook her head. Neither of them had seen Des since, three nights before, he had been summoned from the bar by an irate and dangerous looking Evan. Sonia had traded a few texts with him about the evening. It had been his idea to come, since Sammy The Speedster happened to be on the ticket and, because of the wedding video, he had become convinced that he and Henry were now the best of friends. Sonia had acquired the tickets and emailed Des his confirmation. He'd promised to meet them there. If he could.

"He'll be here," Sonia said, sounding less than convinced.

The crowd rose again, both to their feet and in volume, as two more gladiators bounced into the ring. This was a lightweight contest, the division before Sammy's. His fight was to be the main event of the next series of bouts – making it, Henry realised with a touch of frustration, a long evening ahead. Although, as the fight seemed to be over within moments of starting, perhaps not as long as he'd originally feared.

Then, as the next fight came on, a strange feeling came across Henry. At first, he couldn't quite put his finger on it. His stomach seemed to contract. His legs stiffened, along with his neck, and he leaned forward. As one of the men hit the canvas, having been dealt a series of left jabs followed by what Henry thought was going to be a right hook but turned into a grapple, pulling them both to the ground as the one with the stronger hold finished off the other with a series of knee kicks to his chest, Henry heard himself shouting. Felt his own cheer of excitement. The rush. The trigger.

The next pair of warriors specialised in fists and kicks. No holds – although Henry was fairly sure that there was nothing in the rules to stop either of them changing their minds. It made for a bloodier and more savage affair, Henry thought. More exciting. Their fists, sheathed in only the flimsiest of fingerless gloves, moved at terrific speeds. Each one seeming to connect with a harsh crack and send out a red spatter – or at the very least a fine, pink mist. The one who Henry decided to support, for no reason other than he immediately seemed to have the upper hand, took a sudden step back, spun around and brought his bare heel into his enemy's cheek. The crack could be heard over even the loudest of cheers. Including Henry's, who accompanied his raucous scream by waving his own clenched fists.

The fights went on, one after the other. Each faster, bloodier and more brutal than the previous, until Sammy and his opponent came into the cage. The first thing Henry noticed was the sheer quantity of tattoos Sammy had acquired since the videos Des had shown him. Including a blood red, broken heart on his chest. 'D' on one side of the cracked symbol

126

and 'S' on the other. As he bounced around the ring, the way only a confident champion can, Sammy pointed at the new artwork and screamed, "Di, Di, Di!" Then Henry wondered if, actually, he was gesturing towards his opponent, only accidentally pointing at the broken heart as he swung his arm to-and-fro, while shouting, "Die! Die! Die!"

The second thing Henry noticed was the sullenness and seriousness of Sammy's adversary, who Sonia had informed him was called Mac. Mac was a relative newcomer and so had yet to earn a nickname. Although, going by his enormous height, Henry guessed it would end up being something along the lines of Big Mac. Or Mighty Mac. Or perhaps, as Henry also took note of his wide-eyed, unblinking stare, Mad Mac. As the two faced each other Mac lunged forward, teeth glistening and bared, and attempted to take a bite out of Sammy.

Mad Mac it is, Henry decided.

The third thing Henry noticed, just before the referee let them have at each other, was how desperately he wanted Mad Mac to win. He didn't know why, but every fibre in Henry's body, every ounce of his soul, wanted Mad Mac to lay Sammy The Speedster flat out and paint the canvas with his blood.

Mad Mac did not get off to a good start, finding himself pushed back against the cage as, within a split second, Sammy sprung forward with a barrage of punches. To call Sammy a speedster struck Henry as a colossal understatement. Mac brought his arms up defensively and moved to the side, swivelling backwards, and – in a moment that brought a collective gasp from the entire crowd – managed to get beside Sammy, catching him off guard, and land three mighty blows into his midriff. As he did so, Henry's thoughts began to blur. To fracture. Then to coalesce again, bringing a collage of thoughts from the back of his mind together with those in the front. Instead of watching Mad Mac and Sammy The Speedster fighting, he was watching himself and Drew. But instead of him being Mac and Sammy being Drew, it was the other way around. He could only see himself as Sammy and Drew as Mac.

He watched Drew towering over him, landing a series of terrible, devastating punches. Bloodying his left eye. Bruising his right cheekbone. Cracking his ribs. All as he stepped back against the cage – raising his arms and looking utterly dumbfounded at the strength of his opponent. Terrified. Then he heard the boos. The screams of anger and hatred towards Drew. And he saw himself being spurred on by the loathing. Strengthened by the hostility towards his enemy. He saw himself balling his fists and, with unimaginable speed and strength, hammering into Drew's solar plexus, throat and face. Pushing him backwards and down until he was on his knees. Then finishing him with one final, ruinous kick. Henry's face felt on fire. His eyes burned. His throat was raw from screaming as he watched Drew fall backwards. Onto the canvas. Out cold.

They shifted back from being him and Drew to Sammy and Mac. Henry was, again, just a spectator. Although he felt as if he had been in the fight himself. Exhausted and exhilarated. As the crowd roared and cheered Sammy's victory, Henry turned to Sonia and screamed, "Let's do it!"

"Do what?" she shouted back.

"Kill him."

Sonia smiled.

"Let's kill the fucker!"

Sonia beamed. She leant forward, put her arms around Henry, pressed her lips close to his ear and whispered, "Bloody hell, yes."

Henry turned back to the cage. He watched Mad Mac being helped up and Sammy stand tall, victorious, holding the belt he'd just been given. He watched Sammy then leave the ring to join his brother, Ron The Tat Man. He saw them embrace each other. Brothers in a moment of victory would.

And then, standing next to Ron, he saw Marion. Staring back at him.

Chapter 19: A Brief History of the Sonia K Gallery

Sonia wasn't sure exactly when the warehouse was built. Definitely during the height of Britain's trading years, when the East India Company was more powerful than the Empire and canals were the life blood of the country. The building was set apart from the surrounding structures as, where most were for imported goods such as silks, spices and cotton, shipped over from the colonies and then sent up the Regent's Canal from Limehouse Docks, the building destined to become her gallery was designed to house livestock. The flat Sonia now lived in was originally a hay loft, and the remnants of the winch used to lift bales could still be seen just above her bedroom window – which, as did the old hay door, ran from floor to ceiling. The animals, mostly cattle or sheep, would have been housed on what was now the main gallery floor. Back then Sonia's gallery and her three neighbouring businesses would have been one, long space. A massive barn with the animals held in pens on either side. The beasts would be brought in on the hoof from various local farms and held there until they were taken to be sold at the market.

That was the fate of all these short-term residences until the building's owner and builder, a Mr Colin O'Connor, whose name appeared on the farmyard animal themed mosaic above the modern gallery's front door, saw an opportunity to purchase and kill some of the livestock himself. He would then have the carcasses taken further up the canal to

Paddington where a colleague of his would collect them to distribute around new food halls in London such as Fortnum and Mason and Harrods, among other high quality, West End butchers.

The plan was a great success. O'Connor made sure to select only the best of the livestock that came in and quickly gained a reputation as one of the finest purveyors of meat in London. However, this led to some local resentments as, on a daily basis, they watched the highest quality beef and lamb being shipped away from them to the gluttonous West End. Heeding his neighbours and, being a man fond of a fine steak himself, O'Connor decided to convert the Northern end of his warehouse-come-abattoir into a local butchers. The ground floor he had tiled and fitted with various cold rooms and larders. But realising he had no more space for a room in which to carry out the extra butchery required, he looked downward.

The basement was designed and built specifically, and expertly, as his in-house butchery. The entrance downwards was large enough for the stairs, and also a winch with which to lower the carcasses. The walls were brick lined, then plastered, then tiled, as was the custom, for easy cleaning and to brighten the space. The finest decorated enamel tiles, patterned in traditional green and white, still adorned the walls even in Sonia's time. Everything about the space was spotlessly clean and designed to be kept constantly so. Including the floor, which was constructed in an almost imperceptibly shallow 'V' shape towards the centre where, under the central butcher's block, there was a large, square grate over an outlet. Where all of the day's blood, stray sinew and fleshy detritus could be easily washed away – at the time of its original construction into a rudimentary network, or possibly open ditch, that ran down into the feted canal.

"Why are you telling us this story?" Henry grumbled. He was sure he had other places to be and better things to do. He wasn't certain where or what they were, just that they were elsewhere and better.

"All in good time, Henry."

"So, he did alright for himself, then?" Des asked.

"What?" Sonia sighed.

"This O'Connor fella. He did alright for himself. I mean, with his own butchers."

"Yes, Dizzy. He did very well for himself. But it doesn't really matter."

"Yeah, alright. No need to be stroppy."

Sonia shook her head but refrained from further criticism. Neither she nor Henry had seen Des since he'd left The Bald Monkey with Evan. He never made it to the cage fight or the pub afterwards, where Sonia had ended up having to nurse Henry as he sunk into a vortex of angry binge drinking after seeing Marion with Ron. It shouldn't really matter, he'd repeatedly slurred to Sonia. It wasn't as if there was anything between them or ever would be.

A thought he continued to mull as he tried to listen to Sonia's tale. A thought that kept shifting to a perplexed, Ron The fucking Tat Man?

Now, the following day, they sat together in the basement of the Sonia K Gallery, sipping lunchtime hair-of-the-dog Bloody Marys while Sonia delivered

132

her, Henry thought, highly spurious history of the building.

"Des, this is for your benefit more than any of ours. A little background so you can fill in a few blanks and lend your expertise to the feasibility study on my proposed plan," Sonia continued with her history lesson.

In answer to Des's question about the entrepreneur's fate, Sonia went on to tell how O'Connor retired, sold his business for a King's ransom, then squandered his hard-earned wealth in the East End's gaming and whore houses before shuffling off this mortal coil in a state of syphilitic, abject poverty. In other words, according to Des's interpretation, he died happy.

Shortly after his demise, and by no means associated with it, London suffered what became known as The Great Stink of 1888. In response, the brightest minds and most talented civil engineers of the time were tasked with the vast undertaking of retrofitting what was then the most populated and important city in the world with a state-of-the-art sewage system. An elaborate network of brick lined tunnels, enamel tiled pump houses and iron pipes. A system as efficient and effective as it was overengineered, ornate and, in many places, stunningly beautiful. All so that, instead of simply running downhill though open ditches and drains to eventually end up gushing into the River Thames, London's effluent would be directed and guided through a labyrinth of underground pipes, tunnels and catacombs – before eventually ending up gushing into the River Thames. Just a few miles further out of sight and, more importantly, out of stench.

The area around and under what was to become the Sonia K Gallery constituted one of the very outer limbs of the fractal design. It was neither ornate nor beautiful – apart from the trunk sewer through which Arabella took her last and fatal journey.

The extra space for the winch was long gone. As was the butcher's block and the grate. In place of the latter was now a metal plate. Similar to the outside manhole cover, but square, and covering a parallel shaft that also led directly to the sewer.

"Yep. That looks and sounds about right," said Des, now crouching on one knee and peering down the open shaft. He held his torch in one hand and, straining under its weight, supported the iron plate, which leant towards him at a forty-five degree angle, with the other. "This one's square, though. That's unusual. Most of the old ones are round. You know why?" While speaking he stood, slipped and stumbled forward. He tried to regain his balance by leaning on the plate, thereby twisting it out of its groove so that its axis slipped across the wider diagonal of the hole. The plate dropped through and, with a series of receding clatters and bangs echoing from the shaft, plummeted into the depths of the sewer – ending with a distant splash. "Fuck."

"So that that doesn't happen?"

"Not funny, Henry. Des! You bloody moron!"

"Well, it's not my fault!"

"Whose fault is it, then?"

"Oh, this is off to a terrific start." Henry refilled his Bloody Mary, sat down and decided that, for a while, he'd let the other two get on with things while he'd just sit and watch. Watch and mull.

Sonia stepped forward and, along with Des, peered down into the open shaft. "At least we know it leads to the main tunnel. Did you hear that splash?"

"Yeah. But we're never going to get it back up here. Awkward fucker and it weights half a ton. We'll have to get someone to make a new one."

"Well, that may work in our favour."

"Why's that, then?"

"So that we can control when and how it collapses instead of allowing that to happen." Sonia pointed at the hole.

"I'm going to need more than that."

"Okay. But first, what do you make of that?" Sonia directed Des's attention to a pipe, about eighteen inches in diameter, which ran across her ceiling.

"Hard to say with all those layers of paint. Might be fairly old. Most likely put in when these buildings were converted into flats and the like. There's a lot more bogs around than there was, you know."

"And how easy would it be to sabotage?"

Henry smiled, finally catching on to Sonia's idea. He glanced over at the rickety stairs, the only way into the basement, and could see how easily they could be 'accidentally' collapsed. If, at the same time, the pipe above were to crack, then catastrophically breach, it wouldn't take long for the room to fill with sewage. And if the hatch leading to the trunk line, perhaps eroded and weakened after years of neglect, were to then give way, a vortex of sorts would be created. Sucking all in the room down into the sewer. Just as the flood did Arabella.

"Yeah. Not sure," Des sounded more sceptical. He moved closer and squinted at the pipe, then smiled. "There." He pointed at a connecting collar, which showed signs of discolouration and was slightly damp. "That's the weak spot. But I can't do this kind of work. Not making it look like an accident, which is what we're going to need."

"True. But you do know someone who could." Sonia sounded tentative.

Des couldn't recall.

"Someone who knows about metal restoration and therefore, I would assume, degradation?"

Des still couldn't recall.

"An old drinking friend of yours?"

Des recalled. "Oh, fuck no!"

"You know he could do it, Des. And he can deal with our sudden need for a replacement hatch."

"Absolutely not. He can't be trusted."

"Oh, you don't need to trust him. How much shady stuff do we know about him, back in the day? And, look at it this way. If he does help us then you've made him an accessory to murder. It all goes sideways you could stitch him up like a kipper!"

"If it all goes sideways we're all stitched up like kippers so let's have no more of that talk," Henry interjected.

Des let out a loud groan. "Frank bloody Roberts." He huffed. Then chuckled. "Chief of the Fat Fucks."

"Ha!" Sonia cried, before joining Des in
uncontrollable laughter.

Chapter 20: King Of The Belly Men!

"We are the Belly-Men!
"We are the Belly-Men!
"Belly-belly-belly-belly,
"Belly-belly-belly-belly,
"Chug! Chug! Chug!"

Following the traditional opening chant, during which each of them hoisted their shirts to bare and jiggle their protruding abdomens, the Belly Men would skull their pints and order refills. The keg – which, it was decided during their inaugural meeting, is the collective noun for Belly Men – had been meeting in The Bald Monkey on the third Thursday of every month for the last twelve years. The keg had formed three years previously and, in those early days, would gather in their founder's local pub in West London, just off the Edgware Road. However, their weekly events – and, perhaps more importantly, abrasive personalities – clashed with another regular drinking group of ostentatiously moustachioed gentlemen. After one altercation too many, when a Belly Man decided what fine sport it would be to carry out "a bit of a tash-bash", the keg was invited to find another premises for their monthly furores. The decision to choose a new regular meeting place fell upon the then King Of The Belly Men, Frank Roberts. Frank had recently moved to Camden and, on any evening that wasn't a third Thursday of the month, could be found sitting at the bar of The Bald

Monkey with his new friend, Des. The choice for a new venue was a simple one.

Des was a natural fit to join The Belly Men. He was a bloke and he sported enough of a beer belly to draw notice. Perhaps not as impressive a tank as some of the other members, Des was still a reasonably fit and active man in those days. But a tangible gut, nonetheless. And that, along with a capacity to drink, which Des had in abundance, were the only criteria required for induction into the keg.

Des would join Frank and the Belly Men every month. They would begin with their ritualistic chant, The Belly Man's Anthem, while showing off their extended paunches before drinking to excess. At some point in the evening the nominating ritual would take place, in order to see who should be inaugurated King Of The Belly Men. The present king would produce his extra large tailor's measuring tape, each girth would be carefully assessed, and he with the largest waistline would rule.

It was always Frank – for Frank Roberts was a truly stout man, and only getting stouter. Standing a modest five-foot eight, when he and Des first met Frank was verging on twenty-five stone. The only reason they continued with the nominating ritual was for the sheer fun of jiggling their jelly-bellies en masse. It was once proposed that, in the interests of fairness, the bellies should not be judged by girth but by recent expansion. Then one of the keg's more logical members pointed out that by the time those proceedings of the evening were reached they were not in a fit state to make such complex calculations and, anyway, Frank would still be a clear winner.

The riotous Belly Man meetings became the high point of Des's routine. A chance to break free from the rigidity of work life and, when he became involved with Angie, constraints of domesticity. A monthly opportunity to let off steam with a group of like-minded friends.

During his time in prison Des longed to be back at The Bald Monkey drinking, laughing and waggling his paunch to the Belly Man Anthem. He found it much easier to think of his stretch, not in terms of weeks or months, but by counting down the Belly Man meet-ups until he would be free to attend. Des was released ten days before a third Thursday and, still ashamed of his predicament, didn't dare cross the threshold of The Bald Monkey until he knew his portly palls would be there to lend support. On that day he waited until shortly after nine o'clock, knowing that most of the keg would be in session, and slipped into the bar. As Des approached the group Frank turned to face him, looked him up and down and, rather than offer the expected smile, frowned. Almost scowled. He then coolly pointed out that Des had lost weight on the inside. There was no place for a skinny ex-con like him in the keg.

Des looked down at his paunch, still reasonably rotund in his opinion, and flushed red with embarrassment. With shame. With disappointment and hurt. It was when he turned to leave that Sonia, then just a passing acquaintance of Des's, furiously interjected on his behalf. Telling Frank that, far from being of any sort of king to any kind of men, he was nothing more than a half-arsed Chief of the Fat Fucks. She then took Des to the far end of the bar, his former spot, and bought him copious amounts of alcohol while brokering a truce with Michael – who also held reservations about Des's return. Des was welcomed back, just not while the Belly Men were meeting – Michael didn't need that sort of trouble. And he had to start watching his language. Michael was now trying to attract a family clientele.

Frank stormed out, swearing he would never cross the threshold of The Bald Monkey again. However, the rest of the keg insisted that the meetings continue there and so, on the third Tuesday of every month, that was still where Frank Roberts, King Of The Belly Men, was sure to be found. And, until this day, Des and his cohorts were not.

"Fuck me. He's got even fatter."

"Desmond!" Michael rebuked, before looking from Des to Frank with a squint of trepidation.

Frank, sitting at the bar with the use of two stools, one for each of his massive buttocks, turned to face his former friend. He made no effort to leave his seats, although Des suspected that might have been more due to the effort it would have required than any sort of slight.

"Frank," Sonia politely smiled.

"Sonia. Des."

"Your majesty."

"Oh, for God's sake." Frank returned his attention to his pint, which looked more like a shot glass nestled in his swollen fingers.

"Where's the keg?" Des asked.

"Ain't no keg. Hasn't been for a couple of years, now."

141

Des quietly sidled up to the bar and took the seat next to Frank. "Why's that, then?"

'Well, you know what our parents used to say. It's all fun and games until somebody loses an eye." He drained the rest of his pint and picked up the next, one of two lined up. "Or has a heart attack. A stroke. Needs a new liver. Jack's still hanging on after his triple bypass. Doing alright, I hear. But Dan. Jimmy. Both gone within six months of each other. The others didn't see much fun in it after that. Nor me, really."

"So, what you doing here?"

"Having a pint, Des. What the fuck does it look like."

"Frank! For the love of God, you're as bad as each other."

"Sorry, Michael."

"On your own?" Des asked quietly.

"Yeah. Well..." Frank spoke with quiet embarrassment, "You never know when an old friend might drop by." Then he mumbled into his pint, "Even if he is a skinny fucker."

"Okay, that's it –"

"Oh, for the love of God, Michael!" Sonia finally snapped, "What is it with you and this puritanical stance against the occasional rude word? And don't give us that tired old chestnut about this being a family establishment. This is not a family establishment, Michael. I mean, take a look around you. How many children do you see in here? How many pushchairs or strollers? How many inanely grinning mummies and daddies with their shit-stinking, mewling babies and drooling, grubby

142

toddlers do you see? None, Michael. None of any of the above. What you can see are lonely, solo drinkers staring into their pints. The occasional assignation between couples, most of whom are meeting for the first time via some unsavoury app or another and are, quite obviously, married to other people. A few suits escaping from their office for a lunchtime swift half to get them through their miserable, meaningless day and, later, several to sign off on the end of their miserable, meaningless day while bracing themselves before having to get back home to their equally miserable, meaningless marriages. Let's face it, Michael. This is not a family establishment. This is an establishment to which people come in order to avoid their fucking families!"

Half an hour later, Frank sat opposite Des and Sonia in the booth which Sonia had only just managed to negotiate in lieu of a two week ban for her outburst – although a three-week restriction would apply to the long bar. Frank sat back staring at the other two, while digesting the bucket of chicken wings he'd been snacking on and the information which Sonia and Des had divulged. He'd listened to Sonia hold forth about the dastardly Drew's murderous act and ongoing obsession with Henry, who's life he had infiltrated for reportedly noble but, Sonia asserted, surely nefarious reasons – just as The Bastard Canadian's were when he'd insinuated himself into Sonia's.

Frank had nodded patiently while Des explained the minutia of their plan. How the basement of the gallery so closely resembled an oversized bathroom

143

sink – perfect for flushing away unwanted vermin. He took on board the happy coincidence that there was a sewer line with a degraded collar running overhead. Already on the verge of giving way so all Des would have to do was give it a little help. But some advice on how to do so undetected would be appreciated. He'd laughed heartily when Des admitted his schoolboy error of dropping the square cover into the shaft – then sat up, as best as his cumbersome physique would allow, while Des explained that it was with the replacement for this cover that they required the most assistance.

Finally, he'd listened to Des's flattering pitch. Frank was one of the best metal workers Des knew. The best he'd ever met. The work Frank had done for him had always been top notch. When Des had needed a new, bespoke collar to join a pair of Victorian pipes together, Frank had always matched the metal in order to ensure the minimum corrosion and maximum authenticity. When Des had needed a replacement for a sluice part that hadn't been made in well over a century, Frank had always been able to source an original replacement and refurbish it or, failing that, manufacture an almost indistinguishable reproduction. He had an encyclopaedic knowledge of period plumbing, a knack for acquiring rare parts and an unsurpassed skill in either repairing or reproducing almost anything made of metal. He was also a master of logistics for site work. Something else with which Des knew they would, undoubtably, need support. It was all of these that Des now asked him to utilise in order to help them with their, admittedly villainous – but most certainly justified – scheme.

The first thing they needed him to provide was a matching metal plate, identical to the one that Des had dropped into the sewer – but perhaps not of the same quality. One that had degraded. Corroded. One which had edges that, under just the slightest of pressure, would give way. Des also asked for his advice on the overhead sewer pipe. He could tell that the connecting collar was already corroded. Thick with rust under the paint but, he reckoned, still had a bit too much life in it for their needs. But how could they give it that last, gentle push?

Des had intended to ask Frank to come and have a look at it but, sitting opposite him, realised this wheezing, obese man was in no fit state to manage the stairs down into the gallery's basement – and the stairs were also in no fit state to manage him. They needed to last until the same moment of the sewer pipe and the sewer plate's collapse. The planned domino effect: pipe burst, stairway toppling, and the metal plate collapsing.

Frank listened patiently. Then, when Des and Sonia sat back, he pushed his empty chicken bucket aside, beckoned to the bar for another pint, grinned and asked, "Are you having a fucking laugh?"

Chapter 21: Tomahawk Steak

"Jesus, Henry. Do you ever check your messages? We've met with Des's portly pal, who it turns out is a very decent chap, and he's in. Sort of. Where are you? We haven't seen you for days!"

"End of second message. To delete, press…"

Henry pressed.

"Third message."

"You'd better delete that last message. You know, just in case. God, maybe we should get burners. Dammit. Delete this one too!"

"End of third message. To – Message deleted. End of new messages. To listen to your saved message…"

Henry pressed three.

"Hi. It's Marion."

Henry listened to the message for what must have been at least the fifteenth time. He had called her back as soon as he'd heard it – which, due to his woeful mobile phone habits, was a good thirty-six hours after she'd left it. This would annoy most people, but Marion seemed to take it in her stride. Perhaps because she'd known him well enough in the past and remembered his disdain for the electronic leash. She'd appeared pleasant but a little stiff on the phone, Henry thought, and seemed to speak very softly. Had he woken her up? Surely not, it was well past ten in the morning. Even he'd been awake for almost an hour. They'd decided to 'do lunch', as she'd irksomely phrased it, in a steakhouse on Dean Street. It wasn't licensed, she'd added. Would that be a problem? Of course it wouldn't, Henry had snapped. What did she take him for? There had then been a loud noise in the background, something like a series of thuds followed by a few cheers, after which she'd made a rapid and hushed goodbye. Where on earth was she? Nowhere. Just at a work meeting. She'd see him in Soho tomorrow.

A day later, with his mobile phone pressed to his ear, Henry sat on a bus stuck in traffic on Oxford Street. Were it not for the fact that he'd managed to bag the best seat – top floor, front driver's side – he would have been cursing the retirement of the Routemaster, which allowed people to exercise their own autonomy as to when to jump on and off the back in thick traffic instead of having to sit waiting for fifteen minutes while the bus crawled towards the official stop. Today he was content to enjoy the busy, London view beneath while listening to, ignoring and deleting the messages from Sonia – then returned to the saved one, left by Marion before they'd spoken.

"Hi. It's me."

A bit frosty, he thought. Or even annoyed. Vexed. Why would she be pissed off with him?

"Bit of a surprise to see you at the cage fight the other night."

A surprise for her?

"And with Sonia, no less. Is she a fan?"

No less. What's that supposed to mean? Why shouldn't he be with Sonia? They'd been friends forever. Or does Marion think they're more than good friends? And why does she care? And why do I care if she cares?

147

"Anyway. Henry, we need to sort out this Arabella business."

Arabella. Hearing Marion say her name caused Henry to shiver, even after listening to the message so many times. A strange, unfamiliar shudder. Cold to the skin yet bizarrely warm in his diaphragm. Almost comforting.

"I know it's not something you want to do."

Soft.

"Henry, it's not something I want to do."

Even softer. Kind. He smiled.

"But, it has to be done, so let's just get on with it."

Hard as nails.

Then a sigh, which made Henry lean forward and frown. Frustration? Exhaustion? *Is there someone else in the room?*

A loud clunk from the background.

There is someone else in the room!

"I have to go. Look, let's meet up, shall we? Tomorrow? But not at The Bald bloody Monkey. I have to go in to Soho. Well, I don't have to, but there's a sale on at Liberty, so I want to. If you like we could do lunch?"

'Do' lunch. 'Do' fucking lunch. Who really says that?

More background eruptions. A series of thwacks, a louder thump, and a small chorus of distinctly male sounding cheers. "Okay, call me back." The sign-off was particularly rushed. Almost breathless, and she didn't even leave enough time to finish the last consonant before hanging up. "Call me bac–"

148

All most perplexing, Henry decided, as the bus finally came to a rest and released its prisoners.

Ten minutes later he sat in a booth pursuing the Steakhouse's menu.

"Anything good?" Marion said as she appeared and sat opposite him.

"Lots of steak," Henry replied. "Sirloin from Argentina. Entrecôte from France. Kobe from Japan. Although it looks to be that it'd be cheaper to actually fly to Japan and eat that one there. Nothing appears to be local, though."

"Local meat? Henry, we're in Soho."

"You know what I mean," he grimaced with a squint.

Marion gave a laugh, that snort again, and the waiter arrived with a bottle of red wine.

"And I thought you said this place was unlicensed?"

"I was joking. How cruel do you think I am? Towards either of us."

"Are you ready to order?" the waiter asked.

"Do you have anything local?"

"Not really, sir. This is Soho," said the earwigging waiter.

"You know what I mean," Henry replied, a mite more tersely than he had to Marion.

The waiter smiled and, winking at Marion, turned the menu over to reveal a selection of Best British Cuts.

"What's a tomahawk steak?"

"That's for two."

"We'll have that," Marion interjected.

149

"Rare. Sear Sous Vide. And skin on the chips. Please." Henry handed the menu back to the waiter.

"Sear soz what?" Marion asked.

"I don't know. Sonia told me about it, apparently it's a thing."

Henry and Marion sat back, regarded each other with a moment of relaxed affection, and sipped their wine.

"So," Marion finally said, somewhat tentatively. "Shall we get into this before or after the food?" She gestured towards her bag.

"That's okay," Henry said. He opened his tatty leather satchel and removed a manilla envelope. "I signed the copies you emailed me."

"You check your emails?"

"Drew..." Henry faltered. He drained and refilled his glass. "My assistant. He checks my emails." He slid the papers across the table and smiled. "So. There you are."

Marion sat still for a moment, just staring at the envelope. Then she smiled to Henry and said, "Thank you."

"You're welcome. So. What do we do now?"

"You don't have to do anything. I go to Camden Council and file the paperwork. I mean you can come, too. If you like. I'd like that. But you don't have to. But for now, let's just enjoy our wine and our steak sozzle video."

"Sear Sous Vide."

"If you say so. How is Sonia?"

"Sonia's very well. How's Ron?"

Sonia put down her glass, looked at Henry with wide eyes and asked, "Oh, you are joking," before collapsing into a heap of laughter and snorts.

After what seemed like an epoch Marion's convulsions came to an end. She dried her tears, then broke into a minor relapse while gesturing towards Henry to bear with her. Finally, she regained her control of her paroxysm, dried her fresh tears, sat back and caught her breath while regarding Henry with an expression he gauged to be somewhere between disbelief and pity. Henry wasn't sure how long this process had lasted, but it had been long enough for him to require a top up of wine.

Marion then asked Henry, with as much lofty rhetoric as she could muster, exactly what he thought she had been doing at the cage fight with Ron? Henry couldn't, or wouldn't, answer, so Marion filled in the blanks for him. Work. Ron and she had, indeed, hit it off at the otherwise disastrous wedding, but not in the way that Henry had obviously thought. She had found his business interesting and, although not in the market for a tattoo herself, could see how his artwork was far superior to the average pale green scratches and scrawls and found them aesthetically fascinating. She also had the feeling he was a keen businessman with a savvy take on how to sell himself. The QR tattoo told her that – as well as showing his dedication to his business.

Marion was, and had been for some time, rethinking and, if she was honest with herself, regretting her career choices. She was looking for ways to branch out from or – rather, break free of – her current professional limbo, and had a feeling they could probably do some interesting work together. It was at least worth a meeting or two.

Henry responded with a nod and, eyes glazed over, an uncertain smile which caused another thought to strike Marion.

"Henry," she asked, "Do you know what it is that I do?"

"Well," Henry replied. "... It has been quite a while, Marion. You know. Since we've spoken. Properly spoken, I mean."

"Yes, it has. But, I mean, even before that. While Arabella was still alive, and you were with her all those years. Even back then, did you know what I did? Or, at least, what I was trying to do and what I actually ended up doing?"

Henry had no reply, at least none that he wanted to voice, because the truth was he didn't. Throughout their marriage Henry and Arabella's conversations about Marion had focused purely on the social and personal. Whether or not they were spending Christmas with her. If she was going to attend whatever party Arabella was planning next and, if so, would she be bringing a boyfriend this time. Occasionally, Arabella would say that Marion was having a difficult time at work, or was doing very well, and Henry would ask for elaboration. But Arabella usually – always – shifted the conversation elsewhere. As if Arabella's professional life was some sort of off-limit subject. Either uninteresting or unfathomable. And to his shame, Henry now realised that he had been just as uninterested. Worse: disinterested. To him, Marion was still the diligent photographer's assistant who could clean and pack a camera bag, specific to any assignment, in record time. Even faster and with better care than Drew had ever mustered.

Drew.

He shuddered. Pushed that dark thought back to the furthest recess of his mind, then focused back on Marion. And his shame, and his guilt and his embarrassment.

"Bloody hell. Is that the entire cow?" Marion rescued Henry from his discomfort as the waiter arrived with what did, indeed, appear to be a significant section of bovine midriff, hanging by a rib bone from a metal gallows. "Thank God, I'm starving."

They both watched with glee as the waiter had at the meat with a blowtorch using a technique that provided a spectacular sideshow and created a thick, crisp crust on the surface. He then expertly carved the steak away from the bone into small, manageable slices, revealing a tender, pink centre.

Henry salted his beef and, absentmindedly, threw three pinches of spilt salt over his shoulder, then knocked three times on the table. He then picked up his wine glass and looked up to toast Marion to find she was grinning back at him, on the verge of laughter.

"What?" Henry said.

"Nothing," Marion replied, clinking her glass against his.

As they ate, Henry mostly sat and listened while Marion, in light and breezy tones, elaborated on her career cul-de-sac and resulting frustrations. To Henry's ear, she seemed remarkably forgiving for his

153

lack of interest throughout his years with Arabella and beyond. As she began, he smiled, remembering the early days of her career when they first met.

Chapter 22: Smile and Dial

"Smile and dial," she'd said to him on their first encounter in the Soho pub, with a sing-song voice and a wide-eyed grimace. They'd exhausted the topic of his inside-out shirt and various superstitious ticks, he'd bought a round of drinks and so the conversation had moved on to Marion. She was studying fine art at St Martin's College. The same course Sonia had taken, as it happened. Also, the one Henry had considered but decided against on account of his profound lack of talent. To him, life's primary colours were most definitely the red, blue and green of the photographer as opposed to the red, blue and yellow of the painter.

"Smile and what?"

"Smile and dial. There's a sticker, on every phone, of an inane happy face with a speech bubble that says, 'smile and dial', in what Douglas Adams would call big, friendly letters. According to our supervisors, the person on the other end of the phone can hear it if you're smiling."

"And can they?"

"Probably. I'm pretty sure I can hear the death stares on their faces when I ask them for eight to ten minutes of their time so that I can subject them to a series of excruciatingly dull questions about health and safety in the workplace. That's this month's topic of disinterest. And I can certainly hear it deepening as the estimated eight to ten minutes drags out into a solid twenty to twenty-five."

"Well, if they know it's going to be excruciatingly dull then why would they agree in the first place?"

"Oh, don't be ridiculous, Henry." Marion had laughed, touching his forearm rested on the bar.

That had been the first time she'd touched him, Henry now realised as he revisited the distant yet suddenly vivid memory. He wasn't sure if he'd ever registered that. He was pretty sure he hadn't.

"We don't actually tell them, or even hint to them, that it's going to be in any way dull. Quite the opposite. Our intros are half a step away from neurolinguistics programming. Carefully crafted, using buzz words like 'important' and 'essential' to try and make these poor sods feel like they're a part of some crucial government policy in the making and that their input is going to help change the course of today's society. As opposed to the reality which is that it's a complete waste of their time and will hold no statistical value whatsoever."

Marion then went on to explain the banality and meaninglessness of her part time job which saw her spending approximately sixteen hours a week sitting in a cubical, surrounded by fifty or so identical cubicles, calling strangers from a list. At the time she met Henry she was on a government survey for the Department of Health and Social Care and would greet the person at the other end, always while smiling, with a scripted introduction that read, 'Hi. My name's Marion and I'm calling from SFA Marketing. We're speaking to a carefully selected group of business owners and executive managers in your sector about the impact and importance of upcoming changes in health and safety regulations. Would you be willing to help us out for ten minutes or so by becoming a part of the consultancy process for these new government proposals?'

She estimated that about one in fifteen people she called agreed to go along with the surveys. These could be divided into two categories. The first were the bored office managers who just fancied a chat. More often or not these were men, no doubt enticed by her soft, feminine lilt, so she would ask the questions in as sultry a timbre as she could muster.

The second category were the disgruntled, angry business owners. Many, she found, with a hard-line libertarian stance, who very definitely had views they wished to express on the issue.

"Health and safety?" they would reply. "Health and bloody safety? Let me tell you what I think about the Government and their new proposals about health and bloody safety!"

"Well, that's exactly what we'd like you to do." Marion would say, with utmost earnest. The sincerity in her voice assuring the angry businessman that she was most definitely on his side, as outraged by big government overreach as him, and ready to get his, and only his, message across.

Henry smiled, remembering how he had then smiled when Marion had first said this, with a wry wink and a second touch to his forearm.

"Would you like to continue?" she would say to the angry mark.

"Would I like to continue? You're damn right I'd like to continue! And I hope it's not anonymous.

157

Because I want these interfering bastards to know exactly who I am!"

"There is a section at the end when you can offer to give your details and any suggestions you may have. Now…"

And, Marion explained to a highly amused Henry, she would carry on with the survey. It was when they started to see through the third of the three lies in her introduction that she could hear the scowl deepening on their faces. When they began to realise that "it'll take ten minutes or so" actually meant "I'm afraid you're in for the long haul, mate. I hope you have a fresh pot of coffee in front of you".

"How much longer is this going to take?" would come the inevitable question instead of a one-to-ten answer, usually at about minute eleven or twelve.

"Oh, we're nearly there. It shouldn't be more than three minutes. Maybe five."

"Five? Five more bloody minutes?" The anger towards the deep state turning in her direction. "I thought you said the whole thing wouldn't take more than ten!"

"Well, it usually does. But most people don't give such well explained and detailed answers as you."

"Oh, I see what you're doing there," Henry had interjected, offering Marion as wry a wink as she'd given him. "That's very good. Very clever."

"Sneaky, I would say."

"Does it work?"

"Nearly always." Marion finished her drink and motioned towards Malcom, the octogenarian bartender who managed to simultaneously appear both grumpy and jolly, for another round.

"And what are the other two lies?"

"Come again?"

"You said that 'ten minutes or so' was the third lie. What are the other two, and when do they discover them?"

The first, Marion explained, was that they or their business had been carefully selected. This was purely a numbers game with a scattergun approach and these market research companies would pay handsomely for as many business details as they could get their hands on regardless of the source. They needed thousands, in the case of this project over twenty thousand, participants in order for it to be considered statistically significant. And by statistically significant they meant that it would have enough responses backing whatever agenda the government was pushing – leading to the second lie. That they would be "part of a consultancy process". What they were being part of was a public relations exercise to help the regime justify whatever plans they were pushing that season.

"In a recent government survey eighty-two percent of business owners agree that at least two workers must be in attendance when a ladder of more than fifteen feet is being used."

Well, sort of. In the early days of the survey the question read, 'on a scale of one to five, five being very important and one being not at all important, how important do you think it is for a second person to hold a ladder if it's fifteen feet or more?' Most people tended to reply one. Not at all important.

159

They'd then scoff and ask Marion, "What winging moron thought that one up?"

Then, in about week three, that same question read, "on a scale of one to five, five being extremely dangerous and one being not at all dangerous, how hazardous do you think it is for a person to climb to the top of a fifteen foot a ladder without a second person holding it?" The fear factor fed the participants' inner anxieties and the answers dramatically shifted.

"Never trust a government, or any other kind, of survey," Marion had advised Henry. "They're all based on emotionally manipulative bollox."

She'd then gone on to explain to him the other absurdities of her place of employment. It seemed to amuse her enormously that this was the only workplace where the pyramid of competence was inverted. In most areas of life, skill and experience drives an employee upwards. From worker, to supervisor, to manager. In market research, it seemed to be the opposite. The people on the phones, the smilers and diallers, were mostly very talented and bright individuals. Part time workers who were bettering themselves in other areas. At the time she met Henry she'd been there for six months. She'd met lawyers studying for the bar, several PhD students and, naturally, a plethora of actors on gardening leave. Most came and went, there for a few weeks or months until their studies were complete or opportunities in their chosen fields appeared.

Above them on the pyramid were the supervisors. All of them started out as smilers and diallers, but perhaps were not as talented or bright as

160

they'd hoped. What had started out as their part time job had become their full-time employment. One of them, Marion had been alarmed to discover, had started as a part timer – an actor waiting for a break = and had now been there as a full-time supervisor for just over ten years. A decade. The very thought had horrified her.

What horrified Henry, as he sat on the bus back to Camden following their blowtorched tomahawk steaks, was that Marion had just told him that she had now been there for two decades and had sunk to the rank of a senior manager. Then he smiled and looked out of the window, allowing the colours of London – the blues and greys of sky between buildings, splashes of green parks and flashes of red busses – fade away as he thought of the more recent example she had chosen to regale him with. The one which has finally pushed her to rethink her life and career. And which she had told him partly, he also suspected, to explain her presence at the cage fight.

"Tell me, Henry," she had asked, as the empty steak plates were removed, "Do you know anything about big data?"

Chapter 23: Big Data

Marion rarely sat in on the briefings, which were a scarcity in themselves and only took place for projects that were considered overly complex. But, having taken the previous day off to play at being Henry's assistant at the aborted wedding, she felt she should be seen to be busy and active in the workplace. She was the boss, after all. Second in command. Although she had no idea how that happened – a question she often contemplated, and increasingly lamented, in the wee hours of the morning. She stood in the corner of the room, a long, soulless vacuum with eight trestle tables pushed together to make one, massive surface. The two writers sat side by side in ultra-casual poses at the head of the table. The head writer with the chair reversed and her crossed arms resting on the back. Her co-writer at a twisted angle so he could drape his forearm on his chair's back and dangle his relaxed hand. To Marion's eye they both looked remarkably uncomfortable. Most of the other seats were occupied by twenty-five operators, the employees who would be making the cold calls and carrying out the survey. As always, a collection of artists, advanced students and, on the older end of the age spectrum, recent divorcees – all just trying to get by while focusing on their further ambitions or resuscitating their lives.

"Okay, guys," the head writer said with faux American undertones while removing her jet-black, knock-off Prada shades, "So, Big Data. We hear about it all the time but nobody really seems to know what it means. And the people who think they do seem to think it's a bit scary, or untrustworthy, or, you know, they just don't like it. So, the Department of Economic Development have asked us to look into it so they can come up with a way of making people feel a bit more comfortable about it all. Because, you know, let's face it. It's here to stay. Am I right?" She addressed the question to her unsmiling co-writer who, as if given some sort of cue, rose from his seat, took a stack of A4 scripts and began to slowly circle the room, placing one in front of each caller.

"So," the head writer continued, "I know we don't usually do these read-throughs, but this one really is pretty complicated stuff with a lot of technical terms, so you guys really are going to have to stick to the script and really be on the ball. Now, we reckon it should take about fifteen to twenty minutes, so we'll time it now as we go through it. Then you can ask us some questions, and I'm sure you'll have a lot of them. Okay. Ready?" Again, the question was addressed to her co-writer who, with perfect timing, was lowering himself back into his seat.

Did they actually rehearse that? Marion wondered as she started the stopwatch on her iPhone.

"Question one," read the co-writer, who had clearly attended the same mid-Atlantic elocutionist as his superior, "On a scale of one to ten, ten being extremely well and one being not at all, how well do you understand the term Big Data? Question Two."

It was at this point that Marion allowed her mind to wander, absentmindedly hearing that the second

163

question had something to do with fears and anxieties around large corporations collecting personal data. She remembered that when she met the writers during the early scripting stage, she'd suggested that perhaps instead of ten being 'very anxious' it should probably be 'fucking terrified'. Neither of them found the quip particularly amusing. Then again, none of her copywriters seemed to find anything terribly amusing. Probably because, she hypothesised, they only worked for her because they'd failed to make the cut for any decent advertising agency. She glanced down at the fake Prada glasses and allowed herself a smirk.

Real copywriters wear real Pradas.

She then looked around the room to see what sort of individuals comprised this collection of worker bees. Two of them she knew well. Both actors who had been working there on and off, in one case mostly on, for the last four years or so. There were a couple of new, very young faces whose bright smiles were only outshone by their brighter wardrobes. Both had joined her hive together and appeared inseparable. They were art students attending her former college, she'd learned from an overheard conversation, which gave her more than a slight shiver.

In the middle of the group was one man who sat very much alone. He had arrived early and taken a place at the head opposite the writers and rearranged the chairs so as to get rid of the chair that was beside him.

A man who likes his personal space. Marion silently related with staunch approval. His designer glasses, which were prescription and only slightly tinted, were most definitely not knock-offs. From the rest of his carefully sculpted and mostly black ensemble she guessed he was either in music, the production as opposed to performing end, or fashion. Guessing the actual work and passions of her worker bees was one of Marion's favourite pastimes. She'd make little bets with herself and, invariably, she was right. In this case, she decided that this guy, in his mid or perhaps late twenties, was definitely in the music world. And no doubt highly diligent as he seemed to be taking today's assignment extremely seriously, jotting several notes in the margins of his script. She decided that her bet today would be that, if she was correct and he was in music, she would return Ron The Tat Man's messages.

Ron had already left her three since they had met the previous day. A little bit keen for her liking but perhaps, she thought, that's just the way young single men do things these days. Marion estimated that Ron was about fifteen years her junior. Not that the age difference would make any difference to her. Serious, long term relationships were no longer of any interest to Marion. She thought they were until, a couple of years ago, she'd met a man and been almost convinced he might be worth making the big jump with. They went out a few times, went to bed several times and began to stay at each other's flats on a regular basis. Marion quickly found that she much preferred going to his place to him visiting hers. At first, she though it was just because he had such an amazing flat – he was a very successful stockbroker. It was several times the size of her place, with high ceilings and a balcony that looked over Tower Bridge.

After a few weeks, she realised that she much preferred her flat. His might have been bigger with a better view, but it was cold. Antiseptic. She would wonder if it had been designed and decorated by the same people who brought us such aesthetic masterpieces as the executive suites in the Marriott Hotels. Marion realised that the only reason she preferred staying at his place was that she could leave whenever she felt like it, whereas it was a lot more difficult to find a way of expelling him from her home when she grew weary of his company. Which seemed to happen far more quickly in month ten than it did in month two. It was in month eleven, however, that she realised the truth. He suggested that, since they had been together for nearly a year, she give up her flat and move in with him. Instead of feeling elated and excited at the prospect, as she genuinely thought she might have, she felt nothing but sheer panic. She rushed home, double locked the door, wrapped herself in her favourite blanket on the sofa and, while binge watching whatever American drama had caught her fancy that week, came to the realisation that the idea of sharing her personal living space with anyone else had become unimaginable. Not out of worry of it all going wrong, or fear of being hurt if she was left, but because, quite simply, she had yet to meet anyone whose company she enjoyed as much as her own – and, at this point in life, really wasn't interested in trying to. If there was such a potential partner out there then it certainly wasn't the stockbroker.

Ron, charming and handsome as he may have been, she could see wearing pretty thin after a very short time. He didn't, Marion suspected, have any appreciation of silence. Stillness.

But she was very interested in his tattoos, at least from a professional aspect. She appreciated the artwork. Some of them, both on the website and on the living canvas that was Ron, were quite beautiful. More importantly, they reminded Marion of her own artwork. Over the years she had kept up with her sketching and painting, mostly using pencil and acrylics, and her home studio was now crammed with fantastical characters and dreamlike landscapes from the depths of her imagination. None of which she had shown to anybody. Would, she wondered, they be suitable as templates or ideas for a high-end tattoo parlour such as Ron's? Her recent series of angels, in soft pastels with wispy wings and ethereal expressions, reminded her of a few of the examples on the Show Us Yer Tats website.

"Question twelve: How overwhelmed do you feel...?" The question drifted towards Marion as if it were a conversation overheard as opposed to one with which she was supposed to be professionally engaged.

Overwhelmed. A definite ten on the 'fuck, yes' scale. Permanently. About everything. But that's my business.

Marion glanced back at the suspected music producer, who continued to doodle on his script, and set the bet in her mind. If she was right, and he was a sounds man, she would call Ron and arrange a meeting. If not, she'd forget about the idea.

167

"Okay." The head writer chimed in as her colleague closed his script. "That's the whole survey."

Marion stopped the stopwatch on her iPhone. Twenty-nine minutes. *Twenty-nine bloody minutes!* How were her worker bees going to convince anyone to stay on the line for that long. And that was a dry run with no responses.

"So, does anyone have any questions?"

Marion felt her back straighten when her suspected music producer raised his hand.

"Go on?" the head writer said with an encouraging smile.

"Yeah, hi. I just thought I'd say that this is actually my area of expertise. I've got a BA and an MA in computer studies and I'm doing my PhD on this exact subject."

Damn. Lost the bet. Oh, well.

"Ooh. That's interesting. So what are your thoughts?" the head writer asked with a wide, excited grin.

"Well, I hate to tell you this, but everything you've written here is wrong."

Marion attempted to disguise her grin by sucking in her lips.

The head writer's smile remained fixed, but her eyes widened. "I see. Um. Well, just what do you mean by everything is wrong?"

"I mean, everything. As in nothing is right." The PhD student scanned his notes. "Even your terminology is... I've got to ask, did you make these words up? Because I've never heard of most of this jargon and I've been dealing with this subject for

168

over a decade. I've made a few notes along the way and I'd be happy to share them if you like but, really, as it is now, it just makes no sense and you're gonna get nothing out of this."

While Marion suppressed her laughter and the two writers sat frozen, faces still and eyes fixed on the newly discovered expert, a voice from the other end of the table rasped,

"Nah, mate. You're all right." It was Felix, Marion's least favourite of the supervisors. A scruffy, marijuana reeking twenty-something with glazed eyes and a baseball cap loudly inscribed with 'Victim'. "We're just here to do the calls."

God, how Marion wished she could fire him. But she was only a senior manager of the operation, not the owner – who happened to be Felix's uncle.

"Yes," the head writer agreed. "But thank you for your input."

"Alright, guys. At the desks in three and on the lines in five." Felix nasally droned before leading the exodus with a lazy shuffle.

Once the group had filed their way out, Marion sat down and began to leaf through the discarded script with the PhD student's notes. After a moment she pushed it aside in favour of her phone.

Bet be damned, she thought. And texted Ron.

169

Chapter 24: The Shooter

While Henry was returning from Soho, Des and Sonia had been sitting in their, now regular, booth, running through their usual topics of early evening chit-chat. Where was Henry? What was going on with him and Marion? Would he chicken out of the scheme? This was when Sonia suggested they make a wager – she maintained he'd back out, Des that he'd stay the course. Double or nothing if he leaves it until the big day. As they shook hands on the bet, Evan rolled through the double doors – throwing both of them open so that each clattered against the back wall, as was the little man's habit. His narrowed gaze swept across the bar, searching Des and Sonia's usual corner at the bar, then scanned the rest on the pub – finally locking on Des. Zeroing in on his target.

Evan weaved through the various tables and chairs, stopped in front of Des and demanded, "You. A word. Now." Then he turned, marched back to the doors and, again, threw both sides against the walls as he exited.

Des obeyed, without even looking at Sonia, and caught up with Evan across the street. "Everything alright, Ev?"

"No, Dizzy, everything is not alright. Everything is a long fucking way from alright. You want to know why?"

Des chose to not answer.

"Well, I'll tell you why. I was at Ronnie Scott's last night. You ever go to Ronnie Scott's, Dizzy?"

"Yeah, a few times. Angie used to like a bit of Jazz now and then."

"Did she. Well, good for Angie. Good for fucking Angie. Obviously she has better taste in music than she does in men." Evan lit a cigarette, took a long drag and then took another step towards Des. Close. "I went there with a fit bird last night. Big tall one. Nice legs." His sharp glare flicked toward the pub, then back up to Des. "Not as long as your friend Groucho's, but still. Not bad."

"Easy, Evan."

"Easy. Easy? Don't you fucking tell me easy, Dizzy! I fucking tell you easy! Do you hear me, you mountain of shit?"

Des took a step back, silently looking down at his shoes.

Evan matched him, moving further into Des's space – his size seven, patent loafers toe-to-toe with Des's size fourteen, steel capped boots. "Fucking look at me," he hissed.

Des obeyed.

"So, there I was. Ronnie Scott's. Nice bird. Decent drop of wine. Got a good bit of sirloin on the way. Always got a good steak at Ronnie Scott's. Almost as famous for their steak as they are for their jazz. And last night – what a line up. James Francis top of the bill. You ever heard any James Francis, Des? Ah, sublime. Fucking sublime. What he can't do with the ebonys and the ivorys ain't worth knowing. That's the reason I was there. But we showed up early, you know. For the steak. Soak up the atmosphere. Get a little booze down me bird's gullet, if you know what I mean. So there I am, ordering the second bottle of red. A Malbec, that one. Goes nice with the meat. Yeah. There I am, just about to order it, when a new band gets up on the stage. Local band. Bunch of old cats who've been around for years, and one kid. New guy in the band. A new drummer." Evan lit another cigarette from the end of his first, then flicked away the spent one and hissed, "Can you guess who it was, Dizzy? Can you guess who this new, young, little drummer boy was?"

Des felt his pulse quicken. His stomach contract. Although he didn't notice how dry his throat was until he heard his own voice croaking, "Evan. Let me just explain."

"Oh, please do, Dizzy-fucking-Desmond. Please do explain."

"Look, I knew about it. That's why I let him off. He told me about the show. And how much he was going to get paid. And it's enough to sort him out, Evan. It's enough to get him out from under and in the clear with you. With interest."

"Really. And why did you not share this tiny little tit-bit of crucial information with me, Dizzy-fucking-Des?"

Again, Des held back a reply.

"Because, you knew that wasn't your call to make, Diz. You knew it weren't your place to let him off. And you knew I wouldn't care. You knew it wouldn't matter because he'd already missed his deadlines. It wouldn't matter if he could have paid the whole wedge back the morning after I sent you over. An hour after I'd sent you over. Interest or not. You miss the final warning and you fucking pay with your bones."

172

"For Christ's sake he's a drummer, Evan. How can he make the money to pay you if you break his hands?"

"Yeah. And a damn fine one, from what I saw. It's a crying shame, but it doesn't fucking matter, Des. Those are the rules. Those are the rules and those are the rules for everyone. Coz if the rules don't apply to everyone, then they can't apply to anyone."

Both fell silent. Des still looking down at his boots.

Evan flicked away his second cigarette and continued, "Now. You, my dog-shit-thick friend, are going to make good on this, and mend the error of your ways." He handed Des an object wrapped in an oil speared piece of hessian sack.

Des felt the weight of the object. The shape. And the knot in his belly tightened like a noose. He unwrapped the gun. A small, snub nose revolver. The gunmetal worn and the handle chipped. "Jesus."

"Yeah, Jesus. You're going to take that and you are going to pay the drummer boy another visit. And you're going to shoot him in the head."

"Evan, wait."

"Not only that, but you are going to video this act of redemption on your phone. And you will do this, Des. Because if you don't kill the drummer then, I swear to God, I will kill you. Do you understand me? Dizzy Des."

"Yes."

"Then say it. Say it so I can hear you, loudly and clearly, so there can be no further misunderstandings."

"I understand, Evan."

173

"Well, halle-fucking-lujah."

Des wrapped up the revolver and slipped it into one of his cargo pockets. He looked to Evan and said, "That it?"

"Yeah. That's it. I'll give you some time to get your head around it, just because we're mates. But don't take too long, Diz." Evan then added, "And put a good word in for me with that Groucho bird, will you? You cost me a sure thing last night. I was so fucked off it threw me totally off my game."

Des's hands shook as he brought the second tequila shot to his lips and knocked it back while Sonia, with a look of captivation, examined the revolver under the table.

"I'm amazed. Who'd have thought that an oik like Evan would be a fan of real jazz?"

"Yeah. I did. He had a radio inside and that's all he'd listen to. Turns out he met Tommy at some jazz club up near Broadway Market."

"Oh, you are a plonker."

"Jesus, Sonia. Do you not get this? Either I kill the drummer or Evan kills me."

"Or." Sonia said, handing Des back the gun. "As requested, you put in a good word to me, and I invite Evan to the party."

Chapter 25: Heavy Metal

"Well, hello fucking stranger," Des barked as Henry approached the corner table. "Where have you been, then?"

"Elsewhere," Henry mumbled and took his seat beside Sonia. He threw an uneasy glance towards the corpulent newcomer who, he noticed with slight discomfort, took up the entire bench on the wall side of the booth and had an oxygen tank on wheels beside him. Des made the introductions and explained how Frank, an expert on welding, metal, metal fatigue, metallurgy and, generally, anything with the word metal in its title, including the musical stylings of Metallica and Iron Maiden, was going to help them with their pest control issues. Henry already knew most of Frank's background and role in their machinations from the various and increasingly detailed voicemail messages from Sonia. All of which he promised her he would delete.

Des handed the floor over to Frank who produced a portfolio case. Inside he revealed a series of sketches and plans that, in contrast to the slovenly, wheezing man who produced them, were detailed, precise and, to Henry's eye, quite beautiful. Frank started with the overhead sewage pipe. Although he had been to visit Sonia's gallery, due to his obesity he had been unable to venture down the stairs into the cellar, so he had relied on peering down from the top of the stairs along with photographs provided by Des – which, as further evidence of his meticulousness, he now included in the presentation. As far as he could tell these pipes had not been seen to for decades. This was in the trio's favour. Des had been right about the connecting collar. The metal had already become rusted and brittle to the point where it would need little more than a reasonably hard whack for the desired effect: catastrophic failure. All they would have to do is give it a "right old belt" with a lump hammer.

The manhole cover, however, was a more complicated issue. They would require the one which Des had managed to let fall into the shaft. This led to a minor argument which mainly involved Des bombarding Frank with a series of "are you having a laugh"s, and, "Oh, for fucks sake!"s.

Frank assured Des that he was in no way having any laughs and beseeching all the fucks in the world would not change matters in the slightest. That cover had been in place, Frank suspected, for well over a century. Its chemical compositions would have been built up over those years along with the rest of the room and, in the forensic investigation which might well follow a fatal accident, any decent examiner would be able to tell the difference between the original and a replacement. Apart from that, when the initial investigators found two covers at the bottom of the shaft it would send up a red flag that would be more akin to a solar flare.

When Frank made this last point Henry looked from Des to Sonia. Both nodded in placid agreement with Frank, but their terrible poker faces told Henry that, like him, neither of them had thought of this strikingly obvious point.

Natural criminal minds we are not. Henry shuddered.

Finally, Sonia asked Frank about the stairway, which he seemed to find hilarious. That wouldn't be any problem. A decent shove of the foot would topple it onto the middle of the room. He was amazed it hadn't fallen over before and suggested that all they really needed to do was to use it gingerly and make sure it didn't fail until the appointed moment.

As he chortled and sipped his pint Frank looked past the others with a squint of suspicion and closed the portfolio case. "Hello. Who's this short-arse, then?"

The others tuned to the room as Evan, tatty newspaper rolled up and gripped like a truncheon, marched towards them. His eyes fixed on Des as he said, "We on track then, Dizzy?"

"Yeah. All good, mate."

"It ain't good yet, Diz. It won't be good 'til you make it good."

Des nodded and hunched his shoulders. Then, to Henry's astonishment, Sonia smiled and asked, "Are you coming to Henry's opening, Evan?"

"What's that, then?"

"Henry's opening." She gestured to towards Henry who forced a smile. "A week on Thursday at my gallery."

Evan shifted uncertainly, looking around the table. Frank remained po-faced, Des shrugged and Henry maintained his increasingly aching grimace.

"Should be a good party," Sonia coyly added.

Evan tapped the newspaper against his hip, beating out his thought process, then gave a snake-eyed smile and hissed, "Yeah. Yeah, that sounds good. Cheers." He slapped Des on the shoulder, leaned down to him and whispered, "We'll make that the deadline for that little job of yours. Alright, Diz?"

Des clenched his teeth. His cheeks flushed with a burst of anger, then settled.

"Cheers, Son," Evan said. Then turned and strutted away with an even more exaggerated than usual shoulder roll, as if he'd gained some sort of upper hand.

"Looks like a fly in need of swatting," Frank muttered.

"More like a spider in need of flushing," Sonia replied.

Henry looked to Sonia for an explanation.

"That's right," she continued, "You've missed the last few meetings. We've decided to invite Evan to our little soirée."

"Oh, really? When did we decide that?"

"When you were off romancing the lovely Marion."

Henry leant forward and opened his mouth to protest. Then realised he really had nothing to protest against and turned his attention to his pint.

The following night Henry and Des set about retrieving the fallen plate. Henry, once again, donned his EEK. An ensemble he thought had been permanently retired and which felt strangely comfortable and reassuring to wear again. The preparation for this excursion had been more complex than their previous endeavours due to the salvage aspect of the mission. The plate, Des

178

estimated, weighed a good one hundred and fifty pounds. Not as much as the round, period ones they were used to shifting, which averaged nearly twice that, but still far too heavy for them to even consider hoisting up a fifty foot vertical shaft by hand.

"Were gonna need the big toys!" Des had grinned while they continued their planning in the pub – with what seemed to Henry a slightly inappropriate air of excitement.

The big toys, Henry discovered, mainly consisted of a heavy winch with one hundred feet of steel cable and an inverted tripod of scaffolding. The tripod supported a pulley through which the steel cable would be threaded, Des explained, as they set it up over the open chasm in the centre of Sonia's basement. Then one of them would venture down into the sewer, wrap some Teflon netting around the cover, shout up to whoever's up above to hit go on the winch and up she'll come. Bob's your uncle, easy-peasy lemon-squeezy, job done. Whole thing shouldn't take more than an hour. Hour and a half at the most.

Three hours after they had set up the inverted tripod they were still trying to work out how to get the electric winch, which must have weighed twice as much as their quarry, down into the basement.

"We need another winch to lower the bloody winch," Henry quipped.

"Not a bad idea," Des said. He looked up at the sewer pipe running across the ceiling. "Maybe if we threw a rope over that?"

"You mean use the pipe that's so close to collapse that all we need to do is give it a good crack with a hammer for it to disintegrate."

"Fair point."

"Jesus, you really are a pair of amateurs, aren't you?" Frank, to whom Des had sent an SOS message half an hour earlier, wheezed as he crossed the room – pulling his oxygen tank behind him. He paused at the door, looked down into the basement and then over to Henry and Des. "Put the winch here." He pointed to a spot on the ground floor near the door. "Then get a chair for me next to it and both of you go get your useless, sorry arses down there."

Once down in the basement and under Frank's direction Henry and Des reconfigured the pulley below the frame, which turned out to be a complex group of pulleys, to Frank's specifications. They then positioned the winch near in the doorway and ran the cable down into the basement, where Des threaded it – again, as per Frank's strict instructions.

"Right. Who's going down below?" Des asked Henry.

"Well, you dropped it."

"Yeah, but you're the one wearing the dry suit under all that clobber. Don't think any of us haven't noticed."

"Okay, then. Let's toss for it."

Henry lost the toss and prepared to climb down into the dank darkness – thinking, as they began to take action on what had until now been mere pub jibber-jabber, what a ridiculous and terrible idea this enterprise was beginning to seem. If only Marion knew just how far they had taken things since she was party to their musings. How would she react?

...Badly.

"And just shout up when you've got enough cable."

"Ah. No need for that," Henry said with a boyish grin, and produced from his pocket a pair of walkie-talkies. He'd purchased them earlier that day thinking that, unlike in their previous adventures when they weren't separated, they might come in useful. Also, he confessed only to himself, he'd wanted a set since he was a child.

Des looked down at the device in his hand, which he noted was made by 'the same people who brought you Action Man!' "For fuck's sake," he sighed, "Just get down there."

Once at the bottom of the shaft Henry set about searching for the plate. He narrowed and brightened the beam of his head torch into a searchlight mode. First he scanned the area for anything untoward. The first thing he noticed was the second set of metal rungs about fifteen feet further along the sweating wall. Instinctively, he looked up to the top where the white beam of his light illuminated the round manhole cover. The one outside the gallery. The one covering the hole through which Arabella had slipped.

Fifty thousand litres per second during high flood conditions.

He felt frozen for a moment as the dark, cruel memories returned. This was the first time he'd been down into this stretch since he'd started his futile search all those years ago. All for the sake of a university prank.

Drew.

The anger, the rage, the bloodlust came rushing back. He turned and looked up the other ladder, the one he'd just descended, and his torch beam caught Des looking down and then swiftly retreating.

"Jesus, Henry!" Des's voice crackled over the walkie-talkie, "How about you use that searchlight to search instead of blinding me?"

Henry got to work, turning the beam downwards. As he did so he felt glad of his sturdy boots and dry suit. The water was nearly up to his knees. He also caught the stench, which was even more pungent than on his previous excursions. He wished he'd remembered to bring with him the Vicks VapoRub which Des had offered. Then another thought dawned. He realised that there was no way his torch beam, no matter how many lumens it threw out, was going to penetrate the turbid water's surface. He would have to search by feel.

Damn Des and his clumsiness!

He turned the headlamp to its maximum setting and again, glanced upwards – making sure to be quick and catch Des before he snapped back.

"Henry!"

Yeah. Fuck you, Dizzy, Henry chuckled. Then braced himself and knelt down in the effluent. Once down in the shit he felt around the floor through his, thankfully, thick divers gloves. He then spent what felt like an hour dislodging various reminders of society's less salubrious necessities. Mainly bloated sanitary towels, half rotted nappies and a few loaded condoms – all of which insisted on circling and bouncing against him as he became their centre of gravity. Twice he felt himself retching but managed to force down the urge. Mustering his willpower by telling himself that the only thing more humiliating than being waist deep in Camden's waste would be to become covered in his own. Finally, he felt something. The sharp edge and right angle of a thick, metal plate.

"Blimey. That was quick," came Des's crackled reply after Henry had reported his success. Henry checked his watch, which he cursed himself for not having removed as he wiped a greasy smear from the dial. He'd only been down there for a little over eight minutes.

Perhaps this will go quicker that we'd thought, Henry allowed himself to think.

Half an hour later he was still trying to get a decent grip around the edge of the plate and find purchase on the slippery floor to try and raise the beast. This was not a one-man job. He radioed above for reinforcements.

As he descended the ladder the stream of expletives, grunts and cries emanating from Des echoed around the tunnel – and probably throughout the entire system, Henry was sure, all the way down to The Embankment. The big man landed with an angry splash, waded his way towards Henry and brandished a crowbar. "You lever. I'll pull."

Henry took the crowbar, slipped it under the plate and, sure enough, within a moment or two they had the plate raised onto its edge and upright, sticking out of the water and ready to drop down into the net. Or rather, they had half of the plate. Instead of the large, iron square expected they both stared, somewhat bewildered and confused, at a largish, iron, almost-rectangle.

"Bollox," Des sighed. "The bastard broke."

Almost two hours later Henry and Des, exhausted and soaked through, sat on the floor of the basement – either side of the bisected plate which they had eventually managed to raise, one half at a time, before carefully putting back in place to present as whole.

"This could be in your favour," said Frank, still supervising from above. "If the plate had become so brittle that it broke in two like that, it'll make it much more believable that it gave way in your flood. Anyway. I'm knackered. I'll leave you boys to clean all this up. And yourselves. Christ, you stink." He grinned as he heaved himself out of his chair and trudged away.

Henry and Des stayed still for a moment, staring at the plate while gathering their strength for the clean-up while listening to Frank's footfalls recede. As the door closed behind Frank, Henry thought about his point and, examining the smooth, perfectly straight split separating the plate's two halves, smiled over at Des and remarked, "I suppose you could call it a lucky break."

Chapter 26: Business as Usual

"Oh. Hi."

Henry looked up from his computer screen, wondering why Drew would be so surprised to see him sitting at his own desk.

"Coffee?"

"Yes... Please," Henry replied, then returned his attention to the image on the screen. The photograph he worked on was of a Victorian pump house. He thought it would be fitting to have at least one in the exhibition – even though, to his mind, what started as a retrospective of his life's work had now become nothing more than an elaborate cover for what Sonia has started describing as "the perfect crime". She vehemently denied Henry's characterisation, having convinced herself that the night could also be a glorious triumph for Henry's career. Sonia saw no reason why the show shouldn't carry on as a resounding success while the rats drowned in the basement. In fact, she maintained, it would make for the perfect alibi. For the perfect crime.

Henry had yet to be convinced but, while the day approached, saw no reason for not continuing with his preparations. So onward he marched. Business as usual.

In spite of having succumbed to the age of digital photography nearly two decades ago, under both duress and protest, Henry still couldn't bring himself to use Photoshop. The idea of removing elements of an image you find unappealing, such as erroneous background objects you hadn't noticed at the time, seemed like cheating to him. More than cheating, it was fraud. A lie. To Henry the primary goal of a photograph was to record a moment with accuracy. Purity. Of course, he realised he was in the minority in regard to this opinion and suspected it was a throwback to his war photography days, when to tamper in any way with an image, either while snapping or rendering, was an offence that would see you both fired and blacklisted. But still: to him, the integrity and honesty of everything within the frame was paramount.

Apart from that bloody reflection of Marion. He thought, fully aware of his own cognitive dissonance when it came to his many attempts to alter that one photograph. Amend that single memory. Then he smiled. Somehow, it didn't seem to bother him nearly as much as it used to, even just a few weeks ago.

If he did ever venture into the world of social media, a colleague once said to him, the only hashtag he would ever use would be 'no filter'. Henry had no idea what this meant, but he suspected it was an insult to most and a compliment to him.

The platform Henry used for his photography was the simple version of the one that came with his camera, which he used much the same way he did the enlarger in his darkroom. To straighten a shot, crop where necessary and adjust for exposure. Occasionally, as in this case, he also liked to play around with contrast and boost the colours. The tiles in the pump house were a mosaic of dark green and crimson red. Which, like the copper and brass of the pump itself, had been polished to shine. Henry

186

wanted the colours to pop. He boosted the saturation and darkened the shadows until they did just that. Then he sat back and examined the pump, still fully operational. He wondered how efficient it was.

Fifty thousand litres per second. He winced. He shuddered. He raged.

"Here you go." Drew placed the coffee beside Henry's keyboard.

Henry could feel his jaw clench as he looked down at the mug, which was a novelty item painted to look like a two hundred millimetre lens. A birthday present, many years ago, from Marion. Something else he'd forgotten until recently.

"Thank you."

"What's on the agenda?"

Henry turned the screen towards Drew.

"Nice."

"I've got two more, plus a series of black and whites from the Venice at Night series. I need you to print them and then get them down to the framers." Henry stood and pushed the chair towards Drew. "I'm off to Sonia's to talk details."

Henry moved through the living room gathering his wallet, keys and coat. He glanced over at Arabella's collage – then approached and looked, again, at the engagement photograph with the London Eye in the background. A new print which he'd made the day before after returning from the salvage job under the gallery. He looked at the ring, then at their faces. Their smiles. Then at the reflection of Marion in his spectacle's lens, behind the camera while taking the photograph, which this time he had made no attempt to remove.

187

From the Sonia K Gallery.

You are cordially invited to a private drinks reception

previewing

The Retrospective Photographic Works

of

Henry Glass

on the evening of the 21st October at 18:30

RSVP ASAP

Sonia scrutinised the card, peering down her nose through her half-moon, off-the-shelf reading glasses.

"Good God, Sonia. You're actually sitting at your desk. I thought that was just a piece of set dressing to impress your clients."

Without tilting her head Sonia raised her eyes and looked up at Henry, striding towards her along the length of the gallery. "You're disturbingly chipper," she flatly commented, "and, what did you boys get up to the night before last down in that basement? It's like a bleach factory down there. I don't know how we're going to get rid of the smell before Thursday."

"Trust me, it's better than the alternative."

"I don't want to know." She presented him with the invitations. "These just arrived. You know, as I sit here and look at the general guest list, I can think of quite a few other people we could invite for this little soirée. What about that awful ad man who's always parking you in? He seems to annoy you intensely and I'm sure the wider world would miss him not an iota."

"Yeah, but I don't want him dead. Jesus, Sonia, what's wrong with you? We're not serial killers, you know."

"I know, but it seems such a shame to send out just two of these. And one of them to the staff! They're embossed with raised lettering on pearl card with a satin finish. And I had to order a hundred of the bloody things. Very expensive."

Henry plonked himself into one of the two chairs opposite Sonia, in front of her ostentatious, eighteenth century desk: leather topped and adorned with gold leaf. What Henry had always called her Emperor's desk. "Well, in that case, perhaps we should make a short list. How many do you think you could fit down in that basement?"

"Oh, at least ten. Fifteen in a pinch. But whether they'd all get flushed before that automatic shut off thingy kicks in is a different matter. Des reckons it'll be about eight minutes before the pressure drop registers a red flag. Another three until the pressure actually drops. Let's keep it down to five."

"Okay then. The ad man. Terry. Fuck him, he's in. That means two more. How are you getting on with Michael these days?"

"Oh, bite your tongue, Henry! Michael's a gem. No, serious contenders only. What about that Ron chap you were so vexed to see at the cage fight?"

"Nah, he's alright. I think. But you know who's really been getting on my nerves lately? Cedric."

"Who?"

"Cedric."

"Never heard of him."

189

"Oh, come on, Sonia. Cedric. Shrimpy little fella in his late sixties. Comes into the pub every day around the same time as us. Only sometimes a little before and always, always takes our corner so we end up having to sit in a row and lean around each other to talk."

"Oh, him! Yes, he gives me the pip, too. Even tried to chat me up, once. And, as you say, he is a shrimpy little fella. Can't be much of a swimmer so he's sure to go down quickly. I'll put an invitation aside to bring in. That's three. We need two more. Who else?"

"Your turn."

"Well, there are several art critics I can think of but, sadly, I don't think any of them are replying to my invitations anymore. There is that amoral lothario Magnus bloody James. He'd probably be happy to die looking at his own portrait. And from what I hear the young ladies of Soho would do nothing but rejoice at his demise."

"Christ, really? Okay. Let's earmark a ticket for him. One more."

"Your turn."

"God, I don't know. Maybe I don't have as many enemies as I thought. Wait, I know. Mike O'Connor."

"Who?"

"Mike fucking O'Connor!"

"Who is Mike fucking O'Connor?"

"Never met the man. But he's given me three parking tickets in the last week alone, just because I've been exactly an inch too far over the yellow line, and I want the bastard dead!"

"Along with the bastard who has forced you to park that one inch over the yellow line. Justice is truly served. He's in!" Sonia threw her head back and roared with laughter, as did Henry. As their convulsions slowly calmed, Sonia dried her eyes and added, "It would be spree, by the way. Not serial."

"What's that?"

"A serial killer, generally speaking, kills several people one by one and over a prolonged period of time. Such as those nut jobs you hear about who like to drive across America knocking off prozzies and hitchhikers. A spree killer, on the other hand, kills a group of people in one go. Like that Norwegian fucker a few years back. Regardless. You have to kill three or more to qualify for either category."

Henry's laughter evaporated, as did his saliva. "What would that make us, then?"

"Vigilantes."

Chapter 27: Tattoo Who?

"If I'm getting one, you're getting one," had been Marion's final argument after Henry's hour or so of protestations. She had called to thank him for the steak lunch but really, Henry was pretty sure, to tell him all about her sudden change in career path. Perhaps, also, to garner some moral support – although Henry hadn't anticipated that this support would involve shades of self-mutilation.

"It's only self-mutilation if one carries out the action oneself. I can assure you, this will be undertaken by the most competent of professionals."

"The stickers were right, you know."

"What do you mean?"

"I can hear your smile. And it sounds more than a little wicked."

By way of confirmation Marion responded with a throaty chuckle before saying goodnight.

Twelve hours later Henry found himself sitting on a thinly padded, vinyl bench against a red wall adorned with a variety of framed images: skulls, snakes, spiders, dragons, Disney characters, the golden arches, several versions of the Coca-Cola logo and a plethora of other random, corporate insignias. Along the top of the wall many of the more elaborate tattoos were shown off by a row of celebrities. Mostly cage fighters, boxers and reality television stars, none of whom Henry recognised. Marion, clutching a portfolio case to her chest, sat beside him and they both watched the room before them with wide-eyed fascination. What, to Henry, looked like three dentist's chairs were occupied by two enormous, leather clad men and one waifish girl. The two men were each having their arms decorated, one finishing off what Henry had been told was a full sleeve. In his case mainly themed around red and green snakes coiling their way from his wrist up to his shoulder. The other was having colour added to a Harley Davidson logo that covered his impossibly large bicep. He, Henry noted with a twinge of concern, appeared on the edge of tears as he winced with tightly closed eyes. The girl, on the other hand, struck a disturbingly relaxed pose while she lay with her head tilted backwards and the artist worked on her throat. Presumably adding to the dense rose garden which Henry could see already grew from her chest and over her shoulders.

Henry listened to the pulsing buzzes coming from the mechanised needles and tried to imagine the agony of having the thin skin of one's throat perforated when he heard a sharp, high-pitched yelp. He looked towards a curtain, slightly open, and could see a pair of feet dangling over the edge of a bed. The person was lying on their back with their trousers around their ankles. Above the curtain a sign read, Private Parts Piercings & Art.

Feeling his hands beginning to shake with the possible onset of a panic attack, Henry slowly leant towards Marion and whispered, "What in the name of God's greatest fuck are we doing here?"

To which Marion whispered back, "Don't be such a wuss."

"Alright, Mar?" interrupted Ron, appearing from his office. "Henry. You going to go first, then, while me and Mar talk business?"

The panic attack inched closer and was, Henry felt sure, only abated by his annoyance at Marion's grin as she goaded,

"Go on, then. We won't be too long and I'll be right behind you."

"I'll bet you will."

As Marion and Ron went to the office the biker rose from the chair, his Harley logo covered in translucent clingfilm, and whimpered his way towards the cashier. The artist who had seen to him, a twenty-something whose body art revealed a fascination with 1970s horror films, approached and with a surprisingly warm smile asked, "You Henry, then?"

Moments later Henry sat back in the chair, which he decided was more akin to a Spanish Inquisitor's than a dentist's, carefully watching the proceedings around him. The artist, who had introduced herself as Alice, went about cleaning and sterilising the immediate area with a vigour that both impressed and, in a strange way, set Henry's mind, almost, at ease.

"I like your choice of tat. Small and simple. Perfect for a first one," she said as she snapped on a pair of bright blue, latex gloves.

"First and only."

"Yeah. That's what I said. When I got this." She raised the sleeve of her black T-shirt and pointed to a small, bloodied meat cleaver. Just above what was her second piece – a detailed rendition of Malcom

McDowell donning his Clockwork Orange bowler hat and eye makeup. "Where do you want it, Henry?"

"Somewhere nobody else will ever see it. Ever."

"Best do it behind the curtain, in that case." She winked, then smiled as she watched the blood drain from Henry's face. "Okay. Let's get your shirt off. Top of the shoulder it is."

Henry grudgingly complied while Alice studied the image Henry had chosen. A small, monochromatic depiction of a twin lens reflex camera.

"Does it hurt?" Marion asked, looming over and grinning down at Henry, fifteen minutes into the ordeal.

"You remember when you were a child losing your milk teeth and when one was loose. You'd press it and feel that weird, sharp pain that was almost pleasant and rather satisfying?"

"I do."

"Well, it's nothing like that. Yes, it bloody hurts. How did it go?"

"Swimmingly." Marion told Henry how Ron had liked her work even more than the images she'd emailed him and agreed that they would, definitely, make suitable templates for any parlour under his company umbrella. But, as he'd said to her on the phone, the works were always more valuable when inked by the original artist. They set out a timetable and plan where Marion would be trained in the parlour, by Alice, before opening her own shop with his backing. Meanwhile, he suggested that she choose one of her own images to have Alice tattoo on her today. Unlike Henry, she needed hers to be in a place of prominence that could be shown to potential clients.

"After all. Would you get a haircut from a bald hairdresser?"

"Or trust a skinny chef. A fair point." Henry concurred as he rose from his seat and allowed Marion to take his place. "Which one are you having?"

Alice stepped forward and produced a stencil she had made from one of Marion's angel series. Pale blue and pink pastels with soft, feathery edges. She placed it on Marion's arm where, rather unsettlingly, it reached from the top of her shoulder to the middle of her bicep. Then she said to Henry, "You might want to make yourself comfortable, if you're going to wait around," before snapping off her gloves and going about re-sterilising the area.

'Don't go too far!" Marion blurted, suddenly appearing nervous. She took Henry's hand and gave a gentle squeeze adding, "Please."

"Of course not," Henry replied, taking the seat next to her. Then he felt his face flush as he looked away when Marion, as per Alice's request, began to remove her shirt.

"Oh, relax, Henry," Marion chuckled. "I came dressed appropriately." She removed her shirt to reveal a tank top underneath.

"Does yours still hurt?"
"No, not really. Hardly even noticing it now."
"Rubbish."

"You're right. It stings like hell and I curse you for dragging me along."

"Ha! And yours is about a tenth of the size of mine. Wuss." Marion poured Henry another glass of wine. It had been a little over twenty-four hours since they had left the tattoo parlour, freshly inked, and Marion had shaken hands with Ron to cement her milestone career change. She and Henry had agreed to reconvene the following day to remove the translucent protective wrapping together and reveal their new works of art-for-life – in the flesh, so to speak, and after a decent cooling down period.

"Shall we?" Marion said.

"Perhaps we should open another bottle first. Just in case."

"Absolutely." Marion stood up and exited towards the kitchen while Henry sat back and looked around her living room.

The last time Henry had been a guest in one of Marion's flats it was a single room out in Ealing. She'd recently graduated and was putting together her portfolio for galleries and to look for commissions. In order to save money she'd signed up for one of those Guardian schemes, run by companies who ran security for empty buildings in a state of limbo between their previous use and their next – the next usually involving demolition and site redevelopment. Technically, the tenants were considered security and so had to comply with a clutch of silly rules. Such as no smoking in your room, weekly tidiness inspections and, rather incredulously for any adult renter, no overnight guests. The whole thing struck Henry as being highly dubious and he was sure it had to fall into some sort of double-billing category: the company would charge both the property owners to provide security guards and the tenants to act as security guards. Nevertheless, it had been a good deal for Marion at the time and he remembered being very pleased for her.

That one and only visit he'd made was a few days after she had introduced him to Arabella. She wanted to show him a painting she'd just finished. Her first attempt at using oils. It was a stark, winter scene of St James's Park – frozen over, with a lone figure skater pirouetting in front of Buckingham Palace. Bright whites, soft greys and thick globules of oily blacks.

It was an afternoon Henry hadn't thought about for years. Now, as he again looked at the painting above Marion's current mantlepiece, the memories of it came trickling back. He wondered why she never sold the piece. It was as masterful as many expert oils he'd seen go for hundreds. Then he wondered why she hadn't continued down this route, instead choosing to focus on pastels, acrylics and charcoal sketching.

"Too much like hard work," Marion had laughed when he asked. "Also, too smelly and, at the time, far too expensive."

At the time. Henry had only asked her these questions on this visit, while looking at the painting above the mantlepiece in her grown up, Holloway Road flat. Back when he visited her student, Ealing digs he hadn't been as interested in the work as Marion might have hoped. Mainly because all he

198

wanted was to know more about Arabella. His visit had been to thank Marion for introducing them. They had already seen each other twice more since that first meeting, which seemed to surprise Marion. He now wondered, which he had not then, why this was the case.

No matter. Now, as he studied the painting, he felt more appreciative. The texture alone was superb and the framing reminded him of one of his own photographs, taken around that time. It was one of those paintings that gave Henry a slight twinge of envy. Wishing he had the skill and talent to paint with oils, or even acrylics, instead of just capturing light.

"Here we go," Marion piped, returning from the kitchen and clutching a bottle of Bordeaux. She then held aloft a pair of Murano balloon glasses. "I thought I'd bring out the big guns for this round."

She sat on the sofa and Henry perched beside her. They raised their glasses, clinked and drank. Settling their second bottle, accompanied by some soft cheeses and cured meats. Halfway through, they finally plucked up the courage to unveil their new permanent exhibits.

"Puny!" Marion scoffed with a smile, a snort and a sip.

Henry had to agree. His little, monochromatic line drawing was, indeed, a rather small affair. But, he was relieved to see, still as discreet and almost as tasteful as he'd thought it in the parlour. "Your turn, then."

"Care to do the honours?"

The request came as a surprise, but Henry obliged and peeled the crumpled, opaque plastic away to reveal the angel beneath. He felt a wave of relief upon seeing that hers, which in the parlour looked as if it was going to cover most of her arm, was a more sensible size. And higher than originally planned, now near the top of her shoulder. He found himself impressed at the detail of the face, the expression serene with a quiet smile, and put the fine detailing down to a combination of Marion's original design and Alice's expertise. Then he noted that the depiction had a gracefully long neck, much like Marion's, and bare shoulders meeting the folded, impressively layered robes beneath. Again, the detailing was superb. Henry had no idea that body art could be so refined. The making of it, however, was the wings. How their fine lines of pastel pinks and blues, highlighted by pure whites and deep blacks, feathered and merged into the soft texture of Marion's perfect skin.

"What do you think?"

"Sublime," Henry replied. Then, inexplicably and instinctively, where the tip of an angel's wing diffused into Marion's arm, he placed a delicate kiss.

Chapter 28: An Invitation, a List and a Note

"This is for you." Sonia handed Drew a sturdy envelope.

Drew opened it feeling slightly bemused, as it had been he who had made the order, picked up the invitations and then stuffed the envelopes. "Thank you. And for the VIP party, no less."

"Yes, don't get smart. Or overly excited. I'm afraid we're having some problems with the catering staff so you might have to, in fact you will have to, handle the bar downstairs."

"I see."

"Well, look on the bright side. I'm going to be reduced to handling the food. Or at least Tesco's Finest will. Regardless – we're all going to have to muck in. Wade in the same shit, so to speak." Sonia bit her tongue to stop herself smiling at her inside joke for one.

Drew carefully slipped the card back into its envelope, tucked that into his pocket and returned to the task of hanging another picture: a modestly sized print from one of Henry's earlier portfolios. Snapped in black and white film and printed by Henry in the darkroom, with all the gritty grain and untouched flaws intact. The Serpentine frozen over in the snow with a lone, mad dog walker in the centre.

"Is that okay, Drew?" Sonia didn't think much of Drew's attitude at the best of times, especially now that she knew him to be a psychopathic murderer, but in recent days his casual superiority had been particularly irksome.

"Yes. Everything's fine."

Sonia nodded and, satisfied that everything was indeed fine, pushed her spectacles down to the centre of her nose and peered at her paperwork.

"It's just."

Shit.

"Well, it's just that, lately, it feels like I've been working for you and not for Henry."

"Technically, we're both working for Henry."

"Yes, but you've actually seen him. Every time I go to the office to pick up new prints, or catch up on the day-to-day stuff, he's either out or busy in the darkroom. I don't think I've actually seen or even spoken to him for well over a fortnight. Is he upset with me for some reason?"

To this, Sonia's response took much thought. Probably too much as she could feel herself sitting utterly still while unblinkingly staring at Drew as he waited for a reply. *Is Henry upset? For some reason? No, Drew. He's furious. Enraged. Wrathful. Murderously vengeful in the true sense of the phrase.* "No, not at all," she finally replied with a bright smile. "Just a bit busy, that's all. He's got a lot riding on this show. As do I, Drew. So, if you don't mind?" The bright smile stayed fixed as she gestured towards her desk.

Drew gave a dissatisfied shrug and returned to his work. Sonia clicked her pen, again adjusted her glasses and thought, *Christ. He knows. He bloody knows.*

202

"He doesn't know," Des sighed. "You're just being paranoid."

"Why would you say that?"

"Because you're always fucking paranoid." He knocked back the shot and picked up his pint glass, readying himself for the last sip and swill. "Now. On to other matters. Coz the day's not done yet, Groucho. Not even by half."

Sonia offered a nod of agreement. Having been spooked by Drew's questions she had sent Des an SOS text to meet at the pub. Michael was just opening the doors for the day when she and Des arrived at the same time.

"You're probably right. Sorry."

"Ha! Well, it was worth it just to get a sorry from you, Sonia. Besides," Des looked around the empty pub from their vantage point at the bar's corner, "it's nice being here when the place is quiet, like this."

"Does it always smell of disinfectant in here?"

"It's either that or the fine aroma of stale slops," Micheal interjected, "Are you having another?

"May as well while we're here."

"Nah. Got to be getting on."

"Really, Des? My treat. By way of apology for interrupting your oh-so-busy-day."

"My day is busy, as it happens. Look." Des held up a scrap of paper. "I've got all this to get through. Shopping. I hate shopping."

"For Evan?"

Des leaned forward and whispered, "Frank."

"Give." Sonia snatched the list, gave it a quick peruse and then threw Des a wicked grin. "Michael. May we have one of Des's God-awful snakebites,

203

along with his customary shot of gut-rot, and a bottle of your cheapest rosé."

"Sonia, this is a bad idea."

"Oh, my dear Dizzy. If you think this is a bad idea, wait until we adjourn to the corner."

Once they did sit down in what she had started to refer to as Conspiracy Corner, Sonia poured herself a large glass of wine, took out her phone and dialled, "Drew." She grinned.

"Oh, Christ." Des lamented, prematurely downing his shot.

"Do you have a pen and paper? There's one on my desk. I need you to go to the shops and pick up a few things. Mostly cleaning supplies, but a few bits and pieces. Ready? Good." She sat back in her seat, looking into her wine while swirling the glass, and read out the list of items from Frank's list. "Three wooden wedges, picture hanging wire, a firm rubber mallet, gaffer tape, and a Prochem Birchmeier five litre stainless steel pressure sprayer. Yes, I agree, that is a large and unusual item. Probably quite expensive. But there should be plenty of petty cash in the biscuit tin in the kitchen. Make sure you get receipts. Has Henry been in yet?… Okay. Well, on you get and let me know when you're back." She rang off, then said to Des, "I hope this is all completely necessary. That's my booze fund tin I've just sent him to. And why gaffer tape?"

"It's mostly for the clean-up. The wedges and the wire are to fix the cover so it splits and separates, then falls down the shaft, exactly when the stairs topple. Frank reckons those are items you'd find in a gallery so wouldn't cause any fuss with any sort of investigation."

"Frank would be correct."

"You know, I always knew he was a bit shady but I'm beginning to think his past was truly fucking murky. This definitely ain't his first rodeo. And never mind that. What the fuck are you thinking sending Drew, Sonia? You're gonna get us all well and truly kippered!"

"On the contrary, Des. Drew is the perfect errand boy. He will be in possession of the receipts for the tools of his own demise, and his fingerprints will be all over them. Not only that, but we have the perfect alibi during the time of their purchase as we are in here getting riotously drunk."

"Riotously?"

"The day is young and we must make sure to be remembered by as many witnesses as possible."

"Jesus Christ. Criminal mastermind, Groucho. That's what you are."

"Do you know, Dizzy? I think I might be. And, look. Here's Henry, just in time to avoid the round. What brings you here so early?"

Even after all these years there were mornings when Henry opened his eyes and, in that stretched, foggy moment between dream and reality, still thought that Arabella lay by his side. This was one such morning – made all the more vivid when, while emerging into full consciousness, he saw the perfect outline of her shoulder. Half-covered by her thick, black ringlets.

205

Then he saw the angel, whose wingtips he had kissed the night before.

He wasn't sure how to describe the feeling that gripped him. Paralysed him. Clutched him by the gut – then squeezed and twisted. After a few lost, immeasurable seconds he concluded it had to be guilt. The guilt and shame of a man who had just betrayed his love. And not just betrayed, but cheated in the most heinous of ways. With her own sister.

While Henry poured over his sin Marion took a deep, lazy breath. As she exhaled she shifted backwards, pressing against Henry. His paralysis eased and instinctively, involuntarily, he brought his hand forward and placed it on her naked hip. Again, Marion took a deep breath – perhaps in her sleep, maybe awake or, more likely, in that limbo between the two from which Henry had just emerged. As she exhaled, she shifted again. This time, taking Henry's hand in hers. Pressing it against her thigh. Henry felt a warmth as, through her exhalation, he could hear, could feel, her smile.

For a moment the grip on his gut relaxed and he shifted closer to her. Squeezed her hand and moved to nuzzle her neck. Then he caught sight of her jawline, silhouetted against the blue dawn through a frosted window, and an image of Arabella's profile, almost identical, flashed before him. But not smiling, as Marion's did now. Glaring. The edge of her mouth turned down into pursed edges. A grimace of disapproval. Disappointment. Accusation.

The grip on his insides returned, tighter than ever. Twisting. Pulling. He could hear Marion's breathing quicken. He moved away.

Marion's breathing again slowed and then deepened, settling into a low rhythm of deep sleep.

Carefully, silently, Henry let go of her hand. And as Marion slipped back into a slumber, he quietly rose and dressed.

"Did you at least leave a note?"

Henry shook his head.

"Oh, Henry. What a consummate coward you are." Sonia, sounding bitterly disappointed, poured the dregs of the rosé into her glass. "And, FYI. She wasn't asleep."

Chapter 29: Terry and Terry

"Thank you for shopping at Sainsbury's. Now, fuck off."

Henry's mind's ear always heard the second phrase following those hollow words spilling from an automated teller, but this time they felt particularly barbed. Sonia's unfiltered opinion on his character, which he should have been well used to, had hit a particularly raw nerve. And her further suggestion, that he spend some time placating Drew, had done nothing to improve his temperament. Especially since she had expressed it more as an order than a request.

"All I'm asking is that you try and give the impression that it's business as usual," she had finally implored, trying to penetrate what Henry thought was nihilistic brooding but which Sonia and Des read as a petulant sulk. "It's only for a few more days. Then – Adios, Drew!"

"And adios, Evan!" Des had added with a raucous laugh.

Henry had attempted to force a smile, then finish his drink with them, but he couldn't stop brooding. Simmering. Sulking. He'd decided to leave them to their afternoon session – which stuck him as a premature celebration. "Perhaps you're right," he'd lied, "I'll go home and play nice with the murderous weasel."

He'd then left the pub with the intention of returning home and avoiding Drew, who he knew to be working in his office, by retreating into the darkroom. On the way he'd stopped off at Sainsbury's and recruited a bottle of Famous Grouse to accompany him and lend some much-needed moral support.

After paying the offending machine he shuffled his way home. He walked slowly, all the way harbouring a deep-seated hope that Drew would have found more items to take to the gallery. More work setting up the exhibition which, as he dragged his feet and mulled, he was now seeing only as a sham. A ruse. His life's work had been corrupted and contorted into nothing more than a cover story for a ridiculously elaborate crime. A plot from which he now saw no way of extracting himself.

Henry pushed the thought to the back of his mind and, instead, focused on the wide, pristinely painted houses and the oak, ash and plane trees with their browning leaves, most of which had now shed. Stacks of them had been carefully raked and piled into a nook of one of the larger, gnarled trunks. Henry veered towards and waded through the mound, petulance giving way to arrested, teenage angst, as he kicked through to the other side. He felt his sullenness momentarily quelled as he watched the swarm of leaves rise, flutter and chaotically float down the avenue.

Freedom, he thought with a smile as he rounded the corner on the approach to his front door – when he saw his parked Land Rover. Again, his mood deflated. Drew would be there. Then he noticed the other car. He stopped in the middle of the road, his house keys dangling from his hand, and stared at the Jaguar. Sheathed in its protective cover and parked in front of his Land Rover. Nose-to-nose. A mere two inches between them.

Henry pocketed his keys and, feeling his cheeks burn, about faced, marched up to Terry the Ad Man's house and repeatedly slammed his fist against the door until it opened.

"Henry, mate. Everything hunky and dory? I've been meaning to have a chat with you. Come in and have a cuppa." Terry stepped back and appeared to gesture towards his front hall.

"Terry. Will you, for the love of God, find somewhere else to park your fucking car."

"Come again, sunshine?"

"Oh, you heard me." Henry turned and strutted back to his own front door.

"Henry!"

Once inside Henry glared across at The Ad Man, who gormlessly stared back at him, and slammed the door.

God, that felt good.

"What felt good?"

Henry leapt in the air as he spun around, slamming his back against the front door. "Jesus, Drew!"

"Sorry. Didn't mean to scare you."

"Yeah. Well. What are you talking about, anyway?"

"Nothing. I thought you might have been talking to me but I think you must have just been muttering to yourself. Everything okay, then?"

"Yes, yes. Just having a word with... whatshisname. The neighbour with the bloody jag."

"Terry."

"Terry. God, he's a tosser."

"Oh, he's not that bad. I've got to know him quite well over the last few years, actually. By the way he said he'd move it after lunch so I can get to the Rover. There're still a few last-minute pieces to pick up from the framers before tomorrow."

"Oh, are there." *And you couldn't have got on with that this morning?* Henry made sure not to mutter.

"There are. Anyway. You spoke to Terry." Drew looked down, shuffling his feet and, Henry was almost sure, slightly blushed. He couldn't be entirely sure as, in all the years he'd known Drew, it was not a reaction he'd ever witnessed.

"I did. About the car."

"Oh." Drew replied, looking back up. Another strange reaction. As if he'd been expecting Henry's conversation to have been about something different.

"Yes. I didn't realise that you'd spoken to him first." Henry took a step back to gauge Drew's expression, which had returned to his slightly unnerving resting face, with a half-smile and eyes opened a bit too wide for comfort.

What had he been expecting me to talk to the fucker about? Henry pondered the question for a few moments as they stood staring at each other, then recalled the way Terry had stepped back with the welcoming gesture. Had that, in fact, been his action? Henry replayed the moment in his mind and noticed, or remember noticing, a large, black case leaning against the wall, to which Terry could have been gesturing. A portfolio case. Drew's portfolio case? Could his previous, paranoid thoughts actually be

211

true – that Drew had, indeed, been building up a portfolio over the last few years and, now, decided to share it with Terry the fucking Ad Man instead of him? *Does this boy's betrayal have no end?*

"It seems I may owe Terry an apology," Henry continued, hearing a new slow, almost syrupy resonance in his own voice. "I tell you what." He moved passed Drew and reached to a cardboard box on the table, from which he removed one of Sonia's VIP invitations. "Why don't you take this over to him? Tell him I'm terribly embarrassed, especially since you'd already spoken to him, and that we'd very much like to see him at the opening. Especially the VIP preview reception. Downstairs. He is, after all, very much a VIP."

"I think he'd really appreciate that."

"Oh, I'm sure." Henry opened the door and stepped aside. Once Drew had passed, he closed it and, in order to consciously avoid his, apparently new, habit of accidentally talking to himself, said loudly and clearly, "Adios, Terry the fucking Ad Man!"

"What do you mean you're resigning?" Marion's portly superior, who also happened to be named Terry, asked with an expression as equally gormless as that which, across town and at exactly the same moment, Terry the Ad Man stared at Henry. "Aren't you happy here?"

"Of course I'm not happy here, Terry. Nobody's happy here."

"I'm happy here."

212

"Really?" She looked at him, massively overweight and wearing an unwashed shirt that stretched out across his belly so the buttons looked like they were about to pop off. Sitting behind a desk strewn with as many empty snack packets as unchecked piles of paperwork. "Are you sure about that?"

"Of course!" He sat back and dabbed his increasingly sweating forehead. "Well, I mean, not while I'm actually here. But that's work, isn't it. I mean, nobody's happy when they're actually at work. That's why it's called work."

"I don't think that's necessarily true, Terry."

"Of course it is! And that's what's great about his job. Yes, it's a bit miserable. A bit shit. But it's easy. Okay, perhaps it doesn't pay as much as some other jobs. But it's proper nine-to-five. And you can just coast through it. Bit of overtime if you need it, but nobody's forcing you. And you still work the phones sometimes, don't you?"

"Very occasionally."

"So you get all those great bonuses as well!"

"You've never worked the phones. Have you." It wasn't a question.

"No. How did you know?"

"The bonuses aren't that great. Look. I'm moving on, okay?"

"You'll have to serve out your month's notice."

"It's a fortnight."

"Jesus, Marion. How am I going to find someone to replace you in two weeks?"

213

"Well, I'd suggest you just go down to the floor, ask if anyone's interested and then get all who are to draw lots."

"What?"

"As you say, it's an easy job. Let's face it, it's beyond easy. A trained monkey could do what we do. And I'm not even sure if you'd have to train it for that long."

"Okay, now you're taking the Micky. Aren't you."

"No. I mean, we train our new recruits for three hours on day one. And, let's face it, there's really nothing more to learn after that."

"Okay, you are taking the piss. You've been here longer than me, for God's sake."

"Yes, I have. Twenty years I've been here, Terry. Twenty bloody years. Gone. What a waste of fucking time."

"Careful, Marion. You're on thin ice, here."

"What? What are you talking about? What exactly do you think is going on here, you utter dilettante?"

"What did you just call me?"

"Interesting question. What, exactly, do you think I just called you?"

"Right! That's it, Marion. You're sacked!"

"Are you sure about that?"

"I'm sorry, but I am. Go and clear out your desk. You're done."

"Well, all right, then. If that's what you want. Just make sure that my severance pay is included with the final pay package, yes?" She retrieved her resignation letter from his desk and, without

214

bothering to go to her office, left the building. As she walked through the small park opposite her former place of work she looked up and saw a cloud of brown leaves released from an oak tree by a gust of wind. She smiled, watched the leaves dance away from each other and each float its own way, and thought, freedom.

Chapter 30: Five Hundred and Eighty-One Pounds

"My life has become entirely too fucking complicated." As he had been doing since the day before, Henry spoke his thoughts aloud. His rationale being that if he's going to talk to himself then he may as well do it on purpose instead of as an accidental mutter. That latter would, quite obviously, make him a lunatic.

'Are you accompanying me to the courthouse?' read the text, which had arrived while he had been in the darkroom printing old memories and drinking whisky. 'Tomorrow morning at ten am. Picnic. Spanner. Radishes.' There was also a map below, with a blue dot near St Pancras Square. Henry felt his jaw clench slightly. Did Marion think him so useless that he wouldn't be able to find the offices for Camden Council on his own? Then he looked again at the strange, random words at the end of the message. Picnic, spanner and radishes. What in the name of God was that about? Some sort of half-arsed shopping list she'd accidentally added? Did she want to go on a picnic afterwards? Perhaps. For the most part, it had been a fairly mild autumn so far and there were those steps outside the new St Martin's College by the canal.

Henry replied with a guarded thumbs up emoji and put the phone aside. Then he poured himself another generous whisky and returned his attention to the photograph he'd just developed. Another print of Arabella sitting in the booth of the floating

Chinese restaurant, smiling back at him while showing off the charm bracelet. This copy he'd printed with a narrower aperture than usual. Dark and with a higher contrast – angular, silver lines and sharp edges leaning forward with a piercing stare and a half-smile. Exactly seven years ago. Her final moments. Seven years ago, tomorrow.

He put the photograph aside, finished his drink and padded his way to bed.

"What's in that?" Marion asked, pointing at the old Fortnum and Mason wicker basket dangling by Henry's side.

"The picnic."

"The what?"

"The picnic. Your text message said you wanted a picnic."

"It... I... It said what?"

"Didn't it?"

"No. Oh!" Marion clicked. Then smiled. Then broke into a cacophony of guffaws and snorts which, for a moment, Henry thought might knock her over. Once she'd regained control and righted herself Henry said,

"I take it I'm missing something."

"You are, but I'll tell you later. And I'm glad to see you've come dressed for the occasion."

Henry looked down at his funereal black ensemble – then back to Marion, who wore simple jeans and her old biker's jacket. "Too much?"

Marion replied with a shrug and a sideways glance. They moved towards the revolving doors.

"This building belongs in the ninth circle of hell." Henry's statement bore a tone of caution rather than realisation. He had spent an horrendous day there some years previously, photographing self-satisfied bureaucrats and minor politicians. The event had been billed as an exhibition of young, local artists but, in reality, was more an excuse for the North London government suits to gather, scoff and quaff on their constituents' dime. Henry remembered wondering why an event promoting young painters still in school was serving champagne and crab puffs. Although what he remembered more, as they emerged on the other side of the revolving doors and were stopped in their tracks by a cacophony of echoing conversations and splashing water, accompanied by the pungent stench of stale sweat and chlorine, was how much he'd hated this building.

A Neo-brutalist nightmare housing the Camden Council offices, the first two floors had been designed to be a 'welcoming public space where people could gather and socialise'. An open plan Swiss Army knife of a building intended to suffice as many local needs as possible and ending up serving none. The enormous concrete cell in which they now stood served as the much-publicised welcoming space, with a mezzanine level about half the size of the ground floor referred to as a library. These two levels had housed the exhibition Henry had photographed, and he still found himself seething as he remembered how the library didn't actually have many books. Instead, it was home to several rows of computers and about as many hot-desks. These, Henry was sure, would have been extremely useful, were it not for the fact that it was nearly impossible to acquire a decent Wi-Fi signal. Even if you could, with the constant chattering emanating from below, then bouncing around the concrete walls, floors and massive windows, concentration would surely prove to be a near impossibility.

"Is that chlorine?" Marion asked, inhaling through her nose with a wince of distaste.

"Yes," Henry replied, before briefly outlining his previous visit and adding that, in order to maximise their inefficiency and idiocy, they'd also installed a swimming pool and a gym in the basement. The result was that the entire welcoming space possessed a permanent aroma of chlorine and – due to the network of corridors and lift shafts having, Henry suspected, been designed specifically for the purposes of amplification – the added sounds of splashing and screaming.

"I think you were wrong, Henry. I think this building is the ninth circle of hell."

They approached the nearby reception desk where Marion produced a printout of her appointment confirmation.

"You need to go to the third floor. Office number eighteen," the receptionist said in a strange tone that was both charming and yet thoroughly deflated. "Around the corner and take the last lift on your right, against the back wall."

"Why only that one?" Henry asked.

"The one ahead of you only goes up to the library and down to the swimming pool. The first one around the corner is an express and only goes up to the top floors." She gave an apologetic shrug.

"I'm sure you could have done this over the internet."

"No, I couldn't. And you know nothing about the internet."

"True. But I'm still pretty sure you could have."

"No, I couldn't. Some things, believe it or not, still have to be done in person. You'd know that if you'd done anything to actually contribute to this nightmarish process."

They'd spent well over the last hour sitting in a waiting room which, in complete contrast to the downstairs lobby, was tiny, windowless and oppressively stuffy.

Henry sulked for another moment or two. Then mumbled, "Everything's online these days."

"Jesus, Henry! Why are you being so bloody difficult?"

"Well, you're the one who kept begging me to come."

"Begging is a bit strong."

Referring to the heat, which he had complained about several times over the preceding sixty minutes, Henry then said, "I just hope the sandwiches don't spoil. I made them myself."

Marion rounded on him and was about to let loose her tongue when, catching them both off guard, the office door finally opened.

"So sorry to have kept you," said the blue suited official with a cheeriness that grated on both Marion and Henry's fraying nerves. "Got caught on a video call. Do come in."

Once through the door, and their eyes had adjusted to the sudden blast of natural light, both Henry and Marion looked around the office in abject wonder: spacious with a ten-foot desk at one end and a sofa area at the other, along with floor to ceiling windows offering a panoramic view.

"What a lovely office," Marion flatly commented.

"It is, isn't it? You should have seen the one I had before we moved into this building. Yes, I'm afraid I really have been in this job that long. Don't let my youthful looks fool you. Anyway, the old office. It was a real shoebox."

"Rather like your waiting room," Henry said.

"Well, I wouldn't go that far! Please, do sit down." He gestured towards the seats at his desk and immediately settled behind his computer. "Now." He tapped various keys. "Let's see what I can do... Ah." As if suddenly noting the seriousness of the meeting he measured his tone, looked back at them and quietly said, "My condolences. I am sorry for your loss."

"Thank you," Marion replied, "Although, as you can see, it was a while ago."

"It wasn't that long ago."

Marion flushed slightly, shifting in her seat.

The official gave an uncomfortable smile and continued, "Well. Do you have all of the documentation with you?"

"I do." Marion removed a folder and passed it over.

The official put on his wire rimmed glasses and read the top document – the original police report.

221

"Mm–hmm." He licked the tip of his finger, turned the page and read the next document. Marion's declaration, as the sister, that Arabella had not been heard of since the disappearance. "Mm-hmm." Again, he licked his finger, turned that page and read the next: Henry's declaration, as Arabella's husband, which Marion had finally managed to get him to sign. "Mm-hmm," came the third approval. He then looked up at them, peering over the glasses, smiled and asked, "And do you have your proof of advertising?"

"Proof of what, you say?" Marion asked.

"Proof of advertising."

"Advertising what?"

"Well. Your sister's disappearance. All of this paperwork is in order but, in order to declare a missing person officially dead, even after the seven-year threshold, there need to be public adverts asking if anybody has seen them or knows of their whereabouts."

"This is the first I've heard of that," Marion said.

"Ah. Well, you should have been advised otherwise."

"But why?"

"Well, you know. Just in case the person is actually out there and, for their own reasons, wishes not to be found. To give them a chance to come forward. A bit like the public request for objections before a wedding."

"A wedding."

"Oh, for the love of God!" Henry snapped, reaching into his satchel and removing his thick, battered file. "Here. Just look at these." He flicked past his maps and lists to the back of the file, where there were various newspaper cuttings. "It was in all the papers. Evening Standard. Metro. The Times, even the bloody Guardian. I mean, some of these were written years afterwards." He shoved several of the articles across the table. Most were from the days and weeks following the accident, with increasingly gaudy and sensation headlines: Shock Disappearance In Flood. Missing Manhole Mayhem. The distasteful, Flushed Away, from a red top.

Marion watched intently as Henry frantically leafed through the file to find some later pieces.

"And here. Look at these ones."

Two of them were interviews with Henry. A One Year On article, asking if her body would ever be found – and Henry insisting that he fully expected her to be found alive and well. 'Perhaps she's in a hospital somewhere with amnesia', he'd suggested, 'Or on the streets.' He'd asked them to print a photograph, that last one from the Chinese, in case anyone had seen her.

"And here!" Henry continued, beginning to rant. "This was just a couple of years ago." The headline read Five Years Later and was, again, accompanied by the photograph – just in case. "I mean, it was seven years ago. Seven years ago during the worst storm for decades. Do you know how fast that water was going through the tunnel when she was swept into it?" He leafed back to one of the earlier articles. "Here. It's right here. Fifty thousand litres per second. Fifty thousand. From Camden all the way to The Embankment. Is she dead? Of course she's fucking dead!"

Marion watched Henry as, finished and exhausted, he sat back in his seat. She wondered if he realised that he'd been shouting. Screaming. Almost raving as the words spilled out of him. That he had been raging with anger and grief while tears streaked his flushed cheeks. Marion smiled softly and placed her hand on his, which shook, while the last words of his rant echoed in her mind. Of course she's fucking dead.

Finally.

The official pursued the articles, gave Henry a mild, caring smile and said, "I'm sure these will suffice. I'll scan them and get the originals back to you. Now. All that remains is for you to pay the processing fee of five hundred and eighty-one pounds."

"How much? I thought it was a tenner for a death certificate!"

"Nineteen pounds, actually. But that will be on top of the processing fee for the declaration."

"Jesus."

"That will be fine," Marion interceded, reaching into her handbag.

"Oh, I'm afraid you can't pay me. That department's on the fifth floor. Or, if you like, I can send you a link when I've processed it all and you can pay online."

"That would be much easier. Thank you."

"You're welcome." The official smiled, stood and gestured for them to follow suit – then nonchalantly added, "Actually, I'm rather surprised you didn't just scan the documents and do all this online yourself. That's the way most people do it these days."

Chapter 31: Small Talk

"So. It's an imagined grid, across the entire planet. One metre squares, I think. Or maybe it's two. Anyway, you tap on the map and it gives you three words. Like this." Marion tapped the map on her phone's screen, the size of which verged on the cinematic, and three random words appeared: table, tomato, and giraffe. "Now. If I send you, or anyone, these three words then they can go onto the app and it'll give them this exact location. Clever, yes?"

"Well, yes. But why not just use a pin on the actual map? What do you need these extra three words for?"

"I suppose that's all very well if you're somewhere civilised. But this works worldwide. Even out in the middle of a desert or up in the tundra. As long as you've got a GPS tracker you can be found."

"Fair enough. Although, I must point out that we're in neither a desert nor the tundra. We're in fucking London, Marion."

Marion stopped chewing and gave Henry a long, stern look. Then she swallowed, smiled and said, "Henry. What is going on with you?"

"What do you mean?"

"I mean… You're a little punchy lately."

"Well, we have just finally declared your sister and my wife officially dead. It's not exactly an everyday occurrence."

"I don't think that's it."

"What do you mean?"

"I mean, I think it's something else."

"I don't know what you're talking about."

"You know exactly what I'm talking about. Or, rather, what we are not talking about."

"Ah. That." Henry looked down from Marion's gaze. He took a bottle of Chablis from the basket and topped up their already full cups.

"Perhaps we should?" Marion touched the back of his hand, gently stopping him from overfilling her wine.

"Perhaps," Henry smiled, "Or, perhaps not. Perhaps later. Yes?"

"And what would you suggest we talk about until later?"

"How about these excellent cucumber sandwiches which I got up at the crack of dawn and fought off the mother of all hangovers to prepare?"

"And which managed to survive the stuffiness of Camden Council's bizarrely tropical temperature controls. Yes, they are good, I'll give you that. The smoked salmon and cream cheese ones are excellent, too."

"It's the cayenne pepper and lemon juice."

"Is it, now."

"It is. And how do you like the wine? I thought a crisp white since it's so unseasonably warm." He topped up his own which, in spite of speaking at twice his usual speed, he'd managed to almost finish in under three sentences."

"Well, Henry, it is certainly crisp. And, might I add, perfectly chilled. How ever did you manage that? Ah. Now I see." Marion purposefully lifted the silver cool bag from its section of the basket. The spread was an impressive one. The wicker basket along with the pewter cups, housed in a worn leather case giving away their vintage, had been a lovely touch. Along with the perfectly prepared selection of sandwiches, box of mixed nuts, packet of crackers to accompany the soft cheeses and, Marion noticed last of all, a generous portion of foie gras. She pointed to the last item and added, "I take it you included this to scare off the natives?"

Henry looked around with a wicked grin. They sat together in the middle of a set of oversized steps, resembling stadium seating, overlooking the canal. Behind them was the, for them, new campus of St Martin's College. A long way, both in terms of time and location, from the bohemian incarnation Henry and Marion had attended two decades prior. He looked around at the current crop of students: many wearing the same sort of bright, garish clothes or monochromatic, Goth ensembles that he, Marion and their peers had sported – but they appeared somehow more contrived. Cleaner. Put together by outside designers rather than individual inspiration. Even the wild hair colours which many of them had – pastel pinks, bright greens and vivid blues – seemed a little weak. As if, instead of proper dye, they were temporarily washed in so that they could be just as easily rinsed out – just in case one of their economics major friends was having a party they needed to attend without offending the market traders in training. The future rulers of the world on whose patronage their lives would depend. It all lacked any real commitment.

Of course there were exceptions: Henry squinted at a nearby group, one of whom could easily have been mistaken for one of the punks from the King's Road of the late seventies. Proper nose piercings and a foot high super-glued Mohican.

At least one of them's the real deal.

"You're muttering again, Henry."

Shit.

"And I know what you're thinking. And I really don't know why. You've worn nothing but tweed jackets and button-down shirts since the day I met you."

"I did once have an earring." He looked back at the Neo-punk, whose earlobes had been stretched out with three-inch diameter discs – and who displayed a crop of jagged tattoos. "Looks like a potential customer for your new vocation."

"Jesus."

"What?"

"You, Henry. You hate small talk. I hate small talk. And, what's more, we're both bloody useless at it. So, for the love of God, let's talk about this. Because, I know it's awkward. And I know it's unexpected. But I, for one, am glad it happened. That said if it's really upsetting you this much and making you so uncomfortable then maybe we should just forget about –"

Henry leant forward and kissed her. She kissed him back. The two sat silent for a moment, their lips together and eyes closed, and then separated. Smiled. Relaxed.

"Don't you have your opening tonight?" Marion asked.

"That's tomorrow."

"Oh. I thought it was the same day as the anniversary."

"So did I. I forgot about the last leap year. It's tomorrow." *Christ. Tomorrow.*

"Okay. Well, in that case, what are you doing for the rest of the day? I've got something I'd really like to show you."

The previous tenant had been a barber which, Marion enthused, gave her a fantastic head start. The layout was already close to meeting all her requirements. The space was bright, with floor to ceiling windows facing out onto the busy thoroughfare of Camden High Street – albeit the less fashionable end. Six of the hairdressers chairs had been left behind and would perfectly suit Marion's purposes. She even liked their design: black vinyl with chrome tubing and an Art Deco flare. Marion planned to design the rest of the parlour's aesthetic around the same style. Lots of chrome, lots of mirrors and, of course, lots of photographs.

That's where, she pitched, she wanted Henry to come in. The wall nearest the door and the waiting area would display Marion's designs. Framed in simple, perfectly aligned clip-frames. Dispersed throughout the rest of the shop she envisaged large, glossy portraits. Glamorous people displaying Marion's, and her future employees', work. She'd also need a respectable headshot of herself, showing off her own tattoo, both for the front window and for her planned publicity and advertising campaign.

Speaking of which, Marion segued, she was planning on a local and online promotion in the build up to opening, which would also require some images. Could she entice Henry into that? She'd pay, of course. She wasn't asking for special favours just because they were friends. Or, possibly, more than friends, now. She got the impression that neither of them were too sure about that one.

Regardless. Marion had a strong vision for her new enterprise, the first in her life that had truly been her own, and was now looking for allies. Would, she asked, Henry be one of them?

Henry looked out of the window. The weather, as the afternoon darkened, had become more typical for the season. The wind gusted, swirling brown leaves down the street and into the faces of pedestrians – who now hunched forward and pulled up collars as they walked into the zephyr. A few heavy raindrops began to fall and one or two people, perhaps fearing a storm, ducked into the establishments across the road. A smart, independent coffee shop and a high-end tap-and-bottle shop sandwiching a vintage clothing store. It may not have been the fashionable end of Camden High Street for the younger sets, but it was definitely the more expensive stretch – more popular with the well healed. Henry wondered how they'd feel about a branch of Show Us Yer Tats blighting their swanky boulevard.

This was Marion's hook, she explained. She pointed to a few of the passers-by. All wearing expensive, designer clothing and striding with purpose to their high-powered meetings. And almost all, if you looked closely, with at least one tattoo peeking out from under their garments. The forked tongue of an adder flicking out from a hedge fund manager's double-cuffed sleeve. The edge of a Celtic cross just visible above the waistband of a business skirt. And these were just the ones you could see. Tattoo culture, Marion explained, was no longer the purview of the boxers, the heavy-metal rockers and greasy biker gangs. Today's body art was just as likely to adorn the flesh of a wealthy banker as it was that of the downtrodden unfortunate on whom he's just foreclosed. It's just the former could, and would, pay far more than the latter – in the right place and if serviced by the right talent. And especially if the artwork was just that. Art. Beautiful, fine art. This was Marion's marketplace. Her target to exploit. Marion had every intention of doing for tattoo parlours what Nikki Clarke had done for hair salons. Although it would be a franchise of Show Us Yer Tats, with Ron's backing, training and him providing her talent pool, she planned to convince him to start a new brand, for her. Renaissance Ink was the current name proposed = although she was open to suggestions. Again, she asked – her excitement building further as she paced up and down the old barber's shop, flailing her arms while spouting out new ideas – would Henry help out? If nothing else, it should be great fun.

"That it would," Henry agreed. "But there might be one possible fly in the ointment."

"What could that be?" Marion asked.

"I'm about to become a triple murderer."

Chapter 32: Serious Talk

"You know, from the inside, this place doesn't seem nearly as flashy as it does from the outside."

Marion held her glare, refusing to reply to anything Henry said that didn't have a direct bearing on her initial question: what the fuck was he thinking? It had been a little over an hour since, in the middle of her enthusiastic patter, he had casually informed her of his plans to become a serial killer. Marion had immediately taken him across the street, ordered triple strength coffees for them both and demanded an explanation.

Henry began by pointing out Marion's error in confusing serial killer with spree killer and explained the difference as Sonia had to him. This did little to quell Marion's dismay or her anger, the latter of which was beginning to vastly outweigh the former.

"You knew about this, Marion. You were there when we first came up with the idea."

"Jesus, Henry. Do you honestly think I took any of that seriously? I assumed it was the shock talking. Fuelled by the alcohol. So, don't you bring me into this as some sort of retroactive accomplice. Don't you bloody dare! I told you, there and then, when you first found out about Drew and his abominable secret you should've gone to the police. Either that, or you do nothing. Fire him. Get him out of your life and move on. But this? I mean, how far down the road are you?"

Pretty far, he was careful not to say. Opting instead for, "Then you, at least, agree that he's abominable?"

"Yes, of course I do. But that's not the point. And it certainly doesn't mean you have the right to kill the man. And, what do you mean, *triple* murderer? Who else is on you and your idiotic friends' hit list?"

Henry told Marion how Des had met Evan in prison, then became so indebted to him on the outside that Evan was about to order him to kill a boy over a mere thousand pounds.

"Once again," Marion pointed out, "A matter for the police."

"People like Des can't go to the police, Marion," Henry said, with as world-weary a tone as he could muster.

"Oh, don't be so thick-headed, Henry! Of course they can! Jesus, I can't believe we're actually discussing this. I can't believe that you've been sucked into this. I mean, you've always been a bit of a gullible twit, but really. This is beyond the pale. Even for you. What am I saying – even for anyone. It's just… it's just… it's just absurd. It's nonsensical. It's absurdly nonsensical. And who, pray tell, is the third invitee to your little VIP party of death?"

Henry paused in his reply. He looked out of the window, to the empty shop that was soon to be Marion's tattoo parlour, and took a long sip from his, now cold, coffee. The adjournment lengthened until it became a noticeable evasion tactic. Terry the Ad Man, he finally admitted, before listing his enemy's many misdemeanours and citing his suspected collusions with Drew.

"Henry. Are you listening to yourself? You've just told me that you intend to kill a man, to *kill* him, because of his inadequate parking skills."

"Oh, no. It's much more than that."

"It really isn't."

"But it is. He's a wrong-un, Marion. A bad dude who's been up to all sorts of shenanigans for years."

Marion held her stare on Henry, trying and failing to think of a sensible reply. Then she realised that she couldn't possibly come up with anything sensible or level-headed to say because there was nothing sensible or level-headed about what Henry had been telling her. It was insane. It was unreal. It couldn't possibly be real, she decided, and she smiled. She sat back, smiled, then gave a single laugh and said, "Oh, Henry. You had me. You really did have me there."

"Marion."

"Come on, Henry. It's banter. Pub banter shared between three friends who have been spending entirely too much time together drinking heavy spirits in The Bald bloody Monkey. Fantasies, Henry. None of it's real."

"Marion, I can assure you, this is all very real."

"No, Henry. It isn't. None of it is. It's all fantasy and make-believe and I want you to stop. Because if it is real, if you are actually planning on doing this, then you have truly become unhinged and I cannot have that, Henry. I simply cannot have that. Now," she gathered her bag and coat together and stood, "I am leaving. Tomorrow evening, I shall be attending your exhibition at Sonia's gallery. And I expect it to be just that, Henry. An exhibition."

"Marion."

"I shall see you there." She leant down and kissed him lightly on the lips. "Coffee's on you." She moved to step away, but Henry grabbed her wrist.

"Marion," he said again, firmly. Then he clenched his teeth and his eyes burned. "He killed Arabella, Marion. He killed her. And then he watched me grieve. He watched me grieve, and mourn and search for years. For seven years, Marion. How can I not do this?"

Marion held his look, her own eyes welling as she recognised the determination and commitment in his. Her face flushed, her jaw clenched and, with two decades of aggregated rage, Marion slapped Henry across his cheek.

Marion sat in her car, gripping the steering wheel as tightly as she wished she could grip Henry's throat. To throttle and talk some sense into him. Her right palm still stung from the slap. She hoped his face was pinpricked with infinitely more pain.

The tapping on the window didn't come as a surprise. She'd half-expected Henry to follow her and had spent the last twelve minutes watching the dashboard clock creep towards a quarter past the hour. That was the arbitrary deadline that she'd given Henry to catch up had he followed. He'd made it with two minutes to spare. She looked over at his wide eyes under sodden hair, a confused face peering through a rain-streaked window, which she rolled down.

"Get in. I'll drive you home."

The first few minutes passed in silence, apart from the occasional gasp from Henry as he gripped onto the handle above him while Marion zigzagged through various alleyway shortcuts she'd learned over her years of London driving. She took a ninety-degree corner at what felt like sixty miles an hour. Then swerved around a skip, emerged on the other side and accelerated into another right-angle turn onto the street.

"I do wish you wouldn't do that."

"Do you. Well, I wish you wouldn't commit mass murder but, hey. I guess we're all in for a disappointing week."

"It's not that simple."

Marion fell purposefully silent.

Henry did not. "I'm sorry, Marion," he said. Then, in spite of physically feeling the anger wafting towards him from the driver's side, he continued, "I'm sorry that things worked out the way they did, all that time ago. But that's just the way it did, and I couldn't help it. I couldn't help how I felt. I'm sorry that Arabella fell in love with me. And that I fell in love with her. Instead of you."

"Jesus – H – Christ!" Marion throttled forward, ducked down a dead-end alley and slammed on the breaks. She rounded on Henry, who was clutching his chest where he'd been bruised by the seatbelt, and shouted, "Is that what you think, Henry? That you, me and Arabella were some grand love triangle where you two were the glamorous romantic couple and I, poor Marion, was the tragic, rebuffed sister – left to mourn my great love for years on end while I

237

had to watch that which should have been mine blossom and bloom before my sad, lonely eyes?"

"Well, I wouldn't –"

"Shut up, you deluded fuckwit! There was nothing between us other than friendship, Henry. At least not back then. I mean, yes, there was the potential for it. I thought there was the potential for it, and I thought you might have, too. Which is why I introduced you to Arabella. To ask her opinion of you because, back then, I was as naive and unaware of her character as you managed to stay throughout your entire marriage and, God love you, beyond. Back then I still thought that my sister was everything a good sister should be. Kind, loving and giving. Everything a good partner should be. So, yes, I was a little shocked when she suddenly started pursuing you. And don't for a minute think it was the other way around, Henry. It was very definitely she who pursued you, while doing her best to steer me away from you. And do you know why? Because she could. Because she was not kind, loving and giving. She was cruel, hateful and selfish. And watching you with her for all those years broke my heart. Not because I was oh-so-in-love with you that it made my heart crack just a little bit more every time I saw you together. But because every time I saw you together I saw my friend, the man who I might have ended up falling in love with, being crushed. Humiliated. Subjugated. And you're still doing it, Henry. You're still falling for her bullshit, even though she's been dead for seven years. You still haven't seen through her. Christ, just look at some of those photographs you've got pinned to that shrine to her you've made

238

– which, by the way, is more than a little creepy. Just look at some of them and how she's looking back at you. How she's *really* looking back at you. And how she's looking at a few of the other people, too."

"What do you mean?"

"You know what I mean, Henry. Deep down, you must know. And if you don't then you really need to take a long, hard look at those photographs and yourself. Work it out. God knows, you've had enough time to do that. Do you know why you shouldn't kill Drew tomorrow night, Henry? I mean, let's forget the legal, moral and ethical issues, and the sheer madness of your drunken scheme. Aside from all that, there's one, key reason for you not to do it. It's that Arabella isn't worth it. To you her death may have been bad luck because she stepped under a ladder. Or the result of an idiotic university prank. You might even see it as murder. But to me? Sometimes, God help me, I really do think it was just karma." Marion, red faced and shaking, wiped her eyes and sniffed back her tears. "Who knows. Perhaps it was all of the above."

Henry felt paralysed. Like he was halfway through waking up and, although his thought processes were fully functional, almost working at double speed, his motor functions were lagging behind. He could feel his arms, his legs, his hand still gripping the handle above the door. But he couldn't move any of them. He couldn't even speak. All he could do was stare at Marion as she stared back with unburdened fury. Then he managed a blink. Finally, summoning his will power, he released his grip from the handle and, fingers trembling, eased his hand down to the door handle. As he reached to pull it open Marion caught the movement and snapped,

"Don't you dare."

He stopped. Frozen again.

"I said I'd drive you home and I will."

Henry alighted and walked towards his front door while fumbling with his keys and listening to Marion drive away. As soon as he heard her tires screeching around he turned and marched down to The Bald Monkey. As he strode through the door, he could still feel his face burning from Marion's slap while his shoulder, wrenched by the seatbelt, stiffened. He spied Sonia sitting in Conspiracy Corner, picked up a pint of ale at the bar and joined her.

"Jesus, Henry. You look like hell."

"Yeah. I'm not sure, but I think Marion just beat the shit out of me."

"Really? Do tell. Actually, save it until later when Des gets here. We should talk about him first. And go through the final plans for tomorrow night."

"Yeah." Henry said. "About that. Look... Are we really sure we want to go through with this?"

Sonia laughed and shook her head while topping up her wine. "Well. That's a bullseye Des owes me."

"What's that?"

"Des owes me fifty quid. I knew you'd turn chicken at some point. I thought it'd be sooner, to be honest. Although, it's a shame you didn't wait until tomorrow because then it would have been double-bubble."

"What's going on here?" Des interjected as he sat down.

"Henry's trying to chicken out."

"Oh, for fuck's sake!" Des produced his billfold and ceremoniously peeled off two twenties and a ten.

"Thank you."

"You're welcome." Des knocked back his tequila shot, turned to Henry and added, "Fuckwit. It's your round."

"Why is it my round?"

"Because you just cost me mine. And, by the way, we ain't backing out now."

"Look, I just think we should talk it through one more time before we pass the point of no return."

"We are past the point of no return, Henry." Sonia chimed in.

"All I'm saying is –"

"Henry, old chap. There you are." The interruption came from Terry the Ad Man – who appeared over, and leant on, Henry's shoulder. "Drew dropped by the invitation, and your message. No hard feelings, of course. None at all. And I'm very much looking forward to seeing your work, matey. And the drinks do. Your gaff, is it, Sweetheart?"

"Um. Yes." Sonia replied – for the first time in her life feeling utterly perplexed.

"Outstanding. Outstanding. Well, I'll see you then. Sonia K." He gave Sonia a wink, Henry an effusive slap on the shoulder and adjourned to his table – where there waited a nineteen year old Insta-model.

241

Des and Sonia turned their gazes of incredulity on Henry, who could only reply with a defeated shrug and say,

"My round again?"

Chapter 33: Thursday Morning

When his phone pinged in the morning Henry had yet to fall into any kind of slumber. He'd left the pub soon after Terry's surprise visit, which had taken him off guard. Especially following his mooted suggestion that they reconsider their diabolical plans for the coming evening.

Christ. This evening.

He had left with the intention of getting an early night in the interests of managing a clear head for the spree. Des and Sonia both said that they would follow his lead after one last drink. Henry had his doubts.

His phone pinged again. Probably a reminder to check the first message, he thought. Which would, undoubtably, be from Sonia with some last-minute reminder for the evening. Or from Des, asking for clarification on a similar issue. He closed his eyes and, again, tried to will himself to sleep. Even just fifteen minutes would suffice. Within seconds his eyes popped back open. Instantly focusing on a crack in the ceiling which he'd never noticed until that morning's dawn light, and which he'd now been staring at for the last two hours. Was it just the paint? Or the plaster. God, he hoped it wasn't structural.

Maybe the message was from Drew, wondering if he should come to the house today or just go straight to the gallery. Today. *His last day.*

Or perhaps it was from Marion, again trying to get him to see reason. Well, her idea of reason. Maybe even threatening to go to the police.

Oh, for Christ's sake! Henry checked the message and repeated, this time as a shout, "Oh, for Christ's sake!" He deleted the NHS reminder that he was now overdue for an MOT. At the top of the screen he saw the time. Six fifty-nine.

Seven in the fucking morning! he sighed, resigned himself to the day and threw the covers aside. *Coffee.*

By the time he was on his fourth mug Henry was beginning to feel the caffeine jitters. Not something that he usually experienced but that extra mug, along with zero sleep and the anticipation of the evening's impending slaughter, would, be supposed, be enough to make anyone a little anxious. His phone pinged.

Message from Sonia: 'Don't forget to wear a suit and tie. I hope you're well rested.'

Henry replied with a thumbs up then rose from the kitchen table. Clutching his mug, he padded his way into the living room. As he neared the sofa his phone, again, pinged.

Message from Des: 'Any idea what we should wear tonight? Wish I'd left when you did last night.' He'd signed off with two yellow-faced emojis – one with a crooked mouth and goggly eyes, the other expelling green vomit.

'Jacket and tie, apparently', Henry replied. He smirked at the predictability of his, now literal, partners in crime.

As he sipped the, still just a little too hot, coffee, Henry looked up at the collage. He stepped towards it and scanned a few of the images. Early memories of him and Arabella. Still young and affectionate with their arms wrapped around each other. Wide smiles and bright eyes. He looked towards the centre of the collection. An area he rarely explored, apart from when he printed them. The one that caught his eye was from their first wedding anniversary. A group shot with him and Arabella centre frame surrounded by a collection of friends – the men attired in fine suits and the ladies in finer dresses, raising champagne glasses and smiling. As he studied it, he realised that he had not seen any of these people since Arabella's disappearance. He couldn't even remember any of their names. In fact, he doubted he had ever even known most of their names. Strange, as the photograph had been taken in his own garden. His and Arabella's. The only other person in the frame he recognised was Marion, who sat off to the side clutching a red wine glass in one hand and the bottle in the other. That made him smile – and then he wondered who had taken the photograph.

Another ping.

Message from Drew: 'Should I go to the house or just straight to the gallery?'

"Ha!" Henry said, with a strange feeling of triumph. Then he replied, 'Gallery', and turned his eyes back to the collage. Forgetting the group photograph which, moments before, had piqued his curiosity, his focus shifted forward a few years. To one of the few holidays abroad he and Arabella had taken. Christmas in New York. Henry had, earlier that year, scored one of the most lucrative assignments of his career. A high-end fashion shoot for a glossy magazine which Danny had taken over as guest editor. At first Henry had declined on the grounds that it was a one month shoot that meant travelling to Morocco and Arabella didn't want to go. She said the extreme heat wouldn't agree with her. Never mind all that sand.

"Jesus, Henry!" Danny had berated him, "I'm not just throwing you a bone here. I'm chucking you a fucking steak!"

The money was very good, so Arabella eventually suggested he go alone. She would miss him terribly. But she wanted to spend more time with Marion so perhaps this was an opportunity to do so. Then he could make it up to her by taking her away for Christmas. After all, he'd be able to afford it for once.

And it was a wonderful Christmas. The photograph he examined was of Arabella standing on the ice rink in front of the famous Rockefeller Christmas Tree. The edges of her flouncy dress and flyaway hair were blurred as she'd just completed a pirouette with surprising dexterity and ease. Until that day Henry had no idea she could even skate. He had snapped the shot with a slightly slower than normal shutter speed, entirely by accident, but managed to capture a moment when all in the frame was a blur except her face, which was lighting up with an excited smile – just on the verge laughter. Henry felt himself on that same verge as he recalled why she was so amused. She had spent most of that morning trying, with hilariously little success, to teach him how to ice skate. It had, for Henry, been a cold, frustrating morning of stumbles and tumbles. He was still wearing the skates when he took the photograph and, as he had bent his knees to get the angle he wanted and snapped the shot, was just in the process of falling on his arse.

A perfect moment, he thought. Then he felt the smile give way to clenched teeth. Another good reminder as to why Drew was getting what was coming to him.

Ping.

"Oh, for the love of God."

Henry checked the phone. No message. It sounded again and Henry realised it was not a ping from his phone, but a ring from the front door – which he went to answer.

"Marion." Henry pulled the dressing gown cord tighter around his waist.

"Mind if I come in?" The question was rhetorical. Marion was halfway through the door before she'd finished asking. Once in the living room she turned and said, "Come to your senses yet, then?"

Henry was poking his head out of the doorway and looking down the street.

"For God's sake, I haven't brought the police."

"I didn't think you had."

"Yes, you did. Because you're paranoid. And you're deluded. And, honestly, Henry, I really think you're having some sort of breakdown. I mean, your two lunatic friends coming up with this kind of idiocy I can believe. But you, Henry? That I can't fathom. This is not you." She sat down on Henry's sofa with a heavy thump. Then threw him a look and snapped, "Well? Coffee?"

Henry came back in, closed the door and obediently headed to the kitchen.

"How do you know, Marion? How do you know what is or isn't me? I mean, up until a few weeks ago we hadn't even seen each other for nearly seven years." Henry spoke with a calm, measured timbre as he emerged from the kitchen with a fresh pot of coffee. He'd occasionally been peeking through the kitchen door and watching Marion sitting in silence, her furious face staring into nowhere, for the fifteen minutes it had taken the coffee to brew. Well, ten to brew. Another five for him to pluck up the nerve to face her again. He now sat down beside her and poured two generous mugs. "And before that, well. I don't know where you went once Arabella and I got together."

"And whose fault do you think that was?"

"Well, it wasn't only mine."

"No, Henry. It wasn't only yours. And it only wasn't mine." Marion looked away from him. Back to staring blankly forward.

Henry followed her gaze and realised that she was not staring into nowhere, but at the collage. He tried to work out which of the photographs she was studying. "You know, you said some pretty awful things about her yesterday."

"Yes, I did. Terrible things. Things I've never said out loud before, but which I've often thought. I mean, don't get me wrong. I did love her. But only because I had to. A hard-wired instinct between siblings. But, the truth is, I'm not sure if I ever really liked her. Would you like to know why, Henry?"

Henry shook his head. He'd really rather not.

"Jesus." It came out as a cross between an angry hiss and a resigned sigh. Marion sipped the coffee, winced and put the mug down. She stood, approached the wall and walked up and down – surveying the photographs. She stopped. "This one." She snatched the photograph of Henry and Arabella announcing their engagement. "This is the one I took, yes? The famous first photograph of you and her as an engaged couple."

"As you can see from the –"

"Yes, yes. The reflection. The bloody reflection. Jesus, Henry. You're not still going on about that, are you?" She tore the photograph in two and let the separated halves fall to the floor.

"Hey!"

"And, this one." She selected another. One of him and Marion reunited after her two-week winter holiday to Hawaii and California. Her, Henry and the American friends who came back with her. "Do you remember this crowd, Henry? Specifically this guy?" She pointed to the tall man standing directly behind Marion. Her host in both states on the trip. "Ever notice how many of your photographs this old friend of hers crops up in? How often he used to visit London?"

"Well, they were friends before I met Arabella. You know that."

"Oh, boy, do I know that. And, boy, were they friends."

"What's that supposed to mean?"

"What do you think." Marion tore that photograph in four and let the pieces fall next to the

249

first. She took a third from the wall. "And let's talk about this one for a moment, shall we?"

"Marion, that's enough.' Henry stood and took a step forward but she glared at him with such ferocity, with such incandescence in her eyes, that he stopped. He looked at the photograph. The last photograph. Marion smiling, holding up the charm bracelet, just minutes before she would vanish forever.

"How many times have you told me, told everyone, about this one? The final image of poor Arabella's last night after your, oh-so-romantic anniversary dinner."

"Well it's true, Marion."

"It is not true, Henry. It's a fabrication. It is a lie. It may be a lie you have come to believe, but it is a lie. Sheer, utter fantasy."

"How would you know?"

"Because every time you tell that story you tell it with me in it. That I was there, on the other end of the phone as you left your perfect dinner, wishing my perfect sister a gloriously happy birthday. But I wasn't, Henry. I didn't speak to Arabella that night. We hadn't spoken for months."

Marion held the photograph high, brandishing it like a weapon, then ripped it into quarters and let the pieces fall to join the rest of the torn memories. She stood for a moment, shaking as her eyes reddened and welled, then she wiped her cheeks and repeated, "For months." She turned and marched towards the door. As she walked by the fireplace she saw, resting on the mantlepiece, the boot which Henry had salvaged from the fatberg. Marion turned back to him and, pointing at it, added, "By the way, Arabella never wore Burberry boots. That was me. Arabella said they were low class, for footballers' wives and Essex girls, and that she'd never be seen dead in a pair. Quite prophetic of her, don't you think?" Without waiting for a reply she left, leaving the door open behind her.

After a moment the wind caught and slammed the door closed, snapping Henry out of a trance he hadn't realised he was in. He knelt down and examined the fallen pieces. One piece drew him in. The most precious. The last one. One quarter of it had been severed from the rest to show only Marion's face. Without the bracelet. Without the restaurant behind her. An isolated close up of her face which always smiled back at him. But now, unencumbered by context, she wasn't smiling. It was something else.

Chapter 34: Seven Years and One Day Ago

Arabella looked down at the finely crafted bracelet which Henry had just gifted her. The charms, hand etched by one of London's finest artists, comprised of a crucifix, a Star of David, a crescent moon and a fat Buddha, just to cover any and all religious bases. A four-leaf clover, a horseshoe, a baby elephant, a happy pig and a tiny rabbit's foot, to bring as much luck as possible. A club, an ace, a diamond and a heart because, apparently, as well as being a fine artist, the creator was also a notorious poker player. And, finally, a tiny disc inscribed with the number ten. This Henry had asked to be added both as a commemoration and because the number of original charms totalled thirteen. Which, he thought, rather defeated the purpose of them being lucky.

"Is it silver?"

"Nope," Henry grinned." Guess again."

Arabella gave him a cockeyed look.

"What metal is for tenth?" he prompted.

She shrugged: dunno.

"Tin! It's tin!"

"Tin," she sighed. "That's so you." As she looked up at him, Henry raised his old Minox spy camera, his own lucky charm which he had carried with him since his teenage years, and snapped a candid shot.

The final shot.

"Aren't you going to put it on?" he asked.

"Here," Arabella shoved the box towards him, extended her wrist and said, "Knock yourself out."

Henry carefully fastened the bracelet around Arabella's wrist. Then, holding her hand in both of his, he softly kissed the back of her wedding ring finger. As he did so a thunderclap shook the empty glasses on the table and Arabella snatched her hand away. They both looked towards the window, which was streaked with beads of heavy rain. "I'm afraid it's going to be a wet walk home if we can't find a taxi."

"That it is." Arabella replied as the waiter arrived with the bill, "Of course, you could have ordered one ahead of time." She turned her attention to her mobile phone, scrolling through missed calls.

Once the bill was settled, Arabella walked ahead of Henry with her mobile phone pressed to her face. "It's tin. Can you believe it? Apparently, that's the metal for a tenth anniversary. I mean, tin! ...No, Chinese. I can already feel the MSG coursing through my arteries."

Henry caught up with her as a head waiter opened the door for them. Outside the black sky sparkled with streams of heavy rain caught in the streetlights.

"No, he didn't bother ordering one. We're walking back. ...Cats and dogs. My new Jimmy Choo's are going to be ruined! I'll see you soon. Yeah? ...Bye, now." Arabella hung up and pocketed her phone.

"Marion?" Henry guessed, linking his arm through hers.

253

"Come on, let's get a move on." She pulled up her coat's collar and dashed out into the storm.

Henry and Arabella made their way through the flooded streets of Camden. Wading uphill through torrents and splashing through puddles. An occupied taxi came past, its pavement-side wheels catching the edge of a pool and throwing a wall of water over them.

"Bloody HELL!" Arabella cried, finally having enough and running towards the nearest temporary shelter: a small scaffold outside the Sonia K Gallery. As she attempted to brush water off herself, she looked into the front window and saw a row of black and white photographs leaning against the blank walls, ready to be hung. "Oh, of course," she laughed. "We had to come by here. Didn't we."

"Well, it's on the way and I just wanted to see –"

"Is that why you didn't order a taxi, Henry? So that we could take a nice, romantic walk back home and gaze lovingly at your great achievements on the way? For the love of God, get under here before you drown!"

Henry was still standing out in the torrential rain. He took a step forward, then stopped and moved to one side.

"What are you waiting for?"

Henry glanced at the ladder, leaning against the scaffolding outside the first floor window. Set up for Sonia to mount the sign advertising his latest, and biggest, exhibition.

"Really, Henry? The ladder?"

"Well, it's bad –"

254

"Bad luck. I know. Bloody. Hell. Henry. You and your idiotic superstitions." By way of making a point Arabella stepped toward the ladder and waded through the stream that ran over her brand-new boots.

"'Bella, please be careful!"

"Oh, be careful! Bad luck! For Christ's sake, Henry! What is wrong –?"

And as she stepped under the ladder, Arabella disappeared into the water. Swallowed by an open manhole and flushed into the bowels of London.

Chapter 35: Desecration

Henry stared down at the shredded photographs. The pieces, with vicious jagged edges, randomly strewn on the floor. Scattered around his knees. Gathering his equally wrecked thoughts he shuffled the pieces, like three jigsaws, and roughly put them back together.

Arabella, again, stared back at him from the Chinese restaurant. Leaning forward into the frame. But what had been the sparkle in her eye had now become a glare. The smile a contemptuous smirk.

Henry turned his attention to the second of Marion's targeted memories. That of Arabella, Henry and the group of Americans she had brought back from her impromptu holiday to Hawaii and California during that harsh winter of ice and snow. Two years before the flood took her. Henry bent down to further inspect the group. He focused on the man who Marion had pointed out. A tall collection of muscles with blow dried hair and a chiselled chin.

What was his name? Todd something? Harrison? No. Bradley. Brad.

Bradley B Winchester the Third. A name as ludicrously American as his phosphorescently white teeth – which, even in black and white, Henry now noticed caused an inordinate amount of lens flare. He also saw how close Bradley stood to Arabella. Slightly behind her. His manicured fingers just visible, creeping down from her shoulder. His arm casually draped across her back. And Arabella,

Henry realised with a twist of his gut, leaning back into him.

Henry glanced up at the collage. He scanned for various other group shots. The ones taken at the parties they'd held or attended over the years to meet this group of American dignitaries whose company Arabella had always valued so much more than any of their home-based social circle – particularly those from his side of the marriage. They had been old friends of Arabella's who she had known since before she and Henry had met, so the visitations went right back through the timeline. The first to a thanksgiving dinner which Arabella had insisted she and Henry host for them, about a year after they were married, when Bradley, BB3 to his friends, and his business cohorts had found themselves stranded in London. Henry stared at the photograph of the long, dining-room table laden with roast turkey, potatoes and yams.

His eye went to the head of the table where Arabella sat with BB3 to her right. Both smiling back. Leaning towards each other. Bradley's arm across the back of her chair. Henry could feel his innards give another turn. Then another, until he could look no more.

Henry shifted his attention to the first photograph Marion had torn in half and let fall. That first, cherished image of him and Arabella as an engaged couple. He pushed the two halves towards each other, trying to piece the memory together. He first looked at his own face. Filled with genuine joy and amazement that this beautiful, vibrant woman had agreed to marry him. A pure memory, still. Then

257

he looked at Arabella's. Bright eyed and smiling. And genuinely so – an expression, like his, of happiness. Lacking any sort of malice. Certainly not any of the kind he had finally noticed in that last image. And yet there was something, a certain bearing, which he began to notice. He couldn't quite put his finger on it, but there was something around the edges of Arabella's eyes. The corners of her lips. As he stared, searching his mind for what he now saw, there was only one fitting word he could find. Melancholy. The sadness of a love lost.

He looked back up at the Thanksgiving photograph. On Arabella's other side he saw a woman wearing an expression which he imagined was similar to the one he now exhibited. Her face was turned to the camera, but her eyes looked towards BB3. His wife, Dana. BB3's very rich wife, heiress to an East Coast fortune – one undoubtably guarded by a battalion of lawyers and a regiment of trustees around a fortress of prenuptial agreements. Her face was lined with disappointment, anger and regret.

For the first time, Henry wondered why Arabella had married him. Then he heard her voice echo through his mind reciting some of the mantras he had heard her say to him over the years. Particularly the early ones. How Henry was so sweet. So nice. So caring. How she knew he would stay by her and she would never be abandoned. Never be alone.

"I'll never be lonely," she would say.

To which Henry would reply, "And I'll always love you." Convincing himself that they meant the same thing.

Henry continued to stare at the separated engagement photograph on the floor. He pushed the two halves further together. Now trying, not to reunite the image of him and Arabella, but to reassemble the reflection of Marion behind the lens – which her furious rip had torn straight through. The twist in his gut became unmanageable. Bile bubbled at the back of his throat.

Christ. He began to feel nauseous. *Whisky.*

As he poured his second dram Henry sat at the dining room table – where the Thanksgiving meal had been all those years ago, he had now spread the pieces of torn photographs. Reassembled and, like the shrine, placed in order of chronology. His whirling mind started to settle as new recollections replaced old memories. The old becoming dissipating echoes. The new forming as crystal clear snapshots.

Henry finished the drink, sat up straight and, with calm resolve, picked up the pieces and stacked them in front of him. He started with the last image, the final day, and added the Thanksgiving photograph. Before adding the engagement shot he, once more, pushed the two halves together, ragged edge to ragged edge, in an effort to see the reflection of Marion. But the damage today's Marion had done was too great. For some reason, this made Henry laugh.

He poured himself a third dram. Then calmly rose, took his drink and the stack, and moved into his office. There he switched on his cross-cutting shredder. A heavy-duty model designed for destroying large photographs beyond any sort of recognition. It activated with a low, tantalising hum – which was interrupted by quick, sharp buzzes with each of the pieces he inserted.

With slow purpose, Henry returned to the living room. He went to the beginning of the shrine and, carefully, removed each photograph – one at a time. By the time the wall was bare he had two sizeable stacks on his dining table. He needed two because he feared the first would topple, and the second was nearly as tall. For years he'd pinned layer over layer. There must have been close to five hundred photographs.

He didn't pause to look at any of them as he went about his task. He no longer had any need to. Nor, which he found strange, did he have any desire to.

A fourth dram accompanied the first stack. Henry carried it into the office and, one tainted memory at a time, he fed the hungry, mechanical beast. Henry felt a little more sated with each sharp buzz that accompanying every bite. The larger prints causing longer and louder howls than the fragments from the torn images. Occasionally he'd hit a special photograph which he'd printed on a heavier gauge paper than the norm, and the machine would cry out with a particularly satisfying, agonised wail.

After shredding the final photograph, and finishing the last dram, Henry ambled over to his desk and retrieved his file. The precious file of maps, photographs and notes which had been his life's obsession – not project, or mission but, he now realised, obsession – for the last seven years. He opened it and, starting with the first of the maps, set about its destruction.

Once the last map had been obliterated, he switched off the machine. Its green light gradually dimmed as its steady hum lowered to an eventual silence, with a tone that almost implied grateful relief. Henry glanced at the large, transparent bin underneath the shredder, now filled to the point of overflowing.

I must get Drew to empty that tomorrow, he thought. Then his face became ice cold and his knees weakened. He steadied himself against the machine. He looked at the window. Pitch black. He looked at the clock. Half-past five. *Oh, no.*

Henry ran at a panic to the living room mantelpiece, where he had put his phone after Marion had left, nearly nine hours before. Next to the boot. Thirteen missed messages from Sonia. Twelve from Des. On the screen he could read the preview of Sonia's last message to him, sent minutes before: 'Fuck it, Henry. We're going ahead without you.'

Christ!

Chapter 36: Last Minute Invitations

At around the same time Marion was storming out on Henry, having torn his past to shreds, Sonia padded her way down the stairs from her attic apartment to the gallery's main space. She carried in one hand an oversized mug of coffee and, in the other, a half-pint glass of water fizzing with a double dose of Solpadeine Max. Four soluble tablets, each containing five-hundred milligrams of paracetamol and twelve and a half of codeine. Sonia's regular, and to date unsurpassed, hangover cure.

"God bless a country where opiates can be purchased over the counter", her Canadian ex-con, ex-boyfriend would say when he introduced her to the restorative = a rare necessity back in those happier, albeit deluded, days of disciplined domesticity.

She sat at the antique French writing desk which had been moved to the entranceway to face the exhibition. This is where guests would sign in, pick up their brochures and buy a copy of the show's accompanying book. It would also be a place for Henry to sit and sign copies of the book while the rats drowned in the basement before being flushed into the sewer. Sonia had placed a small Christmas tree next to a stack of the books. Even though it was only late November it seemed that every other commercial enterprise in town had already been marketing for the season for what seemed like months. Much as it irked her, she thought she might as well remind guests that a signed copy of a photography book always makes for an excellent present. She flicked through a copy, they had only been delivered the day before, and was pleasantly surprised to find them to be of excellent quality. Especially given the fact that, due to the nature of her current finances, she had gone to the cheapest printers she could find. She made a mental note to use them for any future events she might find herself curating.

Sonia closed the book, placed it back on the display and looked up at the main exhibition. The images nearest to her, all set out on white boards creating makeshift corridors around the warehouse, were from Henry's wartime catalogue. A few stark and dramatic images to attract the punters' attention. High contrast, monochromatic tanks with windswept soldiers atop. Shattered buildings and broken faces in front of serene, azure skies. The photograph for Henry's introductory headshot, chosen by Henry and appearing both by the gallery's entrance and in the book's inside cover, was from this period. A self-portrait of his reflection in a Humvee's wing mirror, looking very derring-do while holding his camera at chest level. A convoy of battle-weary US Marines behind him. Henry had always maintained he had taken it by accident. A claim against which Sonia, along with everyone else, held strong reservations.

Past these, along the suggested viewing path, were some of his press shots of the rich and famous. Mostly taken at private events, but some paparazzi snaps: Henry's briefest and, according to him, best paid but least rewarding period. This path led to the far end of the gallery, where most attendees would loop back to view the rest of the show. Circumventing the basement door, which would be cordoned off by a red, velvet rope. The VIP section for those invited, to be firmly closed and off limits for the duration of the actual show.

RIP to the VIPs, Sonia thought, and let out a single, loud laugh. Then sat back, sipped her coffee and surveyed the rest of the exhibition. She found herself smiling with both pride and satisfaction at what she began to realise was probably one of the finest shows she'd put together for years. She had high hopes.

The fizzing stopped as Sonia's restorative cleared. She braced herself for its foulness, drank the entire concoction in three gulps and slammed the glass onto the table while crying, "Christ, that never tastes any better."

"Your morning panacea?"

"Jesus!"

"Sorry," Drew smiled – or perhaps didn't, who could tell. "I didn't mean to scare you." He came from behind one of the temporary walls and, carrying an armful of books, approached the table. "Just thought we could do with a few more of these at the front."

"How long have you been here?"

"Oh, since about seven-thirty. Just tinkering and straightening up a few things. Hope you don't mind. You did give me a key."

"I surely did."

"So. The big day. Any last-minute changes I should know about?"

264

"No. I believe all is in hand."

"Would you like me to finish off the cataloguing?"

"Yeah. That'd be great," Sonia replied. Again, they forced awkward smiles towards each other until Sonia realised that the catalogue to which Drew referred was underneath her coffee and he would need to sit where she was in order to carry out the task. "Oh. Right. I'd better go and get dressed, anyway." Sonia stood and tightened her dressing gown cord, then made her way back to her apartment while sending Henry another text.

About an hour later, showered and changed into her most pin-striped of three-piece suits, Sonia checked her phone while descending the stairs. Still no message from Henry, which came as no surprise. He was never really that functional before his third coffee at around ten o'clock in the morning – although on a day like this she would have thought he could make an exception. She sent him another message asking him to call or text her when he was conscious. She also sent one to Des asking what time he would be making an appearance. Des replied as soon as he could: he had been summoned to meet Evan in the pub at opening time. The news gave Sonia pause, but not concern.

"I've been Messaging and WhatsApping a few of the VIPS." Drew called out as Sonia arrived downstairs.

As if he deserves some sort of fucking medal! Sonia always found Drew's overeagerness to please a highly off-putting trait. It was one of the main reasons she was quite happy to see him done away with. As she savoured this thought, a slight unease set in about the way Drew had phrased his boast. "What do you mean by VIPs?"

"Well, the VIPs. The ones I suppose you sent the invitations cards out to? You know, for the party downstairs."

Oh, shit!

"I just thought I'd take it upon myself to get in touch with a couple of them – you know, the whales – and say how much we're looking forward to seeing them this evening."

Little bastard! She thought, while replying through a fixed grin, "Did you, Drew? Did you think you'd just take it upon yourself?"

"Well, since you put me in charge of the event downstairs I just thought I'd, you know, throw myself into the role. I hope that was okay."

"Well, I didn't *really* put you in charge, I just asked you to work the bar. But, yes. Of course it was okay. It showed great initiative, Drew. Well done. Well. Done. You."

"I have to admit, it's a good thing I did. I've already had a couple of responses from people who hadn't received the card."

"Such as?"

"Well, Magnus James, for a start. Isn't he the one you had high hopes for to buy the portrait of himself? The vain actor?"

"He is, indeed." *Well, perhaps not the worst thing. The world wouldn't really miss him.*

"And Henry's newspaper friend. Danny Thompson."

"Really?"

"Don't worry. They both say they can make it for the reception."

"Oh, good!" *Fuck!* "Anyone else?"

"Not yet. Is there anyone else you'd like me to follow up on?"

"No, that's okay. Don't forget we've got limited capacity downstairs and," she lied, "I've got a few colleagues of my own coming. Critics and the like."

"Oh. Sorry, I didn't know."

"No reason you should. Now, if you could just finish off the last of the cataloguing and print up the last of the pricing labels, that would be ace. I'm off for a decent coffee."

As Sonia left the gallery for the nearest coffee shop, she silently screamed towards the sky. Then texted both Henry and Des to inform them that Drew had entirely fucked up their plan. She would kill him if they weren't already going to kill him.

Chapter 37: Conspiracy Corner

'Little bastard's sent out last-minute invitations to all and sundry for the VIP party. Need to bring the main event forward by an hour'.

Des received Sonia's text just after he'd taken his seat at the long bar in The Bald Monkey – around the same time that Henry was sitting at his dining table and piecing together the torn photographs. "Oh, fucking hell," he muttered.

"For the love of God, Desmond. There isn't even anyone else in here yet." Michael said as he placed Des's pint on the bar. "Are you cursing at yourself while you're drinking by yourself, now?"

"Sorry, Michael. Just helping Groucho out with her event tonight and she's having some last-minute snags. And I'm waiting for Evan."

"Hmm," Michael frowned. "To be honest, I'd feel better if you were drinking by yourself. There's a mean streak in that one."

If you only knew.

"Got one in for me, then?" Evan squawked as, shoulders rolling, he strutted into the pub. "Pint of lager there, Mick. Cheap as you like with a lemonade top."

Michael went about pouring the drink with no further engagement.

"You know he doesn't really go by that. Don't you." Des said.

"By what?"

"Mick."

"What. Think's it's derogatory, or something?"

"No. Just doesn't like it. Or Mickey. Or Mike. He's always just Michael."

"Dizzy."

"Yeah?"

"Come here." Des leaned down and Evan whispered, "I couldn't give a fuck." He smiled at Michael, throwing an array of coins on the table, and blithely said, "Thanks, Mickey. Keep the change," then slipped off the stool while turning back to Des. "Come on. A quiet word."

They moved through the empty pub towards the back where, for no reason other than to amuse himself, Des manoeuvred them to sit in Conspiracy Corner.

"So. Let's see it, then?" Evan said as he settled back, facing Des and the room.

"See what?"

"The video. The video of the drummer boy's final moments. Today's the last day, remember."

The last day. That it is. "Yeah, I remember. I remember I said I'd have it for you at the party, didn't I?"

"What party?"

"The one at the gallery, Evan. Sonia's gallery."

"Oh, yeah. I'd forgotten about that." Evan sipped. His swivelling head and darting eyes momentarily avoiding Des.

Des noticed Evan's hair, not only recently cut but also highlighted, and spontaneously let out a single laugh – spluttering his beer all over himself and the table.

"Bloody hell, Dizzy!" Evan pushed his chair back.

269

"Sorry, Evan," Des coughed through what had become a combination of laughter and mild choking. "Went down the wrong way."

"Yeah, story of your life, that. Everything going the wrong way." Evan stood to avoid any stray liquid running towards him across the table. "Just make sure you bring me the drummer last home movie later on, yeah? And enjoy the work. It's going to be your first of many rodeos, Diz. And you'll end up thanking me. The money's a lot better than the cuts and scrapes jobs you've been on. Like I said. This is a promotion, this is. You're in the big leagues now."

Des felt another rising wave of anger, which he quelled by reminding himself that it really didn't matter. Evan would be down in the depths with all the rest of the drowned vermin before long. "Yeah, no problem," he said. Then as Evan gave him a nod and turned to leave Des also remembered the last text from Sonia. "By the way, I'm going to be there an hour early. Why don't you come along then? Give you a chance to chat up Groucho before it gets too crowded."

"Yeah," Evan replied. "Yeah, alright." Evan put down his lager top, having only finished the first half, and left.

Des finished his drink and, before leaving, replied to Sonia's text, letting her know that he'd arranged for Evan's early arrival while enquiring about Drew and Terry the Ad Man. Sonia instantly responded to say Drew wouldn't be a problem. Now that she'd, apparently, put him in charge of the VIP party he'd probably be down in the basement for the rest of the day. The Ad Man was Henry's problem

– whenever he decided to get out of bed. Des said he'd go and check on him in a while if there was still no word. But first he had to go home, change, and then meet Frank back at the pub to get some last-minute tools for the job. Something about a properly prepared hammer.

An hour or so later – around the same time that Sonia was enjoying her temporary escape to the coffee shop and while Henry, on his second dram, was disassembling his shrine – Des returned to The Bald Monkey. The place was beginning to fill with the lunchtime crowd, through which Des carried two pints – one for him and another for Frank, who had taken Evan's previous seat in Conspiracy Corner. Des crossed the room with an uncharacteristic confidence, straight backed and square shouldered. Partly because of his excited anticipation for the day and partly because he had changed into his evening smarts: a black wool suit with a red waistcoat and black shirt. Angie had chosen the outfit for him, nearly eight years ago. It always felt like his suit of armour.

"Nice threads, Des," Frank said. "Very nice."

Des faltered as he watched Frank wheeze and lift an oxygen mask to his face. An upgrade from the nose pipes he had when they last met. "Thanks, Mate," he replied, feeling a flush of embarrassment, which grew as he saw how Frank's once red, fleshy cheeks and become thin, yellow parchment. "Here you go." He pushed the pint of Guinness towards the once great King, who removed the mask and said,

"Nah. Thanks, but those days are behind me, now. Most days are. On the water with some God-awful nutrient stuff mixed into it." He gestured towards a plastic container with two oversized handles and a thick straw with a corrugated bend. The geriatric version of a toddler's sippy-cup. Then he winked and nodded towards the Guinness adding, "I'm sure it won't go to waste, though."

"No worries on that front, mate," Des replied, pulling the extra pint back towards him. "So. What the fuck is a properly prepared hammer when it's at home?"

"That, my son, is an invention of my own devising." While struggling and stretching to reach into and open his backpack, which hung from one side of his wheelchair, Frank continued, "As we have discussed ad nauseam, the crux of your plan is to give that overhead sewer pipe's collar a good, hard wallop. Thereby shattering it, breaking the pipe in two and causing the biggest flood since humanity pissed off the Lord Almighty so much that he decided to flush away the entire world save that arse-licker, Noah. Yes?"

"Sounds about right."

"Yes, it does. But it struck me that, in doing so, by using a modern hammer of any sort, should there be any forensic investigation, your jig might well come a cropper by the giveaway telltale signs of your usage of said modern hammer. Here. Got it." He finally unhooked his backpack. "So. I have taken the liberty of procuring for you an 'ammer of the correct vintage. That is, ergo, the same vintage what is the sewer pipe you are planning on demolishing. I have

272

also, for the last few weeks, been soaking said hammer in the sewer outlet what is at the end of my garden." He produced an old lump hammer, mostly wrapped in a plastic bag but with the worn, disturbingly moist handle exposed and pointed towards Des. "Forgive me for handing you the shit end of the stick," he added – with the grin of someone who had spent days, possibly weeks, rehearsing what he thought would be the funniest utterance of his life.

"Frank, what the fuck are you on about?"

"I told you. Forensics, Des. Metal fibres and shards. If they do analyse anything under an electrode microscope, and they find that someone's had at the pipe with some rubbish, modern hammer from the local Argos, then all roads lead to you, my son. You'll be up the creek and in the nick before the evening's out! But if you use that, and then you chuck it down into the sewer along with your undesirables, then nobody'll be any the wiser. The metal fibres and rust particulates will match that what is of the right vintage. And, thanks to my soaking it in contemporary bodily wastes and the like for the last few weeks, the antique wood of the handle is now saturated with the appropriate piss and shit, as if it's been lying at the bottom of the sewer for months. Years. Maybe even decades. A secret weapon, Des." He placed it on the table. "Which it is my deepest pleasure to bestow upon you. No need for thanks."

"No need to worry."

Frank only stayed for about five minutes after gifting Des the marinated mallet. Des remained at the table, still looking at the hammer with a mixture of

273

intrigue and disgust, while attending to the extra pint declined by Frank. As he set into it he began to chuckle, both at Frank's increasingly bizarre lexicon, which he now remembered always became more exaggerated when he was excited, and the hammer that sat before him. Perhaps the old King Of The Belly Men was onto something. It couldn't hurt to use it, anyway. He didn't bother telling Frank that the tool he had intended to use was not a rubbish, modern hammer from the local Argos but, rather, the old claw and ball hammer which Evan had given him.

He wrapped Frank's gift up in the plastic bag, hiding both iron and handle from prying eyes, and placed it into the knapsack which Frank had also given him – saying he had no use for it anymore. This last few weeks had been the swansong of his adventures and schemes, and he thanked Des for that. He then called a taxi to take him to, he confided to Des, what he expected to be his final earthly destination. The St Joseph's Hospice in Bethnal Green.

Alone at the table, Des raised the pint given to him by his departed – and soon to be truly departed – friend, took a long draw and checked his watch. Three o'clock. He'd said he'd be at the gallery for four-thirty, with the new early kick-off now set for five. Des settled in to enjoy the extra pint. He sat back and thought, with what should probably have been a lot more concern, *Why do people keep giving me hammers and fucking guns?*

Chapter 38: Marion's Morning

"By the way, Arabella never wore Burberry boots. That was me. Arabella said they were low class, for footballers' wives and Essex girls, and that she'd never be seen dead in a pair. Quite prophetic of her, don't you think?" Marion marched off without waiting for a reply, taking care to leave Henry's front door open.

She did slam her own car door hard enough to attract the attention of Henry's opposite neighbour, who stood on his stoop wearing a silk dressing gown and sipping from his Top Geezer coffee mug. She then let out a long, frustrated scream while dealing Lilith's steering wheel a series of blows – visualising Henry's thick head and giving it a much-needed pummelling.

Marion sat back, feeling some temporary relief from her exasperation, and started the car up. She looked over at the neighbour who was staring back at her. Terry the Ad Man. She wondered if she should warn him about what was in store for him at that evening's party. But that would mean she'd have to admit to prior knowledge of a planned murder. A planned multiple murder. It seemed too absurd and removed from her everyday reality to take seriously. There was no way they'd actually go ahead with it. Not Henry, anyway. *Surely, not Henry,* she thought. *Dammit, here comes the Ad man.*

While Marion dithered Terry stepped down from his stoop and, wearing a broad grin, approached. Marion rolled down the window. Partly out of politeness and partly because she was still weighing up whether she should alert him to the danger – possible danger, unlikely danger – that lied ahead. And if so, how she could do so without incriminating herself.

Terry placed his hand on the sill and leaned down towards her. The other hand he placed on the top of Marion's car, after he rested the coffee mug on her roof.

The increasingly improbable threat was instantly forgotten as the hair on the back of Marion's neck bristled. A hot coffee mug on the top of poor Lilith's freshly waxed roof.

How bloody dare he!

Terry leaned down towards her and oozed, "Hello, love. Our Henry been giving you a hard time, then? You can come in and have a cup of tea if you feel like calming down a bit before driving."

Marion felt her anger violently surge. She glanced past Terry and noticed that, as per Henry's regular complaint, his cocooned E-Type was parked nose-to-nose with Gertrude's grill. She inched her face towards Terry's and said, "For Christ's sake, Terry. Move your fucking car, will you?"

As Terry's jaw slackened Marion threw Lilith into gear, twisted the steering wheel and floored the accelerator. She looked in the rear-view mirror as Terry fell into the street and his mug, slipping from the car roof, hit the ground in front on him. Shattering and spraying him with coffee. For a moment she cracked a smile and allowed herself to find the sight hilarious. Then she felt the tingle at the back of her neck ripple and cursed her rashness. On the off chance that the trio of twits did follow through on their plan then she might well bear some responsibility. Especially since she'd basically just assaulted one of the planned victims.

Bloody hell! Bloody Henry! Marion thought. Then realised, much to the consternation of a pedestrian on a zebra crossing in front of her, she had also shouted. So, she purposefully shouted, "Christ! Now I'm bloody doing it!"

Forty minutes later, having decided to try and put Henry's insanity out of her mind and just get on with her day, Marion arrived at her intended place of business. On the way she had called Ron and arranged to meet him there to discuss various aspects of the venture. After calming down, Marion saw no reason to upturn her life just because of Henry's hare-brained nonsense on which, she had now convinced herself, he would never follow through. She sat in one of the barber's chairs and, while waiting for her new backer, prioritised the topics she needed to discuss with him. She had made a list of nine points but now decided that, in the interest of maintaining focus and getting the most out of Ron's expertise on matters of the greatest import, for today she would narrow it down three.

Artists. Equipment. PR.

She wrote down the three items as column heads, and then proceeded to list various bullets below each one.

Under 'artists', Marion's first concern was how many she would need. She looked around the space and, visually comparing it to Ron's flagship shop, wrote down her estimate of three. Maybe four.

Including me? She thought, and wrote that below – followed by a large, circled question mark. She realised that she would only be in the early stages of training as a tattoo artist and that, for at least the first year to eighteen months, she would mostly be focused on her original designs.

Original designs.

She wondered if there could be a way to get that into the title of the parlour. She flipped the page over, made a note for her own reference later, and then returned to her meeting preparation page.

Marion turned her attention to the next column: 'equipment'. She tapped her pen against the clipboard. Thinking. Tapping. Thinking of a question. Any question. Finally, she laughed and wrote, 'Just ask Ron'. She had no idea what would be needed or how much it would cost. Perhaps she was biting off more than she could chew with this venture. Then she shuddered as she visualised the call centre she'd been marooned in for the last two decades. Smile and dial.

Never again.

She moved onto the next column: 'PR'. Publicity. Advertising. Marketing. These were threads she could work with. The first thing she needed was something to sell. Not just a product, or in her case a service, but a concept. An idea. All the usual marketing buzz words and cliches came flooding into her mind as she looked around the space.

This is a blank canvas. We're going to create something fresh. New. Original – there's that bloody word again! Only unoriginal people claim to be original.

She flipped the page, crossed it out from her shop title ideas list, then returned to the worksheet for her meeting and got back to jotting her train of thought. 'Focus on the artwork. All bespoke. No templates. Fine art for fine skin.'

Ooh, I like that.

Another note in the shop title ideas page, then back to the meeting preparation. 'Examples shown in the photographs on the studio space are examples for inspiration, not replication.' She circled 'photographs'. She drew an arrow from the word and noted, 'Henry Glass.'

If he isn't in jail.

Marion stopped her note taking. Her psyche refused to accept her pushing the thoughts of what Henry might be about to do into the back of her mind any longer. They bulldozed their way into the forefront of her consciousness, reemerging as a strong possibility and then a high probability instead of the vast unlikelihood she had tried to brainwash herself into believing. With a piercing, eye-watering headache, like a needle stabbing her between the eyes, her comprehension of the situation became fully realised. Henry, Sonia K and Des had spent weeks planning this and were taking it very seriously. Not only that but she had just sent one of the intended victims straight into their half-baked trap.

"Dammit!" Marion threw the clipboard aside and checked the time on her phone. Twenty-four minutes past eleven. She opened Henry from her contact list.

Phone or text. Phone or text.

After a moment's consideration she closed the window and pocketed her mobile, knowing that neither option would get her anywhere. She knew that Henry would be avoiding her. He was probably with Sonia and Des already, preparing for their deluded farce. *Strategising, for want of a better word, in their corner table at the Bald Bloody Monkey.*

Besides, if she were to leave a message or send a text then that would definitely implicate her after the fact, at least in regard to her having prior knowledge of a homicide.

Is that what they call it in this country? She made a mental note to stop watching so many American procedural crime dramas.

She checked the time again. Twenty-six minutes past eleven. This day was going to be very, very long. At least until she could work out a way to scupper the crime of the century. She had seven hours. The invitation for the unfortunate VIPs, she recalled, was for half-past six. She reasoned that it wouldn't be too long after before the trio of twits would spring their trap. Then a thought stuck her.

Interference.

Perhaps she couldn't change their addled minds at this stage, or go to the authorities, but she was sure that they would see the monumental idiocy of their folly were their plan to fail. She knew she couldn't stop them from at least attempting to carry out their scheme, but perhaps she would be able to intervene. As her idea began to solidify, Ron arrived.

"Morning, Mar," he said, looking around. "Yeah, I see what you mean. Nice space. Very nice. And I love the chairs."

"What? Oh, yes. Thought you would. Hey, listen. Do you fancy accompanying me to a gallery opening this evening?"

Chapter 39: Early Arrivals

"Where the bloody hell have you been?"

"You said five o'clock," Des protested, "I'm ten minutes early. And why are you whispering?"

"Because Drew's in here," Sonia replied. "Is Henry with you?"

"No."

"Shit!"

"Are there people already arriving?" Drew called from inside.

"Eh, no. Just Des. I'm going to have a quick smoke with him. Be back in a moment." She pushed Des further out onto the street and closed the door.

"I thought you gave up years ago?"

"I did, Dizzy. I'm just buying us a few minutes alone. So you didn't go to get Henry?"

"I thought he was meeting us here?" Des replied as he took out and lit a cigarette.

"So did I but I haven't heard from him all day. And he's not replying to any of my texts. You did say you'd… Oh, for God's sake, give me one of those." Sonia snatched away Des's packet of Chesterfields, threw one in her mouth and lit it. She took a long, deep drag and, while exhaling, sighed with a long-forgotten delight.

"Welcome back."

"Oh, shut up. Henry's gone awol and, all because of Drew's diligence and bloody work ethic, we've found ourselves in a right pickle."

"No, we haven't. Look. Drew's already here, yeah? Evan'll be along in about half an hour or so.

Probably before. He's dead keen to get you alone and I've made sure he thinks he's in with a chance."

"But what about his ad man that Henry's so keen to knock off?"

"Well, that's Henry's problem, isn't it. If he can't be arsed to get it organised, or if he's chickened out –"

"He's chickened out."

"Yeah, he's chickened out. So, that's his lookout, ain't it."

Sonia nodded, considering Des's argument, then replied, "But if Henry's not going to be here does that mean we should still be offing Drew? I mean, that's Henry's fight, too. Not ours. For us to be taking care of him just doesn't seem right to me. Ethically speaking, I mean."

"Ethically speaking? Ethically fucking speaking? Are you having a laugh? It's a little bloody late for that discussion, Sonia. Besides. Ethically speaking, Drew's still a little scrote who's getting exactly what's coming to him. And he's got to be down there pouring the drinks to keep Evan down there. And that nasty little shit's existence ends today."

Sonia took another moment to consider – while stamping out her cigarette and swiping another. "Alright," she said through her first blue-smoked exhalation. She allowed the cigarette to hang from her mouth, a seasoned smoker once more, while sending a text: 'Fuck it, Henry. We're going ahead without you.' She put away her mobile and looked back to Des, again seeming calm about the situation.

283

Then she looked past him, her gaze became fixed and her jaw slackened. "Oh, shit."

"What's up now?"

"A fly in the ointment," Sonia quietly replied. "A big, bloody fly." She forced a wide grin and eased Des aside.

Des turned and saw they were being approached by a silver haired man in his early seventies. Lean and trim with a sculpted, white beard. He wore a brightly patterned, velvet frock coat and carried an ebony cane topped with a silver fox.

"Naughty, naughty Sonia," he oozed. "Back on the ciggies, hey?"

"Well. Only recently. I'm sure I'll be off them again soon. Des. May I introduce you to Magnus James. One of our most illustrious guests this evening."

Magnus gave a flamboyant bow.

"And one of our earliest," Sonia added, looking to Des while maintaining her grimace.

"Oh, I am sorry for my appearing so prematurely, but I just couldn't help myself. And I so wanted to avoid the inevitable throngs. Come along, dear Sonia. Let us peruse these wonderful photographs." As he spoke Magnus linked his arm through Sonia's and walked her into the gallery.

Sonia gave a slight shiver. She hadn't seen Magnus for a few years and had forgotten what a letch he was. How every syllable he uttered had a note of innuendo. A critic, she remembered, had once written, 'were Magnus James to read a nun's shopping list it would sound like hard core pornography. Which would be an asset for a man of

284

his profession were it not for the fact that this is the only way he could read it.'

Once inside, Magnus paused to absorb the aroma of an extravagant display of winter flowers beside Sonia's desk. "Wonderful," he gushed. "All domestic blossoms. I can tell, you know. In another life I was once considered somewhat an expert horticulturist. May I ask from where you procured such lavish and beautifully curated blooms?"

"Actually, the supplier's still standing over there. Admiring one of the portraits which, I have to say, she just bought for significantly more than she charged for the flowers."

Magnus looked at the woman, who struck an elegant poise that appeared faintly stooped by sadness. "I do believe I know why," he whispered, leaning towards Sonia as if he were about to reveal the darkest of secrets. "I've encountered the poor girl before. The subject of the portrait was some sort of celebrity chef, or restaurateur, many moons ago – and your dear florist's lover. I'm afraid he came to a bad end. Murdered on the steps of Claridge's, would you believe. Still. If one is going to be murdered, I suppose it's better to be in Mayfair than elsewhere." He gave a brief, rasping laugh. Then glanced down at the pile of books and, waving his cane over them, added, "I shall purchase a few of these when the maestro is available to sign them for me, of course. Wonderful Christmas pressies. Now. Dare I ask. Where might my likeness be displayed this evening?"

"Downstairs in the basement, Magnus."

"The basement! For shame! Have I been made an outcast? Am I to be shunned?"

"Oh, no, quite the opposite. The best of Henry's portraits have been gathered downstairs. It's a wonderful, brightly tiled space so the light reflects beautifully. The prints are double-sized and in heavy frames so we needed to put them on easels. They look quite spectacular. That's why it's only for the chosen few. It also happens to be where the pre-party is taking place. And where the bar is."

"Oh, the bar! What an excellent suggestion. Lead on, dear Sonia. Lead on."

Again, Magnus linked his arm through Sonia's and, after a gentle pull, allowed her to lead the way.

Des, who had followed them in just as Magnus was pontificating over the books, caught Sonia's eye as they moved out of Magnus's line of sight and mouthed an exaggerated, "What the fuck are you doing?"

Sonia managed a confused shrug so Des thought it best to follow.

As they passed her, the florist turned away from the photograph and, moving towards the door, offered Des a bright smile. Des returned the compliment, doing his best not to be distracted by her eyepatch. A rather beautiful piece of embroidery with a red rose motif, fastened by a looped, black ribbon.

Magnus stood in front of his portrait while leaning against his cane. "Oh, the glory days," he lamented.

Sonia stood a few feet behind him and discreetly stepped backwards to join Des near the bottom of the stairs.

"Well, what are we gonna do about this guy?" Des asked in as loud a whisper as he could risk.

"Don't know." Sonia put down her glass of Prosecco while considering their options. "Worst comes to the worst, I suppose we just chalk him down to collateral damage."

"Jesus, Sonia."

"Honestly, Des, he's a pretty disgusting human being. I doubt anybody would really miss him. Besides. It might look better if there's a random or two on the casualty list. Magnus," she called as she stepped forward before Des could object. "Is it all you expected?"

"Oh, it's marvellous. I remember the shoot as if it were only yesterday – which, as any fool can tell when comparing the youthful scallywag before us with the ragged visage I now wear, it most certainly was not." Again, he ended with his feeble, dry laugh.

Sonia studied the image with him for a polite moment. The Magnus in the frame was, indeed, about two decades younger than its current admirer – although hardly youthful. A charitable observer would have estimated him to have been a well preserved sixty. In fact, he had been a haggard fifty-two. The image itself was, however, quite beautiful. A rich tapestry of deep reds and blues, emanating from the silk kimono Magnus had chosen for the session. The shoot had been in his Soho flat and, Sonia recalled being told by a somewhat bemused Henry, Magnus had insisted on the backlighting favouring a row of lithographs set out on the claret wall behind him: a collection of nudes, by a local artist, which, Magnus would lewdly refer to as his ladies of the night.

"I've never seen a rendition of this size," Magnus enthused, "I've only ever seen it in the newspaper articles it accompanied, if you remember. I must have it. To join my lovely, ageless ladies on the red wall. Where is dear Henry, anyway? Making a dramatic, late entrance, I suppose? Waiting for a crowd to greet him with rhapsodic applause?"

"Actually, he isn't even due here for another hour or so. There seems to have been a bit of a mix up with the times."

"Well, I suppose I'd better pace myself, then," Magnus winked as he tapped the rim of his empty glass.

"But not too much." Sonia obligingly took his flute.

"Might I ask, if it isn't too impolite, for something with a little more pizzazz?"

"Of course, Magnus. What would be your pleasure?"

"Well, I see your boy behind the bar. What's his name?"

"Drew."

"Drew. I see Drew has the makings for a fine, dry martini. Does he, by any chance, also possess the expertise?"

"I very much doubt it but I'm sure you could teach him."

"Oh, it would be my greatest pleasure."

While Magnus sashayed towards Drew and the bar, Sonia turned to face Des – just as Evan came strutting down the stairs.

Chapter 40: Late Departures

'Fuck it, Henry. We're going ahead without you.' Reading the text, Henry felt a surge of panic. He swiped through and scanned Sonia's earlier messages. They began as calm and measured, albeit slightly patronising, requests for Henry to arrive early and dress appropriately. There then followed a series of blow-by-blow updates of how the day was going so swimmingly: Des was meeting with Evan to make sure he got there on time. Then with the King Of The Belly Men for some last minute checks. Drew was already in play.

Shit.

Shortly before eleven o'clock the tone shifted. Drew had scuppered the timing. Everything needed to be brought forward an hour. Des had managed to arrange for Evan to get there earlier, but it would be up to Henry to marshal his Ad Man. And, as a by-the-way, himself. Where was he?

An hour early. Henry checked the time – Drew and Evan, by his reckoning, had about thirty-five minutes to live.

"Shit!"

Henry ran for the door. As he opened it, he realised he wasn't wearing any shoes. He closed it and ran back to his bedroom. Once there he realised he'd left his mobile phone on the mantlepiece. He ran back and fetched it, then darted back to his bedroom. He sat on the end of the bed, dialled Marion's phone number and put his phone onto speaker, resting it next to him as he pulled on his boots.

Marion glanced over at the clock. An hour and a half until the half-wit brigade were scheduled to put their plan into action. It would take her at least twenty minutes to get there. She was beginning to regret allowing Ron to meet her at her flat, but he had insisted. She had made it clear to him that this was by no means a precursor to any sort of romantic interlude. Purely a business outing. She wanted Henry to take all of the publicity and advertising photographs for the parlour and thought it might be useful for Ron to both meet him in a more professional environment than their previous encounters and see his work. It was, in her opinion, a fine pretence of which she was bizarrely proud – and she found the deception uncomfortably satisfying. Perhaps if the three stooges had brought her in on their scheme, she could have come up with a plan that was a little less outlandish and actually had a chance of working without getting everyone involved either killed or imprisoned.

Evil thought, Marion. Evil thought.

Ron remained emphatic that, business or not, he would have considered it ungentlemanly to not pick her up. In the end she had acquiesced but did ask him to be early – implying that it was on account of her insistence on punctuality rather than revealing that the urgency was due to the fact that they were going to be preventing a mass killing.

Clearly, Ron had a more casual attitude towards time keeping. Marion started to think of alternative modes of transport. There was bus from her doorstep to a few yards from the gallery, but to call it

291

unreliable would have been a vast understatement. And even if the tubes were running to schedule things were already looking a little tight. It had to be Lilith. She retrieved her keys and her phone from their respective bowls on the living room table, having decided to call Ron and tell him to meet her there. As she picked up her phone it began to vibrate. An incoming call from Henry.

Marion paused, her finger hovering over the screen.

Answer or cancel. Green or red.

Reckoning that Henry was beyond hope and probably just calling to justify his madness, she hit red. She didn't have time for a debate and needed to call Ron.

"Oh, bloody hell!" Henry cried as his call clicked to Marion's voicemail. He paused in his boot lacing, cancelled the call, opened a text and quickly typed, 'You were right. Bloody fool. Terrible mistake. Must stop them. They're going an hour early. Help!' He then threw the phone aside and returned to his footwear. Another thought stuck him. He returned to his phone and wrote a postscript: 'Me fool, not you. Obvs.'

"Jesus! What the hell is wrong with you?" he said, referring to both the text and the fact that he'd chosen a pair of hiking boots when, next to them, was a pair of pull-on RM Williams that would have seen him out of the house three minutes ago. He pulled the last knot tight, grabbed his phone and, again, ran for the door. Upon opening it he snapped to a halt, finding himself face-to-face with Terry – standing on the doorstep about to knock.

"Terry."

"Henry. Thought I saw you coming in and out. Just wanted a quick word."

"Actually, Terry, it's not a great time. I'm in a helluva hurry."

"Yeah, I know, matey. Big night and all that. You did invite me, remember?"

"Oh, I remember."

"Well. I'm not sure if I should really attend now, Henry. If I'm honest. Not after the run-in I had with your lady earlier on."

"My what?"

"With what's her name. That girlfriend of yours."

"Marion? She isn't my... I mean... What are you talking about, Terry?"

"I mean this, Henry. Look at me."

Henry, having closed his door and navigated his way around Terry, down the stoop and onto the pavement, paused to inspect Terry as directed. He had a bloodied scrape across his forehead and another from his palm up to his elbow.

"Jesus."

"Yeah. Jesus is right. She very nearly ran me over, Henry. Broke my favourite coffee mug, too. And I've got a rip in my silk dressing gown. That was an anniversary present from my wife."

"Was it? Sorry to hear about that. But, really, it'll have to wait."

293

"Well, hang on. Is she going to be there later? Because if she is I'm not really sure if I should be. Not unless she's going to apologise."

"Yes. Yes, she's definitely going to be there later, and she isn't really one for apologies, so you shouldn't be. Bye, now."

"Well. Maybe I should go just to have a word with her."

"No, please don't."

"Why not?"

"Because I don't want you there, Terry." Henry snapped.

"What?"

"You heard me. I don't want you there. I didn't want you there in the first place. I don't like you, Terry. I've never liked you. I don't think anybody likes you. You're rude, you're loud and, quite frankly, you're a narcissistic git." As Henry turned away his Land Rover and Terry's Jaguar caught his eye. He swivelled back and added, "And for Christ's sake, Terry. Move your fucking car, will you?" Then he ran down the street while, again, trying to call Marion.

"Hello, Mar."

"Ron. Sorry to call but I was just looking at the time. Perhaps we should meet at the gallery instead of you coming here?"

"I'm here, Mar. Just outside. Do you want me to —"

Shit! "I'll be right there." Marion shut off the phone, ignoring the new message prompt. She rushed to the door and opened it with a broad smile, which vanished when she found nobody on the other side.

"Over here."

Marion turned towards Ron's voice and responded with quiet, "Oh, good God."

"Sorry?"

"I said oh, good God, what's this?" Marion replied, feigning delight as she approached Ron – who stood tall and proud while holding open the back door of the biggest limousine she had ever seen.

"Thought we could arrive with a bit of style," Ron beamed.

"Did you, now. How thoughtful." She stepped into the car and, while Ron closed her door and walked around to his side, calculated the implications of Ron's irritating act of generosity. There would be no weaving through traffic or zipping down shortcut alleys in this monstrosity, which Marion estimated to be of a size on par with a mid-range cruise ship. Marion guessed it would take them at least forty minutes to get there, and that wasn't taking into account the various road works and diversions they could bank on. Doable, but only just. Far from ideal.

Ron closed the door behind him, smiled and called forward, "On we go, James." He looked back to Marion and laughed, "That's his real name, you know."

"Really. Isn't that a hoot. Look, Ron, this really is very sweet of you but, don't you think it's going to take a long time to drive all the way from here to Camden? We are running a tad late and it would be much faster –"

"Oh, Mar. Relax. Stars need to arrive at these things in a bit of style. And you, my girl, are a star. Or at least you will be once we get your shop up and running." He winked.

Marion clenched her teeth and responded with puckered smile. As the limo hove into thick traffic she felt her phone, again, vibrate with the reminder of a waiting text – while she glanced longingly at Lilith, parked and spurned for the evening, recede into the night.

Marion read the message from Henry. Something about him being a fool as opposed to her. This confused her, then she saw it was a PS. She moved onto the earlier one. 'Terrible mistake...' Marion felt a wave of relief. Perhaps he had seen the light on his own. Perhaps he was going to call it all off. 'Must stop them' and her relief deepened. She almost relaxed, seeing that Henry had finally come to, until she read the last phrase: 'They've brought it all forward an hour'.

"Oh, no."

"Everything okay, Mar?"

She was still looking at the final word of Henry's message. 'Help!'

"Mar?"

"What? Oh. Yes. I mean, no." Floundering, she put her phone away and leaned forward. Her darting eyes spotted the tube station. "Oh, thank God. James, could you pull over, please?"

"Marion?" Ron asked with an uneasy quaver.

"I'm sorry, Ron," Marion said as the vessel slowed. "But it is rather urgent. Henry just messaged and there's... there's... there's a thing. A thing they

296

need help with. For the exhibition. And they need me to do it. So, yes. I'm just going to hop on this tube, it's only a few of stops from here."

"Well, I'll come with you."

"No! No, please, you stay here and come in the car. Everything'll be sorted by the time you get there. And then you can enjoy the exhibition. Admire Henry's work. And perhaps we can all make use of this beautiful vehicle and go somewhere afterwards." Marion threw open the door. "And please don't feel the need to hurry."

"Jesus, Marion! What the fuck?"

Marion jumped ship and ran for the station.

Chapter 41: Martinis, Canapés and a Hammer

"Jesus," Evan said. "These stairs are a bit iffy."

"Yeah," Des replied. "Sonia's been meaning to get to those."

Evan descended, clinging onto the bannisters, and stood close to Des at the bottom. "You got the movie of the week, then?"

Des turned his back to the room, indicating that Evan should follow his lead. The two huddled against the wall and Des removed his mobile. As he moved to hand it to Evan, Sonia, with impeccable timing, appeared between them holding a tray with a single glass of Prosecco on its centre and said,

"It's Evan. Yes?"

"Yeah. I mean, yes," Evan fluffed. "Met you a few times at the Monkey with your mate Dizzy, here."

"We have, indeed. But never really chatted. Would you like a glass of fizz? Or, I do believe there's a mixology masterclass in progress at the bar, if you'd rather something stronger."

"Bubbly's fine," Evan replied as he took the glass. "Grouch... Sonia. Sorry. Thank you."

"That's quite alright," Sonia replied as she relaxed her arm and let the tray dangle by her side. Then she straightened her posture and stepped forward. Forcing Evan back against the wall so he had to crane his neck to look up at her as she smiled, "Evan."

Des looked back and forth between the two with a barely disguised smirk – which morphed into a frown as his focus shifted to the top of the stairs. Sonia followed his gaze and reacted similarly as Sir Danny and Lady Thompson appeared.

"Alright, Sonia?" Danny said as he huffed his way down. "I wasn't sure I had the right place. It's been a right old age!"

Sonia glared over at Drew and, again, cursed his efficiency.

The agitation Marion felt while sitting helplessly on the tube was verging on the unbearable. She'd been lucky when she'd boarded at Holloway Road, where she'd found a train waiting on the platform. She'd leapt on board just as the doors closed, clipping the heel of her back foot, and the train was on its way before she had taken her seat – the one nearest the door.

Four minutes later she was out of her seat as the train pulled into King's Cross and vaulting onto the platform before the doors were completely open. She looked up at the display, praying that the train for Camden would be arriving on a platform near to that she'd arrived on – preferably in two minutes or under. She never knew when switching to the Northern Line at King's Cross – which seemed to take a casual and somewhat random approach to platforms.

What would usually be disappointment manifested as alarm. Her connection was due in two minutes, but on platform six. She stood on platform two.

God, I hate the bloody Northern Line!

Marion knew that platform six was at least a three-minute walk through the labyrinth that is King's Cross Station. Hoping to cut that down to a two-minute run she took off her high heels and ran towards the exit, dodging and darting her way between irate commuters, inane tourists and exhausted families. As she weaved and bobbed she stayed calm by reminding herself that when Transport for London announces that a train is two minutes away they don't mean that it will actually be arriving in two minutes – they mean that it *could* be arriving in two minutes. The train will take two minutes to get to you from where it currently stands, once it actually starts moving. More often than not it's at a standstill, usually in the middle of a tunnel, waiting for the services to even out or for a signal failure, the meaning of which nobody really understands, to be corrected. For the first time in her life, Marion hoped and prayed for a delay – albeit a short one.

As she galloped down the final set of stairs, taking two at a time, Marion could see the train on platform six. She felt a tingle of joyous relief – of which she was instantly robbed by the Doors Closing warning beeps. As the double doors nearest to her moved together she made a last, desperate sprint and lunged forward, one hand outstretched and her body angled sideways. The doors clamped across her shoulder. She did her best to wrestle forward but the rubber edges refused to yield. Defeated, Marion pulled back her arm and watched the train move away. She looked up at the display. The next train was, at best, eight minutes away.

"God, I hate the fucking Northern Line!" Marion screamed, to rapturous applause from a captive audience.

"Perfection, Drew. Perfection. Now, if you continue to make them like this, and especially with that wonderful smile of yours, the ladies will be fawning all over you. Of course, if you make too many for them they'll be falling all over you – but I'm sure the end result will be much the same. My advice would be to find yourself a fine, tall filly, pour three or four of those down one end and – most assuredly my boy – you can fully expect to receive a dividend from the other." Magnus raised his second martini and squealed with lubricated laughter while Drew's marble grimace remained unchanged.

"I see what you mean," Des whispered in a low grumble, "Nobody could miss that tosser." He and Sonia were returning from the bar, to which they had briefly escaped for an emergency tactical analysis.

"Yes, but what about that tosser?" Sonia nodded towards Danny – who stood chatting with Evan near the bottom of the stairs. "And Lady Tosser?"

Lady Thompson stood away from the others and studied one of the five, large scale portraits. She had only casually pursued the other four, including the one of Magnus, but appeared quite transfixed by the last. A ferocious storm of colours surrounding a heavily bearded, smoke-wreathed scream – wild eyed and wide mouthed. He could easily have been mistaken for a vagrant until, on closer inspection, the

301

caterwaul of colours behind him could be identified as a Damien Hirst abstract and, in the foreground, he held the signed head of a vintage Les Paul guitar.

Sonia couldn't remember the name of the musician. Only that Henry was very proud of the image, unlike most of his portraits, and that it had been taken for a photo essay called One Hit Wonders You Thought Were Dead. Sonia also remembered that the essay had been commissioned by none other than Danny Thompson, which gave her an idea.

"Take the drinks over to the men, Des."

"Sonia. This ain't a proper party, you know."

"I know!" She handed the tray to Des and took two glasses.

Des joined Danny and Evan while Sonia went to stand beside Lady Thompson. "You seem quite captivated by this one," Sonia said as she handed Lady Thompson a glass. "Wasn't it one of your husband's commissions?"

"One of mine, actually. I was one of Danny's features editors before I became one of his wives." She looked back to the photograph. "This was my favourite project. Do you have any more from the series on display?"

"Actually, I do," Sonia airily replied. "Upstairs."

Marion leant forward and her leg bounced up and down as her agitation reached what she thought must be a crescendo – then continued to rise. She wished she had a stick of gum to chew. She wished she had a cigarette to smoke, even though it had been well over a decade and a half since she'd given up. She wished she knew what a bloody signal failure

302

was. They'd only been about thirty seconds out of King's Cross when the train had ground to a standstill and, since then, they'd been motionless for what seemed like at least twenty minutes. Just as she was regretting her move of jumping Ron's ship in favour of public transport the driver came over the tannoy to inform them that it had, in fact, only been one minute. For some reason this served to only fuel her concern. She snapped to her feet and moved to the doorway. Realising that there was still one stop between her and her destination she then looked to return to the seat she'd so rashly vacated, only to see that it had already been seized by a skinny suit wearing oversized headphones.

Fucker.

She wrapped her arm around one of the narrow columns, removed her phone and began another text for Henry.

Henry arrived at the canal towpath with a little too much gusto. The steep, downward gradient had added an unexpected momentum to his light jog, turning it first into an urgent run and then a flailing sprint with exponential acceleration. As he rattled towards the end of the cobbled path and saw the water ahead he mentally prepared himself for a drenching. Then he spied the low metal fence. Henry managed to regain control of his hands just in time to reach out and grab the rail – wrenching himself to a stomach-lurching halt. Swinging around to land on both the towpath and his backside.

He sat still for a moment, feeling as befuddled as the cyclist he'd almost dismounted looked, then regained his focus. He pulled himself back to his feet when his mobile phone buzzed.

Text from Marion: 'Escaped limousine. Got on tube but now stuck on the Northern Line. But doing best to rush.' There followed an expression of hope that he can stop things on his own if she doesn't get there on time. Then a mini catalogue of highly uncharitable suggestions as to what should be done with the Northern Line, along with all those involved with both its construction and management.

Henry pocketed his phone and continued at a more controlled jog down the towpath.

What fucking limousine?

As he ran the reference irked him, along with why she'd needed to escape. He was on the verge of a working theory, mostly involving semi-naked and heavily tattooed cage fighters, when his way was blocked by a gaggle of elves and a keg of Santas. Henry stomped to an abrupt halt and surveyed the early Christmas party which had spilled out from Camden's food market onto the towpath and, he could see, across the narrow pedestrian bridge.

He cursed, stepped forward and proceed to wade, shove and twist his way through the crowd, wondering how many minutes the premature revelry would add to what would usually be a thirty second dash.

"Danny."

"Sonia. How are you, then. And when's the rest of the party getting here? i.e. Henry? I thought things had been moved up early on account of his rather special kind of awkwardness."

304

"Not at all. A minor misunderstanding, I'm sure he'll be along shortly. But until he gets here, I was wondering if you and Felicity could do me a favour upstairs?" Sonia had brought Magnus across the room to join them, and proceeded to make introductions as only a seasoned hostess of such events can.

She briefed Magnus on Danny's longstanding relationship with Henry. Gushing about how he had given Henry his early breaks and sent him out to take those haunting war photographs. She even brought Felicity, repeatedly referring to her as Lady Thompson to Magnus's purring delight, into her spin. Telling Magnus, as if it were essential to the history of Henry's work as opposed to information she'd learned only minutes earlier, how she'd been responsible for one of Henry's most interesting and well received portraits.

As she did so, Des cornered Evan and manoeuvred him towards the bar.

"How you getting on with Groucho, then?" Des feigned a toothy smile and a conspiratorial tone.

"Not bad, not bad."

"Des." Sonia called over to him. "Could you and Evan keep an eye on things down here, just in case any more early birds arrive? The Thompsons are just going to give me a little more background information on some of Henry's earlier work. Since he isn't here yet."

"No problem, Sonia." Des watched as Sonia lead the troupe of Danny, his wife and Magnus single file up the stairs. Once they were out of sight, he turned back to look at Drew. Standing behind the bar and filling wine glasses, red and white in equal numbers, each to a uniform level. Then he turned to Evan, who looked around, finally taking note of the photographs. Des felt, for the first time, a quickening of his pulse. A touch of the butterflies. He now had the pair of them, alone, in the trap. Sonia had even managed to remove the 'collateral damage'.

"Not a bad bunch of pics, Dizzy," Evan said. "Your mate Henry's an okay snapper."

"Not bad at all," Des growled.

"Now, maybe it's time to see some of your work. Assuming the job is done."

"Oh, Des," Sonia called, her head popping back around the corner.

Des looked up and, doing his best to make his briefly planned reactions sound spontaneous, replied, "Yes! Sonia?"

"I'd forgotten I'd left some canapés up here. You couldn't come up and grab them, could you?"

"Why. Of course. I shall come up now," Des projected.

Sonia threw him a narrow-eyed squint of disapproval before disappearing.

"Dizzy," the little snake hissed.

"Two secs."

"Alright. But only coz I'm starved." Evan moved aside.

Des lumbered his way up the stairs. Once at the top, he stepped from the wooden platform in the basement to the solid concrete of the ground level. He looked down at the room. Drew, busying himself by polishing glasses at the bar. Evan, helping himself to another glass of wine. He turned and looked

306

behind him. Sonia had led her group all the way down the warehouse, past the front door, to the very far reaches of the show. Well out of sight and out of earshot.

Des reached for and opened a nearby drawer. He removed the hammer which Frank had given him earlier. He leaned down and in a dry, throaty voice said, "Oi. Evan."

Evan looked up. Squinted.

"You're a nasty little cunt. And you're about to fucking die."

"What?"

Des placed his foot on the edge of the board at the top of the wooden stairs and, holding tight to both sides of the doorway, gave a mighty shove. The stairs toppled, fell into the middle of the basement and landed hard on the sabotaged manhole cover. The two parts of which, in turn, separated and fell down into the shaft.

"Des!" The call came from behind him, just as the steps were falling forward.

"Henry. You're just in time." Des replied as he brought back the hammer and dealt the pipe's collar an immense blow.

The pipe cracked. Then split. Then a hole popped as the ancient, rusted metal was forced out by a jet of water that showered the room below.

"Des! What the fuck are you doing?" Evan wailed.

"Henry!" Drew screamed.

"Jesus, Des. What the hell have you done?" Henry said.

"What have I done? What have we done, you mean."

Des and Henry watched as the pipe gave way completely, causing a torrent that, within seconds, had filled the basement to Evan's knees – with a whirlpool in the centre. Pulling at both him and Drew.

"Enjoy the ride, fuckers!" Des shouted. He threw the shit-infused hammer into the centre of the whirlpool. Then he slammed and locked the door.

Marion charged through the front door and ran straight into the first display – knocking over photographs of soldiers, tanks, bombed out buildings, and the one of a youthful Henry looking dramatic in his combat fatigues. Behind the collapsed display wall stood Sonia, Danny and Lady Thompson. The married couple eyed her with confused amusement. Sonia with a glare hovering between frustration and anger.

"Hello, Mar," Danny said. "I never spotted you as the clumsy sort. What's all that racket from down there, then?" He looked to the top end of the warehouse.

Marion looked in the same direction and, from her side of the display walls, could see Des and Henry – nose-to-nose in a crimson-faced screaming match. She straightened herself up and marched towards them.

"Just open the bloody door, Des!" Henry bellowed.

"Not a chance!"

"Christ, we can't do this!"

"We just fucking did!"

"Jesus, Des, just open the door! We've got to get them out of there!"

"They're probably down the pipe by now, anyway. Just like Arabella was. That's what you wanted, isn't it?"

"No. I mean, yes. It was. But it was a mistake. Des, please!" Henry tried to push past but Des blocked him.

"Don't make me belt you, Henry."

"Oh, for the love of God. Get out of the way!" Marion snapped as she stepped towards the door.

Des turned his glower towards Marion. He loomed over her, his fists clenched and swinging at his sides.

"Jesus! What happened?" The interjection came from Danny.

Henry turned to see Sonia standing about ten feet away, staring at him with unmitigated anger. Flanked by the Thompsons on one side and Marcus James on the other. Henry shrugged, looking to Sonia.

Des continued to block Marion, looming over her. Marion stood tall, leaned towards him and quietly said, "What are you going to, Des. Belt me?"

Des maintained cold eye-contact with her. Then blinked, lowered his gaze and stepped aside.

"Thought not." Marion opened the door.

On the basement side, water continued to gush from the broken ceiling pipe. The output, as predicted, was enormous. But the level was now much higher than Des or Frank had estimated, coming to less than an inch below the ground level on which they stood. What Des had also not expected was that the vortex in the centre, which had been pulling their victims towards it with such strength when the level was only at their knee height, was now barely noticeable. A mere ripple from which both of their victims had, in all likelihood quite easily escaped.

Looking pale, panicked and exhausted, Evan clung onto a section of the broken table. A makeshift flotation device which seemed to be only partially successful as he desperately kicked his legs in order to maintain buoyancy, while whimpering, "I can't swim! I can't swim!"

Unlike Drew, who had removed most of his clothing and calmly circled the area using a well-practiced breaststroke.

"Shit," Des muttered. Then he leaned towards Henry and quietly said, "You know, if we just closed the door again they can't last for much longer and –"

"Oh, shut up, Des," Henry replied as he knelt down. "Come on, Drew."

"I think it's Evan we should get out first," Drew shouted back. "Just a moment." Drew swam over to Evan.

"Please!" Evan sobbed. "Please help me! I can't swim!"

"That's alright. I've got you," Drew calmly said as he moved under Evan, caught him with one arm around the neck and swam with a one-armed backstroke towards the door.

Henry helped Evan onto the solid concrete of the ground floor.

Drew, once Evan was safe, vaulted himself onto dry land and popped to his feet with the ease an

Olympian swimmer. He wore only his underwear and proceeded to brush the excess water from his body which, all noticed, was surprisingly well toned and devoid of all body hair. Then he looked over at Sonia and calmly asked, "Do you have any blankets or towels?"

"Upstairs," she said through clenched teeth. "In the flat."

"Evan should get those wet clothes off. Before he dies of hyperthermia."

"Oh, I'm sure."

"Oh, God!" Evan, now shivering like a shaved weasel in the snow, cried. "I don't want to die."

Sonia shook her head. Disappointment clouded her face. Then became thunderous anger as she shot Henry an accusatory glare.

"You'll thank me for this one day, Sonia."

"I very much doubt that."

Then Des stepped forward, an air of curiosity crossing his face. He looked up at the gushing pipe. Then down at the floor. The water was now overflowing from the basement and covering the soles of his shoes. Des tapped his foot. Splish-splash.

Henry followed Des's movements as, his quizzical expression deepening, he again looked up at the pipe. The torrent continued. They both stared it for a good ten seconds before looking back down at the floor. The water was now well over the tops of their shoes and running past them. Down the length of the gallery.

Des emitted a worried, "Hmm."

"Shouldn't that emergency shut-off you told us about have kicked in by now?" Henry asked.

"Yeah. Yeah it should." Then another, "Hmm."

"Des?" Sonia stepped forward.

Des raised his nose towards the basement and sniffed the air.

Henry followed suit and said, "Not as pungent as it usually is. Is that a freshwater line?"

"No. No, it doesn't reek like the usual sewage, but it's still fairly rancid. It's definitely not fresh water. But I don't think it's a sewer line, either."

"Then, what the hell is it?" Sonia demanded.

Des winced and let out a particularly long, I Ain't Seen One That Bad Before, mechanic's whistle.

Chapter 42: A Hidden Amendment to the Brief History of the Sonia K Gallery

When the entrepreneurial Mr Colin O'Conor built the warehouse that was to, eventually, become the Sonia K Gallery, he had no ambitions, or even intentions, of becoming one of the most important purveyors of meat to London's finest butchers and department stores. He was purely a supplier of livestock. A link in the chain between the farmers and the already established butchers – most of whom, in the times before refrigeration, carried out their own killing. As such, when he arrived in Camden and was looking for a suitable location for his endeavour, he had in mind three crucial requirements.

The first was access to both town and country for his customers and patrons. He needed a location which would be suitable for the farmers of Hackney and beyond to bring in their livestock. The place also needed to be convenient for the urban meat sellers to visit with their more modest transports. For this, the nearby main road that would later become Camden High Street was more than satisfactory

His second requirement was a dependable, and economically viable, conduit for his own supply needs. Mostly food and bedding for the animals that would be in his custody until such time as their sentences concluded and execution beckoned. Oats, straw and the like. For this, the warehouse's proximity to the Regent's Canal suited perfectly. And would, as mentioned earlier, eventually spark what he would undoubtably have called his lightbulb moment, had lightbulbs then existed, that inspired his later venture into butchery and wholesale meat delivery.

The final stipulation was that, for the livestock, the warehouse would need to be next to a constant and reliable fresh water supply. This was a time when London was known for, not just one river, but three. The most famous, both then and now, was the Thames: the very reason, with its large estuary and natural harbour, that the original Roman city of Londinium was constructed as an international shipping port. The main artery of this great metropolis, both then and now, providing Londoners with their life blood for over two millennia to date. But in those ancient times, and even in the relatively modern days of Mr Colin O'Connor, London was also serviced by the rivers Tyburn and Fleet.

It was location of the Fleet – or rather one of the Fleet's many distributaries, the river Spike – that provided Mr O'Connor with his final requisite. The Spike flowed within a few feet of the warehouse, easily enabling him to divert a small portion into the building for all of his water needs. He was even able to build a small watermill in order to grind the oats for the animal feed and, indeed, make bread – for both for his own family and, later, a small sideline in his Camden shop.

During the construction of the London Victorian sewer project these rivers were either diverted, incorporated into the sewer's superstructure or, in some cases, simply built over. Quite famously, a great stretch of the river Fleet still flows under its namesake street in the West End. Less famously, the river Spike was diverted through a series of culverts and pipes under, around and through the growing town of Camden – and then completely forgotten about.

Chapter 43: The Spike

"What do you mean, it's a fucking river?" Sonia screamed.

"To be honest, I should have known. You know that big pipe that runs over the platforms at Sloan Street Station? Well, now that I think about it, that one looks a bit like this one. And the one in Sloan Street's a distributary river from the Tyburn. Did you know that?"

"No, I didn't fucking know that, Des. And I don't fucking care. When is the emergency shut-off going to kick in? I mean, for Christ's sake, look at this. At this rate we're all going to bloody drown."

"God, no! Please! I don't want to drown!"

"Oh, shut up, Evan. Right now you are the luckiest man in London and you don't even know it. Des!"

"Well, that's the thing, Sonia. This's been here since the beginning. Back when they started building the old Victorian sewers. Probably why it was so rusted through and easy to break, now I think of it."

"It strikes me, Des, that you're doing an awful lot of thinking now that you should have done quite some time ago," Marion threw in.

"That's not useful, Marion," Henry instantly regretted saying.

"Oh, don't you dare," Marion hissed, validating Henry's immediate self-recriminations.

They both turned their attentions back to the matter at hand. Water now flowed from the basement door at an alarming rate, and the entire gallery floor was now at least an inch deep.

"I don't understand," Henry said to Des, trying to sound calm and measured. "Why isn't all this going down through the manhole?"

"Oh, no chance. See the girth of that pipe?" Des pointed at the river gushing down into the lake that had been Sonia's basement. "Well, that's about twice the area of the shaft's. Twice the area of the aperture, twice the volume of output. So the shaft's only taking about half of what's coming out of that." He looked back at the torrent and shook his head. "Should've thought of that when we were working on the plan."

"Once again," Marion sighed.

"What plan?" Danny interrupted.

Henry, Des and Sonia all turned towards him. All having forgotten his presence. All stumped for an answer.

"He means the building's plans," Marion calmly replied. "Clearly, a miscalculation of that sort would be against all safety regulations. The purpose of the outlet is as a safety net just in case this pipe gave way which, as you can see, it just has. It should have been corrected in the planning stage but it wasn't. Right, Des?"

"Eh, yeah. Yeah. That's right, Marion. Thanks."

Danny nodded, satisfied at the explanation.

Marion gave Henry a mawkish smile and whispered, "Was that useful?"

"Sonia, my dear," Marcus chimed in, "I do believe some of your other guests are beginning to arrive." He gestured towards the front door where a middle-aged couple stood, looking down at the toppled display and the rising water in which it began to float. "Should I tell them to come back in half an hour or so when all this has been taken care of?"

"Half an hour. You think this will all be cleaned up in half an hour."

"You think a little longer? An hour, maybe? That might be a bit of an ask, Sonia. They may well have other plans for later in the evening."

"Go and tell them to fuck off, Magnus! And, while you're at it, fuck off yourself!"

"Well! There's no call for that sort of rudeness! I'm going home!" Magnus whirled around and, lifting his frock coat for fear of wetting the hem, marched down to meet the waiting guests. All watched as he briefly engaged with the couple, who reacted by looking up towards Sonia with horrification before abruptly exiting. "And that's just the first volley, Sonia K!" Marcus shouted. "Your name shall be mud in this town. I promise you! From this day forth, your name shall be mud!" He made a final dramatic turn, this time towards the exit, and splashed his way out.

"What a git," Henry said. "Now. Does anyone else think it's about time to call nine-nine-nine?"

By the time the police arrived the river Spike was flowing out of the gallery's entrance, down the high street and various distributaries of its own were appearing along its path. A few through narrow alleyways but most, rather unfortunately, cascaded down steps and stairwells. Waterfalls had converted several neighbouring basement flats and businesses into subterranean ponds and lakes.

The police, who had insisted on coming alone in order to evaluate what they suspected to be an exaggerated situation, immediately called the fire brigade, Thames Water and, at Evan's snivelling insistence, an ambulance. He was sure he was about to expire from, if not hyperthermia, then most certainly shock. Over the course of the following hours more blue, flashing lights arrived, bringing with them a growing throng of rubbernecked bystanders. All watching with voyeuristic excitement while fire fighters and experts ran and splashed through the water, outwitted by and unable to stop the Spike's never-ending flow.

Sonia, Des, Henry and Marion all sat on collapsable seats, courtesy of a nearby coffee shop, opposite the chaos. They mostly watched Drew and Evan.

Drew stood beside Evan who sat on the back of a parked ambulance. Both were wrapped in silver foil blankets. Both spoke with a senior police officer who kept glancing over at Sonia, Des and Henry. Eventually, the officer snapped shut his notebook and walked away from the survivors.

Evan threw his blanket aside and hopped off the back of the ambulance. Back to his usual form, he marched towards Des – shoulders rolling, brow down and head swivelling. As he neared, he jerked his head, summoning Des to follow. Des sighed and stood.

"Des," Sonia said.

"Yeah, don't worry," Des replied. "He may be alive but now we know he's just a snivelling little shit. Who'd have thought, hey? I'll just get rid of him." Des laughed and marched over to join Evan.

With Des absent from their table, Sonia turned her scowl towards Henry.

"What," Henry finally said.

"Did you know that Drew used to be a fucking lifeguard?"

"Right," Des said, standing over Evan.

"Right nothing," Evan replied with a snap. His harsh, sneering timbre returned. "It was the shock."

"What?"

"The shock. It was the shock. That's what made me act like that. All weak and pussy-like."

"Yeah. It wasn't the shock, Evan. I know that, you know that and, frankly, we all know that. It wasn't the shock, it was just you."

"No! No, it was the shock! But I'm back, now, and you and me are gonna have words. Because I know what you did. I know what you did, and I didn't tell the cops, because I'm gonna take care of you myself."

"You're not taking care of anyone, Evan."

"Yes, I am! I'm gonna take care of you, Des. I'm gonna do you in. Snuff you out, unless you keep doing for me what you've been doing for me. And more. And for half money. And starting with that drummer."

"Evan, stop." Des was beginning to sound tired. "Just stop. Nobody's going to buy it anymore. I mean, what are the odds that if I do a bit of digging I'll find out your sentence was a sham? That you were taking the fall for someone else? Nah. You're done, mate. You're no fucking killer. You're a faker. A bullish artist and now we all know it. Just walk away." Des turned and, with a soft smile, started back towards Henry and Sonia.

Behind Des, Evan flushed bright red. Shaking, he looked small and helpless. With a desperate, high-pitched squeal he shouted, "No! You're done, Des! Dizzy! Dizzy-Fucking-Des! You're done because you're such a useless, dog-shit-thick, fuckwit! Useless and thick. I mean, no wonder your bird fucked off with another bloke!"

Des stopped in his tracks.

"Yeah," Evan continued, seeing Des falter. "No wonder she started shagging him. Shagging around. And he wasn't the only one, you know."

His back still to Evan, Des's eyes burned. His cheeks reddened. His teeth glistened.

"Oh, no," Sonia said, then called, "Des, come here."

"Not by a long shot," Evan screeched. "Became the bike of Camden, I heard. If I hadn't been inside I'd have had a go at her myself."

"You little cunt!" Des bellowed as he wheeled around and rushed Evan like an angry bull.

Evan barely had time to sense any fear before the first of Des's punches flattened him. Striking him square in the nose and pushing the bridge into the front of his brain. He was probably already dead when Des struck the second blow that felled him. Cracking his skull against the pavement. And he was most certainly gone when Des lifted his foot and brought his boot down on his neck. Breaking it with a loud, sharp snap.

Des stood back, released from his fury as quickly as he'd been sucked into it. As the two police officers grabbed his arms he looked down at Evan's broken, silent body. Blood gushing from his crushed nose and ears. Into the flowing water of the river Spike, then washed down a storm drain and into the sewer.

Chapter 44: Stanley

An agreed upon curtain of silence was drawn over the night of the Camden Flood, as the media dubbed it, by all who had been present in the basement. The evening's events were only ever mentioned once between Henry and Drew – and even then the reference was, at best, oblique. Drew had guessed exactly the reason for Henry's attempt to kill him in the same fashion as Arabella had died. When he, to Henry's amazement, arrived for work the following Monday, all he said was, "I'm sorry."

Henry replied with the same, quietly heartfelt sentiment. He then gave Drew a long overdue raise and, some months later, Drew threw himself into Henry's next long-term assignment: the publicity campaign for Marion's parlour.

Marion never saw or heard from Ron again. Her backer's limousine did eventually make its way through the traffic to arrive at the gallery – shortly after the ambulance. Ron took one look at the fiasco and ordered James to take him home immediately.

However, it was only a few months after the event when Henry, Marion and Sonia sat at the bar of The Bald Monkey that Sonia, having reverted to her more disciplined post-work pub regime, announced she had come into a substantial sum of money. She then agreed to, or rather insisted upon, becoming Marion's new backer. It seemed only fair since the colossal windfall was thanks to Marion's observation on the night of the flood. It transpired that Marion's quick-witted excuse for the flood to Danny, that the

River Spike's presence above Sonia's basement should have been in the plans, happened to be true and was very much against building regulations. Between the standard insurance, the extra policy she'd taken out for the show and the settlement from the borough of Camden, Sonia walked away from the night with more than enough funds to pay off all of her debts, rebuild the gallery and become Marion's backer.

Marion secured the former barber's shop, poached several of Ron's best tattoo artists, including Alice who became her trainer, and opened Renaissance Ink by Marion. Sonia also became one of Marion's most regular customers and immediately started acquiring a full sleeve of Marion's angels.

Another year later, Sonia hosted her first exhibition in the refurbished Sonia K Gallery. This a repeat of Henry's retrospective, with an added section displaying his photographs of various models displaying Marion's tattoos. And minus the portrait of Marcus James who, true to his word, never spoke to Sonia again. He did his best to sully her name but it transpired that when mud is slung by shit it rarely sticks. Terry the Ad Man was in attendance, having also entered into an unspoken agreement with Henry, the only condition of which was that he never parked his car anywhere near Gertrude again.

At the end of the retrospective's opening night Marion, Henry and Sonia retired to what had been, for an insane few weeks, Conspiracy Corner, and Sonia braced herself for a moment she had been dreading. Since his sentencing, which had been eighteen years for manslaughter, Sonia had been visiting Des every fortnight. It was mostly she who delivered him news of the outside world and his friends: the inevitable passing of Frank, The King Of The Belly Men. Her partnership with Marion and their newfound success. Henry's dedication to Marion's cause and the painfully slow progress of their burgeoning relationship.

But the last time she visited him, just a week before the show, it was Des who had news for her. Having fallen in with Evan during his last time on the inside Des had decided that, this time around, he would keep to himself. He spent much of his time reading but, being a man with a limited attention span, favoured magazines over books. He particularly liked obscure, foreign publications. Ideally those from warmer climes, so he could imagine sunning himself on hot, golden beaches. Shortly before Sonia's last visit he had been reading one such publication when he came upon an article about an ex-pat, multi-millionaire in Barbados who had been visiting London, some eight years prior to the interview, and living on his Sunseeker in Limehouse Basin. On the day of his departure, quite unexpectedly, the city became the centre of one of the biggest storms in living memory. He and his crew were halfway out into the estuary when it became truly violent. It was too late to turn back, so they simply had to navigate it as best they could – doing their best to remain afloat but making no forward progress.

After several, terrifying hours, when it was becoming light, the seas and skies calmed. He and his captain readied to leave the estuary when a crewman's whistle sounded from the stern: man overboard. They rushed to lend assistance and retrieved from the water, not a fallen member of their own crew, but a stranger. A woman – bedraggled, beaten and semi-conscious, clinging to a navigation buoy.

Rather than turning back, as they probably should have, they took the stranger to the guest quarters and pressed forward. The owner happened to be travelling with a doctor, an old university friend and now business partner, who set her bones, bandaged her wounds and, over the voyage back home, nursed her back to health. When she regained consciousness, she had no idea who she was or how she ended up in the water. The man took her into his home and, over the weeks and months that followed, the two fell in love and married.

The woman's amnesia turned out, at least to date, to be permanent. But she did not seem to mind. She was building a new, wonderful life. She even got to choose her own name, which she and her husband decided would be Fortunata. Partly because of the way they had met, beating such vast statistical odds that they could never be properly calculated and, even if they could, believed. And partly because the only possession that remained of her previous existence, which she was wearing when she was rescued and still wore in her new life, was a beautiful bracelet of lucky charms. Made of tin.

Des had given Sonia the article which, as she sat in the corner facing Henry and Marion, she held under the table. Gripping it with shaking hands while wondering if she'd yet plied them with enough alcohol to show them. As she saw they were, finally, unashamedly holding each other's hands, she decided that they needed at least one more drink. Before rising to get them in, Sonia looked up at the shelves of bric-à-brac, behind the bar and above the bottles, which she remembered Des had once commented upon. She momentarily distracted herself by wondering how long some of them had been there. Little enamel boxes, comical figurines, Toby jugs and German stein mugs.

Had she the eyes of an eagle she would have seen that the oldest and dustiest of the collectables was a bell jar in the centre of the top shelf. Inside – stuffed, smoking a miniature pipe and wearing a tiny pair of spectacles, through which his glass eyes look down upon the pub and watch all its stories unfold – sits Stanley. A red, colobus monkey with a receding hairline…

The End. Thank You for Reading.

Milton Keynes UK
Ingram Content Group UK Ltd.
UKHW020401041224
452080UK00008B/47

9 781786 958976